A Deadly Deal

Simon Fairfax

The current titles are listed below in chronological order:
A Deadly Deal
(formerly published as No Deals Done, *'til it's done)*
A Deal Too Far.
A Deal With The Devil.
A Deal On Ice.

Medieval Series
A Knight and a Spy 1410
A Knight and a Spy 1411
A Knight and a Spy 1412

NOTE: This book was originally published under the title of No Deal's Done 'til it's done

The moral right of Simon Fairfax to be identified as the author of this work has been asserted in accordance with the Copyright, Design and Patents Act 1988.

Published by Corinium Associates Ltd

A CIP catalogue of this book is available from the British Library.

Cover design: More Visual Ltd

© 2017 Simon Fairfax

ISBN: 978-1-999-6551-6-7

www.simonfairfax.com

info@simonfairfax.com

To Elinor, the wind beneath my wings, for all the love, encouragement and badgering. Without whom...

Prologue

Clifton, February 1986

The wind howled through the high wires of the bridge, creating a banshee wail of whistles and shrieks, adding to the eeriness of the puddles of light at the base of the pillars. The couple left the warmth of the George Hotel to walk off their supper and clear their heads, disappearing into the night. The wind and the promise of rain kept everyone else from the bridge. It was late, they'd been the last ones in the hotel dining room.

A number of cars growled past, their drivers concentrating in the gloom. The couple moved slowly, arm in arm, almost staggering. To the interested observer, the woman seemed to be keeping the man upright, as though he were either very drunk or half unconscious. The woman's arm supported him around his waist, holding his left arm firmly to his side. His state worsened as they approached the midpoint of the bridge, away from the main lights of the towers. The man faltered, stumbling against the outer railings of the bridge, recovering a little as he gained some support from the cold steel, leaning into the wiry strength of the woman. She whispered something into his ear as she looked around, the wind pulling at her dark hair, throwing strands of it across her eyes and face. She seemed to relax a little as the final car drove from the end of the bridge and accelerated away into the blackness of the night. The woman cast another glance at her companion and heaved. The man experienced three emotions in quick succession: surprise, shock and fear. From his position at the edge of the bridge, he began a quick cartwheeling flight, his howl of fear carried off on the wind and ending with a subdued splash as he hit the water far below. The woman turned and walked quickly back towards the end of the bridge and the hotel car park, nothing hesitant about her footsteps now. The hazard lights of the Porsche flashed twice as she flicked the key fob, opened the door, removed an envelope from inside her coat and placed it on the dashboard. She locked the Porsche and moved away to her own car, a more innocuous black XR3i.

She drove from the car park and travelled to a secluded lay-by north of the bridge. Here she removed the covering number plates from her car and changed her appearance. The rain began to fall harder, driven horizontally by the wind. She stripped down to her underwear and shivered, goose bumps forming on her stomach as she kicked off the heels and quickly slipped into jeans and a jumper. Next went the hairpiece and the heavy jewellery. She removed the makeup and a ceramic cap from her front tooth. The real one had been cracked and chipped when she was a teenager and she'd never had it formally repaired. Maybe she would now. The trappings of her former appearance went into a heavy plastic bin liner that she threw into the boot of her car. The plain looking brunette at the wheel of the XR3i bore little resemblance to the tall, sexy and attractive woman who had dined at the hotel earlier. She had always been blessed with chameleon looks, like the new breed of supermodels who took to whatever they were given to wear like expensive clotheshorses.

A little later, a woman who'd been walking her dog on the city side of the bridge called 999 to report a body, caught in an eddy of the current in the lee of one of the bridge supports, spinning slowly in the water. The light had been dim and the conditions difficult, but she told the police that she could swear she'd seen two figures up on the bridge sometime earlier.

The woman in the Ford pulled into Leigh Delamere services, just off the M4. It was late now, but the garish lights had pulled in a usual crop of travellers, eager to get a few minutes' rest from the driving rain, and nobody took much notice of her. She was careful, she knew that calls could be traced, even from the blank anonymity of the bright concourse. She dialled a London number, and a man's voice asked a simple "Yes?"

"Everything fell into place nicely," she said. She caught a distorted ghost-reflection of her own face in the scratched Perspex of the booth, and a wry grin broke across her face.

The man thanked her and confirmed the arrangements for payment of the cost of what he referred to as "the project".

The woman walked back to her car, sheltering her face

against the rain. There was a private dental clinic in London that would give her a new tooth in no time. She didn't need any identifying features that could be used to pick her out. Not anymore...

The man replaced the receiver, his chunky gold identity bracelet clattering against the plastic. A few seconds later he picked it up again and dialled another number.

"Simions? It's done. Bristol as planned. The Clifton Bridge, by the sound of it; he fell for her charms quite literally. Yes, suicide note in the car. She has a certain style about her, doesn't she? I wouldn't want to get on the wrong side of her, put it that way. You'd never see the knife coming."

The man fiddled with a silver letter opener, imagining it sliding between the ribs of his rivals.

"Mmm. OK." He heard Simions respond. "We're done. Never could stand his damned morality anyway."

The line went dead.

Part One
The Deal

Chapter One

London, November 1988

She slammed the door to her flat closed with a crash that made her feel slightly better, furious at the departing figure for his betrayal and the insults. She went up the short flight of stairs to the internal landing, stamping her feet in frustration and anger, astonished at his arrogance and assumptions of moral superiority.

She shook her head like a dog would shake water from its coat. Words she hadn't said buzzed through her head, and she wanted to vent her spleen on something or someone. But there was nothing to hand and she'd already hurled the vase at his departing back, so instead she opened the door to the drinks cupboard and took down the bottle. She picked up the nearly empty tumbler and poured herself another stiff whisky. The amber liquid slid down her throat, burning as it went, fizzing straight into her bloodstream. The effect was almost instantaneous, and she felt the tension drain from her

7

muscles as the alcohol entered her system. She brought the cool glass up to her forehead and rolled it backwards and forwards, closing her eyes.

The anger gone, her shoulders slumped and she started to cry. Gentle tears ran down her face as the sobs racked her body. Why now, she thought, when things were just going right? She poured a second whisky and took a large gulp. The doorbell went again, its sharp note jarring into her consciousness. Well, she thought, if he thinks he can just come back and all will be forgiven, he's got another think coming.

She was about to run down to the door, but she hesitated, making him wait one more buzz. The doorbell sounded again. It had to be him as it was the internal bell, inside the building. It went a third time. He was obviously keen to make amends, she gave him that.

"Never liked it much anyway," she muttered, flicking the pieces of the broken vase away from the door with her foot so that it would open wider. Running perfunctory fingers through her hair, she turned the locks and opened the door.

"Well," she said as she looked up. "I suppose you've come to..."

She stopped dead. It was a woman, a stranger; well dressed in a smart two piece suit, early thirties, with a clipboard and a handbag which she juggled rather awkwardly, trying to free a gloved hand. She smiled disarmingly, showing a slightly chipped front tooth and a small scar on her left cheek.

"Good evening" she said. "Have I come at a bad time?"

"Well no... that is yes, but... sorry, I was expecting someone else. How can I help you?"

"Tina Bright, Turner and Ewell estate agents," she offered a gloved hand. "I have an appointment for 7.30pm. It is flat 6 isn't it, Miss Gardner?"

"Flat 6, yes, but I'm not Miss Gardner. You must have something wrong."

The woman's face dropped in dismay. "Oh no. My first time too. Could you just wait while I phone my office?"

"Yah, of course, no problem." The ludicrous situation appealed to her sense of humour. Here she was on the brink of a nervous breakdown and this poor woman seemed to be getting herself into a worse state than her. The agent struggled with her handbag and pulled out a bulky mobile phone.

"Oh don't bother with that, they never work here anyway. The signal is bad, the walls are too thick. Come on in and use my phone."

"That's terribly kind," Miss Bright said. "I feel so foolish, I must have the wrong flat."

"No problem." she said waving her hand nonchalantly.

Miss Bright followed her up the inner stairs of the flat. As she reached the main landing, she removed her gloved hand from her jacket pocket, took a swift stride and reached around in front of the other woman's face, clamping the white pad soaked in diluted etorphine solution over her mouth and nose. Her other arm dropped the handbag and clipboard, before trapping the woman's arms: her victim struggled for a few of seconds, then slumped into unconsciousness.

The woman calling herself Miss Bright caught the

recumbent form, slipping her arm under her legs to support the unconscious woman. She picked her up and carried her to the bedroom, laying her gently on the bed, leaving no friction or scuff marks on the carpet.

Miss Bright went to the kitchen. She saw the whisky bottle and smiled to herself. Picking it up in her gloved hand, she returned to the bedroom. She lifted the unconscious woman into a semi elevated position and poured the remaining contents of the bottle bit by bit down her throat. The woman began to stir, but then dropped back into a fitful slumber. Miss Bright looked at her watch; five minutes so far; another ten to ensure that the chemical was out of her system.

As the minutes ticked by she removed the other women's outer clothes, leaving her in her underwear. She pulled back the bedclothes and laid her carefully lengthways down the bed. She turned on the bedside lights. There was a record player in the bedroom, an old portable one that allowed the woman to listen to music as she slipped off to sleep. No doubt music would be meaningful to her. Miss Bright flicked through the record collection, selected an LP by Everything but the Girl that said all it needed to about mournful late night regret and placed it on the turntable.

She retrieved her handbag from the hall and took a small bottle, a syringe and some cellophane packets from it. She filled the syringe with the solution from the bottle and then placed it into one of the sleeping women's hands. She glanced at her watch one last time and injected the contents of the syringe between the toes of the comatose figure. The woman twitched and her eyes opened briefly at the sharp pain, then she slumped back again, twitched one final time and was still.

Miss Bright switched off the main bedroom light, placed the cellophane packages in an open packet of sugar in the kitchen cupboard, collected her belongings and went down the stairs, closing the door softly behind her.

Chapter Two

London, June 1987

The summer of '87 was going well for Rupert. He had his first deal in the lawyers' hands. Bought on the open market against strong competition from rivals, it was for a small development company specialising in the conversion of large industrial buildings into smaller nursery units. Rupert had been thrilled with his success, especially as it had come to his attention through one of his old university friends, who'd given him an early tip off, which allowed him to place it with his preferred runner, who in turn had proved successful in their bid. It meant that he knew what he was doing, and perhaps more importantly, that he was creating a network that would stand him in good stead for the future

Despite his successful acquisition of the site, he lost interest when it came to the aftermath – dealing with tenants and getting down to the nitty gritty of letting the units. Like Mike Ringer, he had succumbed to the property disease of the 1980s: he had become a deal junkie. He was only interested in the kill and the glory of doing deals, almost for their own sake, despite the fees they generated. As his confidence rose, his character became more aggressive and his reputation in the market grew.

To this end he had started canvassing specific areas in search of suitable sites for development. A time-consuming task, but it was part of the hunt that led to the kill, and a part that he rather enjoyed. Once he'd identified a potential site and discovered who owned the freehold, Rupert would then approach the clients and express an interest buying the site.

The work was speculative, and Rupert often found himself out on a limb, where one fell or rose according to one's own merit. It was the ethos of CR in a nutshell, and Rupert had grabbed it with both hands.

During his last foray, he had found a potential gem of a site in the Golden Triangle between Watford, St Albans and Hemel Hempstead. The problem was that he needed a client to purchase the huge 10 acre site. For the moment, he was stalled in his attempts to come up with an answer. No one seemed willing to bite, and he knew that if he asked for help, he would lose control of the deal.

Sitting in Boswells after another hard day trying to find an answer, Rupert's frustration was threatening to get the better of him. He had arranged to meet Claire for a drink, and he would see if she had any leads or any bright ideas to solve his ongoing dilemma.

Claire's career in retail was flying. Perhaps not on the same scale as Rupert's but she was making useful contacts on the client side, and information was everything. She really was succeeding in a man's world; learning under Tom

Lovich's tutelage how to manipulate, how to use her obvious attractions to her advantage, making them play to her innate ability.

Rupert bought her a drink as she sat down with him, and they made small talk for a while – a task he found easy with Claire. When he got to the point and asked her if she knew anybody who might be interested in making a substantial investment, her answer was direct.

"Well, funnily enough I do actually," she said. "Do you remember that deal I did last year in Watford? We had those two other units that were going begging because Capital didn't want any more exposure in the town?"

"I remember."

"Well, Tom suggested that we put them to MAS Investments. Now, in the normal course of things they would not be looking at such a small lot size, it was only three and a half million. But the owner, Paul Simions, has his own private pension fund and a special requirement for small lot sizes.

"So, I still don't really see how that helps me."

"I think it does, because I met Simions with Tom, just for an initial meeting, almost for the experience alone. Anyway he told me he was looking for bigger projects where he could add value by developing, rather than just pure investment. We know he likes Hertfordshire, he has an appetite for development and he's prepared to take on planning battles. What more do you want?"

"Claire, my dear, you're a star," he complimented her.

"Well, it will cost you. Mine's a G & T."

"Just one thing. Is this Tom's exclusive client, do I have to go through him?"

"I would anyway, it'll give you cover. I guarantee he won't steal your deal, and he'll give you good tactical advice."

"What, like how many buttons to undo?" He grinned at her.

"You don't have the figure for it, darling, trust me," she replied, raising her glass. "And the price has just gone up to dinner."

"My pleasure. But I thought that was Angus's province?"

"Oh, not you as well. Maybe there is some smoke and fire, if you don't mind me mixing my metaphors, but that's one deal that hasn't been consummated yet. Apart from that, no comment."

"OK, OK, only joking," he said holding up his hands in mock surrender.

"Sorry, I just don't want to be another on the long list of Angus's conquests. Let's drop the subject and have a good evening without mentioning the Scottish hooligan again."

"Done."

They moved on to an Italian restaurant around the corner in Dover Street, and not for the first time Rupert wondered what might have been if the relationship had developed further at university. At the end of the evening, they walked arm in arm to get a cab on Piccadilly. Claire spotted one and whistled with two fingers in her mouth. Rupert grinned and did his best George Peppard impersonation

"I never have been able to do that."

"Oh it's easy. You just put your fingers together and

blow," she replied in Audrey Hepburn's inimitable and mellifluous tones.

They both grinned at the old joke between them, fitting easily into the compatible, platonic relationship. They arrived at Claire's flat and stood opposite each other on the pavement outside her door to say goodnight. Rupert politely refused an invitation for a nightcap, sensing for a brief moment a hint of tension between them. He kissed her lightly on the forehead and turned to walk the short distance home without turning around, although he could feel her eyes on his back. He sighed as he heard her door click closed. He still had Kate, and Claire – well, she had Angus, or at least she would one day.

The next day he went up to see Tom Lovich and explained the situation, together with his problem of who to run the deal with. Lovich, as Claire had predicted, was enthusiastic and encouraging. He also thought, not for the first time, that Claire had a good agents' head on her shoulders.

"Ok, here's what we'll do. I'll set up a meeting with Paul Simions at MAS on another subject entirely, which I have to do anyway. That way we'll get our foot in the door, see the main man and not one of his minions, who would probably pooh-pooh it anyway. Also, seeing him face to face will give us a much better chance of succeeding and prevent us from being shafted on the introduction."

"Why would that happen? Aren't we going to offer it exclusively to him off the market?" Rupert asked.

"Paul Simions is a shrewd operator, and he always uses a firm of agents called Shingler Cariss to advise on bigger projects, especially if there's future retail potential. No one has ever got to the bottom of that particular relationship, but it's tight, and while he always pays full fees, he'll wriggle any way he can if you give him half a chance.

"The joint senior partner is one David Shingler, who is a smarmy, arrogant, little shit and I wouldn't trust him as far as I could kick him. If anyone tried to steal the deal it would be him. Also, this scheme will want funding. MAS never bankroll their own developments, and they try to get everything off the balance sheet as soon as they can. So we'll bring out the big guns from the get-go. Hugo Curtiss. You know him, right?"

"Head of investment?"

Lovich nodded. "That way we'll ensure that CR get a share of the whole pie, rather than just crumbs off the plate. It will be a complicated deal, and Shingler doesn't have the same expertise as Hugo."

"I see, it all sounds pretty devious. Would we be better going somewhere else?" Rupert asked.

"No, MAS is a good call and there's no one more tenacious. Once Simions gets his teeth into something he never lets go until he gets what he wants. We'll run it past him and see how we go."

Rupert realised that he was already out of his depth, and despite his enjoyment of life out on a limb he was pleased to have Lovich holding his hand. He was still on the steepest part of his personal learning curve.

The meeting was set up for Friday morning at MAS's offices in Manchester Square. Lovich and Rupert arrived by cab, and Rupert found himself looking at classic

Georgian architecture. White stuccoed buildings of elegant proportions surrounded a small park in the centre, fenced off with newly-painted wrought iron. To the north side was the famous Wallace Collection gallery. A short flight of stone steps led up to the black painted front door.

"Oh, I know where we are now," Rupert exclaimed. "Boswells is just around the corner.

"That's what I like. The mark of a good agent is how well he knows his way around the West End by the bars," Tom commented.

They buzzed the intercom, announced themselves and entered through the main door. The reception area was heavily carpeted, beautifully yet discreetly lit with classically upholstered sofas facing each other across a coffee table laid out with newspapers and magazines together with a press cutting book relating to MAS Investments.

Lovich walked up to the beautiful blonde behind the reception desk, who gave him the full force of her smile as she confirmed the meeting.

They both sat down, and Rupert began to flick through the press cuttings. Lovich had explained on the way over a little about MAS, including the rather unfortunate incident involving Paul Simions' partner, who had committed suicide by jumping off the Clifton Suspension bridge some three years ago, with an odd note left behind and a total mystery as to motive for his action.

"So don't mention suicides," he had advised

There was of course, no mention of it in the press cuttings either, just slick reporting chronicling the meteoric growth of the company that seemed to go from strength to strength.

After five minutes, a smoothly groomed secretary (another long-legged blonde) appeared. She escorted them up to the top floor of the building. On leaving the lift they were faced with the same immaculate décor: deep carpet and light airy space, all exquisitely crafted to impress. The door opened into an office which could only be described as beautiful. Natural light coming from skylights in the roof created a feeling of extra space. Original cornice work contrasted with modern furniture of impeccable taste. It could so easily have clashed with the room, but it was perfectly matched to give the office a mature, professional touch.

The desk dominated the room, reflecting the personality of the figure who sat behind it, almost in profile, backlit by the harsh sunlight. He seemed vaguely familiar to Rupert, who racked his memory, trying to remember where he had seen him before. He put it down to the publicity photos he had seen downstairs.

Paul Simions replaced the telephone receiver precisely, almost delicately, like he did most things in his life. He stood up and walked around his desk in a measured way. He was a man of medium height and build with steel grey hair, gaunt, almost hollow cheeks, startling grey-blue eyes and a smile that never quite seemed to reach them. He was lightly tanned after a recent foreign holiday, and the tan was set off to good effect by his immaculately tailored navy suit.

As he extended his hand he commented; "Good of you to come over, Tom. I hope you have some news for me."

There was no direct menace as such, just a hint of arrogance and the feeling that Simions always expected people to obey him. Lovich introduced him to Rupert, who felt that his soul was being read and analysed before his very eyes.

"Good morning," he said, turning his attention back to Lovich before Rupert could even utter a polite reply. "No Claire today? I am disappointed, she rather brightened up my day when she was last here," he said smoothly.

"Sorry, we keep her for special occasions only. Weddings, funerals, bar mitzvahs, that sort of thing," Lovich joked.

They sat down, and one of the lovely secretaries brought coffee, leaving a trail of expensive perfume behind her as she left. The discussion centred around the business that Tom had come to discuss. Rupert summed up Simions as arrogant, precise and rude beyond belief. He jumped off at tangents, cutting in on a course of reason, overriding arguments with a deprecatory wave of his hand. He was a prize A1 bastard, Rupert decided.

"Right is that it?" he said as things came to an end. "I've another meeting in ten minutes."

"Actually no," Tom answered. "We have another proposition for you, care of Rupert here. It's a good one and I am sure you won't be disappointed," he finished strongly.

Simions raised his wrist and looked ostentatiously at his gold Rolex and then stared at Rupert.

"Ten minutes. Begin."

Rupert had rehearsed this in his head for days; Tom had warned him what it would be like.

"I have found a site in Hertfordshire, within the Golden Triangle, annexed by two major roads, one of which is due to be upgraded to a dual carriageway linking the site to the motorway," he put a copy of the map on the table before Simions.

"It is–"

"When you say 'found a site', what do you mean? Who's on it? What is it used for?"

"Let me explain," Rupert continued, keeping his temper and refraining from being too aggressive. "I canvassed the current owners, Cauldron Domestics, an engineering company who distribute but also have a small wholesale operation on part of the site. They make stainless steel cookware. They trade as Stainless Cook, you may have heard of–"

"How big's the site?"

"Ten acres according to the ordnance survey sheet. But it's all flat, usable land, with good access and a large frontage to the road. I have checked with the Highway Authority and provisions have been made in the new road documents to allow a slip road with traffic lights. It will give perfect access."

"Will the owner sell, and at what price?"

"Yes, he will. Or so I've been told by–"

"By whom?"

"The MD. I have a letter and I've made numerous telephone calls, but he won't release any more information until I name my client, hence the meeting with you today."

"Why does he want to sell?"

"He's been canvassed before, but now that the road is going in he sees pound signs, and doesn't really need to be in such a high profile spot."

"Have you taken this to anyone else?" Simions asked, his eyes boring into Rupert.

"No, I went straight to Tom with it," he said nodding in Lovich's direction, "and we decided to come to you first".

Simions eyed Rupert again, as if reassessing him. "Do you know what Retail Warehousing is?"

"Industrial sheds with planning consent?" Rupert offered, thanking God he had spent so much time around the industrial boys.

"Exactly. Retail sheds with fancy paintwork. The key to this site is planning."

They went over some more details. The more they talked, the more animated Simions grew. A trace of emotion became apparent in his manner.

"Right," he finally said, pointing at Rupert. "You tee up the meeting with the MD. I'll get my people on to it." Simions got up and shook hands, first with Rupert and then with Lovich. "Oh," he said vaguely, as though it had only just occurred to him. "We'll have to bring in Shingler Cariss for the retail warehouse input, alongside yourselves of course," he finished smoothly.

"Of course. We'll send our letter of confirmation across tomorrow confirming terms of engagement and our fees, just to keep it all straight. Usual terms of introduction, especially as we brought it to you off the market?" Lovich finished.

The two expert fencers fought their position, smiling all the time, understanding the subtle nuances that were being made and sought throughout the game.

"Of course. You know we always pay our fees to good agents like yourselves." Simions said. Then to Rupert. "Thank you for this. I look forward to meeting you at their offices."

Rupert grinned. "Indeed. I'll be back to you today, hopefully."

They were shown downstairs by one of the blondes, who gave them her best air-hostess smile as she ushered them out. Once outside and down the steps, Rupert let out a long sigh.

"God, what an absolute bastard!" he said.

Tom grinned. "You should see him when something goes wrong. All the toys come out of the pram. Well done, you handled him well. He always interrupts and baits people to get a reaction of some sort."

"You called it right over the Shingler Cariss issue. Why does he always bring them in, I wonder?"

"We'll probably never know, some dodgy arrangement between them, I guess. OK, we – or rather you – have got some work to do. Draft a letter of confirmation setting out all the information you've provided and we'll kick it into shape and get it off to him ASAP."

On their way back to office they cut through St. Christopher's Place, a new development between Barrett Street and Oxford Street. The open-plan piazza was bathed in sunlight and the various bars and cafés had tables and chairs out on the pedestrianised area. They decided to stop for a beer to celebrate and to watch the parade of girls pass by in low tops and short skirts.

"I'll say one thing for him, though, he's got some great looking women working there," Rupert commented as their beer arrived.

"Mmm, he certainly likes to surround himself with beautiful things. Typical boy done good, straight from the Little

Italy slums, through elocution lessons up to the West End."
Lovich added cynically.

"Really? Not that it surprises me much. He tries too
hard with the accent and the manner. Too precise, too
controlled. What did his name used to be then, Paolo
Simione?"

"Spot on, actually. How did you guess?" Tom looked
hard again at Rupert, considering him in a new light.

Rupert shrugged.

"Yeah, he's done well – but I wouldn't want to cross him
or I might end up jumping off a bridge like his last partner
did. Come on, Rupert, enough maudlin talk, get another
round in," he chided.

Just as Rupert stood up to do as he was told, he spotted a
familiar figure on the other side of the road walking down
James Street from the direction of Manchester Square. It was
the temp with the gold bangles.

"Talking of girls, look, there's that temp who worked in
retail."

They both stared across.

"Oh yes, Nana Mouskouri. Now you listen to your
Uncle Tom and stick with Kate."

"Is that her name?" Rupert asked, ignoring Tom's
advice.

"No idea, that's just what we called her. It's the glasses.
Don't change the subject, how is Kate?"

"Oh, on and off, you know. On and off," he said vaguely.
More off than on at the moment, He thought. He knew it
was his fault, but he had other things on his mind and
couldn't give her the commitment she craved. It would prob-

ably fizzle out like all his other relationships and just fade away through lack of interest.

Simions had his chauffer drive him through the West End. As they glided through the traffic, he picked up the car phone in the centre console and dialled a number. When it was answered, he made no preamble. "David, it's me. I have just had a very interesting discussion with some people from CR. Tom Lovich and a new boy. Rupert something-or-other. He's found a very interesting site up in the Triangle. I know, just what we are looking for. Why didn't your people find it?" he chided. "Well, that's as may be but I have reserved your position and will get the boy – Brett, that's his name – to meet with you. But I want a girl ready to get into them through the agency, OK? Say two or three weeks' time, that should do it. Get hold of Pauline. Start setting up now," he mused, "and maybe get someone in Claire Sewell's team as well. I will confirm as soon as we know more. Good."

He cut off the call and smiled to himself.

They'd sold three properties in Italy in the last six months, netting them half a million pounds in lire. Simions smiled at the exchange rate, the number of noughts on the lire made it look better still. Stupid Italian money. This new venture would swallow it whole, he knew: bribes had to be settled, secretaries paid off and of course Pauline at the agency. But it was worth it. The deals were starting to roll in.

The beauty of it was that he was buffered against it all. It was always done through Shingler, and he never spoke directly to Pauline, the figurehead of Secs in the City. Nothing could be traced back to him, even though he was an offshore shareholder. That was the benefit of corporate espionage, it was all so distanced.

Back at the office, Rupert contacted the MD of Cauldron Domestics and agreed to a meeting the following Wednesday at his offices. He would, in Tom's words, rise or fall on his own merit and no one else could be blamed or praised.

"Just one thing," Lovich offered. "If Shingler goes and plans a meeting, try to avoid at all costs having it at his offices."

"Why?"

"Just trust me. Home ground advantage, more than anything else. You'll be disadvantaged, undermined and shafted. He has some very clever techniques, which seem to work better on his own territory."

Chapter Three

The following Wednesday Rupert went to MAS to sort out a few last details, then accepted a lift to Cauldron's offices in Simions' chauffeur-driven Jaguar.

On the way they discussed tactics and went over plans for the redevelopment. Simions had already got one of his architectural practices to draw up plans showing the site's potential for existing use and retail warehousing. He had run some figures through his own system and told Rupert that they compared favourably with Rupert's own more detailed estimates, predicting a higher capital value per acre for the site. The final set of figures and drawings related to a retail warehouse park. Crinkly tin sheds and much higher rental levels.

"One point still worries me," Rupert said. "The rate we think we need to pay will only justify retail warehouse rents, which means that we'll need planning permission for retail use. The Structure Plan is nearly finished for this area and it only details employment use. How do we get around that?

The last thing we want is for it to be called in by the Secretary of State. They'll bury it for months."

"Just leave that part to me," Simions replied. "By the way, do I recall correctly that you mentioned that home was somewhere in rural Warwickshire?"

"Yes, just outside a small village about 15 miles from Solihull."

"Do you shoot?"

"I do, actually, yes. Father's got half a gun on the local estate. I was up there at Christmas. But better than that, we got some rough shooting in over the New Year in Scotland on the Macpherson Estate."

"Good." Simions said. "I'm arranging a clay shoot not far from here on the Hoo estate in Hertfordshire. I'll get you an invitation. It's in two weeks' time, keep it free." The answer was abrupt and gave Rupert no room for argument.

The car drove into the factory complex, and Rupert immediately saw the potential. A few buildings, a small production unit, weeds and concrete, a mesh fence around the perimeter in which a few pieces of trapped litter flapped in the wind. Patches of brambles and nettles. Rupert shivered for some unaccountable reason at the industrial desolation of it all. The country was moving away from its traditional manufacturing base and relying more on its service industries, and economies of scale meant that the new retail economy was booming. Warehouses, factory shops and supermarkets in easily-accessed parks on the edge of town. And sites like this, for a while at least, were the new goldrush, pandering to economic need in rapidly changing times.

The car pulled up in front of the factory and the chauffeur opened Simions' door, leaving Rupert to let himself out. They were greeted in reception by Cauldron's MD, Graham Carpenter, and the company's Finance Director, Christopher Wall. The offices were one step up from a prefab. Floors creaked as the four men walked through to Carpenter's office. Rupert smiled inwardly at how different the two men were; the MD was short, hard and compact with an innate toughness, honed by many a boardroom battle. His pugnacious chin jutted forward below a strong face with small close-set eyes. Wall, in contrast, was tall and lean with prematurely receding blond hair. Wire-rimmed spectacles perched on the bridge of his nose. They made a very shrewd pair and would not, Rupert imagined, be easy to negotiate with.

"Sit down, sit down please." Carpenter gestured to the chairs. "Kind of you to come in and see us."

Simions introduced MAS Investments and gave a brief, potted history of the company and its objectives. He presented them with a smooth, glossy brochure. His ideas sounded plausible and effective, with no hint of the avarice and aggression that was the real driving force of the company. When he finished, Rupert, as they had agreed, proceeded to give an outline of the events to date and their proposals for the development – subject of course to looking over the factory and land, and to planning consent.

"It seems to me," Carpenter interjected smoothly when Rupert had finished, "that this would be a perfect opportunity for a break. Let me show you around the factory, give you a better idea of what you are looking at."

On their tour, they discussed the layout of the existing

works and the amount of land covered by the buildings in relation to the site area as a whole.

"High site ratio, isn't it Mr. Carpenter? What, nearly 60%? Any redevelopment would only be allowed at 45%, which will play havoc with our figures."

"With respect, Mr Brett, that is your problem. It was you who approached me, after all."

"True," Rupert said, ignoring the rebuff. "But we will have to offer realistic terms, and I only wanted to underline that in order to give credence to any offer we should make."

At that moment, Simions cut across him.

"Would you accept a subject-to-planning deal for say, 6 months? Non-returnable deposit if we fail to get planning."

The change in direction threw both the men for a few seconds. They appeared to reach a decision without actually speaking.

"No," Carpenter replied. "We could not agree to anything like that, even if the resultant figures were higher than those proposed on a speculative basis. We are not gamblers, Mr Simions. In basic terms, we make pots and pans. That is our business. Therefore any offer would have to be free of conditions."

"You are making it very hard for us to give you the best price."

"I reiterate, it was you who came to us. We are simple manufacturers. You are the developers."

They continued the tour in silence. Back in the office they went through various other matters relating to vacant possession and availability. As the meeting ended, Simions added; "Would you be prepared to do one small thing for us?"

"It depends," Carpenter answered warily.

"It's just a small thing, but would you write a letter confirming that you will be relocating in this area and continuing with production? It would help with what I imagine might be a difficult planning battle."

"A battle you want us to be a pawn in, no doubt," said Carpenter, grinning. "I can't see a problem with that."

"Good. Thank you for your time, gentlemen. It has been most interesting," Simions finished noncommittally.

They shook hands and left the building, heading to the waiting car. The breeze had picked up, and Rupert rubbed grit from his eyes. In the distance he could hear the rumble of traffic on the new M25. An artery, bringing lifeblood to the peripherals of London. Blood and money. This was where it happened; the sharp end, far from the cocooned offices with their deep carpets and smiling secretaries. Less than a couple of dozen miles from the heart of the city, but in some ways a whole different world.

The Jaguar moved through the factory gates, and only then did they permit themselves any sign of emotion.

"Well done," Simions said, "You played the injured innocent just right. I knew they wouldn't go for a subject-to-planning deal. What they don't realise is that they are sitting on a gold mine, because the value is all in the planning – and we're going to get it."

"I can't believe how well it worked," Rupert agreed, caught up in the moment. "But we're still taking a massive risk on the planning issue, and there's not many positives in the Structure Plan for the area either."

Hertfordshire's Structure Plan covered the county as a whole, and similar plans were produced by every Local Authority throughout the country every five to ten years, effectively setting in stone the planning designations for any area of the county. This area was designated as Employment Use, which effectively meant manufacturing and distribution warehousing, not retail warehousing, which the planners considered would have a disastrous impact on high streets in the local town centres.

Once the plan had been agreed, fighting it was always an uphill battle. The process would entail a costly planning appeal with only limited hope of success. The current plan was close to being finalised, having already passed through most of the consultation process. It would only be a matter of weeks before it was passed at Committee.

"Leave the planning problems to me. I have consultants working on it as we speak," Simions finished.

They spent the rest of the journey discussing timetables and plans for the proposed scheme, shuffling numbers that Rupert would run on the computer before making an offer. They would adopt two or three scenarios, none of which would make any reference to retail warehousing.

When Rupert finally returned to the office he spoke to Tom Lovich, who called an impromptu meeting with Hugo Curtiss from Investment, Martin Head from Industrial and Claire, who was starting to concentrate more on the out-of-town market that was mostly retail warehousing, moving further away from Angus's orbit.

Rupert relayed the details of the meeting to the others, who were excited at the prospect of a new development and funding but, like Rupert, sceptical about the planning.

"I wonder how Simions is going to pull this one off," Lovich mused.

"He's coming across far too confident to be flying on a wing and a prayer. The bugger's up to something," Curtiss finished. He had no illusions as to the morality of Paul Simions or his methods for achieving his ends. "But whatever he's up to, I'll speak to a couple of fund managers. See what they are looking to fund this at. Somewhere around 7%, I should think. Simions won't want it on his own balance sheet, so they will have to give interim finance as well," he mused almost to himself.

"Interim Finance?" Rupert queried.

"In simple terms, when a developer goes to a fund a project, he can either ask the fund managers to buy him out at the end of the deal, in which case he bears all the risk and they pay him a sharper yield, which means more money. Or he can ask to borrow the money from them from day one. This costs the fund more, and they have more exposure to the risks of development. But the extra risk means they won't pay such a high yield and it will cost them less in the long run."

"I see, but why do we have to tread carefully now? Wouldn't it be better to get it secured and signed up before someone like David Shingler starts whanging it around the market!"

"If we give a fund the exact location, one of Ricky

Barston's moles will hear about it and, as you so delicately put it, whang it around the market."

Ricky Barston, Rupert thought. Even he had heard of him. The man was incredible. He'd come from a corporate background and changed to agency, specialising in development sites. But unlike the others, he wasn't in it for the long haul process of development, he was only interested in buying and selling sites for clients, like a stockbroker or city trader. He offered the non-retained deals around, picking up a fee on the introductions alone, sometimes taking a half or quarter percent just to get maximum exposure to the market. Some rumour had been started that he'd even had a fee on a sixteenth.

His network of contacts was astonishing and apparently endless. No one could pin down where he got his information from, although there were a few astute guesses and the odd discreet finger pointed at corrupt fund managers and agents who sold information for a fee. It was rumoured that he and his sidekick, Steve Reid, were making three quarters of a million a year each on non-retained work – just by broking.

Lovich broke into his thoughts.

"Right, we'll all get to work on the various angles. Main thrust is down to you Rupert. Run the numbers after Simions' input and let's see what you come up with."

The meeting over, they all got up to leave the room.

"Are you coming out tonight?" Claire asked Rupert as they walked along the corridor. "We're all meeting up at Smollensky's and on to a restaurant afterwards."

"Yeah, sure, what's the celebration?"

"My birthday, Rupert. God, you're such a romantic at heart, aren't you?"

"Oh shit, Claire! I'm sorry, it had gone right out of my head. But I'll be there, don't worry," he promised. "I've just got to go over some lease stuff with Martin Sheen."

Claire shook her head in despair. "You might even find time to go and buy me something," she grinned.

Chapter Four

That night Claire was out to howl. All her friends were there and Smollensky's was heaving. Rupert managed to put in an appearance after leaving work late, but he brought a card and a present with him, which he gave to Claire at the start of the evening when she was still sober.

"I know, I know," he held up his hands in mock surrender. "I got Sheened again. You'd have thought I'd know how to avoid him by now," he groaned.

She accepted the present with a hug and a kiss on the cheek, promising to open it later. The party got into full swing and they were already half-drunk when they left Smollensky's for the Italian restaurant in Chelsea near Claire's home. Then an odd thing happened; Angus bailed out and decided that he was not going on to the restaurant. He gave some feeble excuse which didn't seem to wash with Claire.

"Come on, Angus, if I have to be up early in the morning so can you. I'm booked in to ride tomorrow at seven!"

"Ride?" he queried.

"Oh yah, I've been riding out in Hyde Park every morning for the last two weeks before work."

"I knew there was something about your perfume." he chided

She bit: "Ha ha, I use the executive shower in the basement, so stuff you." She changed tack, "Sure you won't stay on?"

"No thanks. I'd better be off."

He offered her a perfunctory kiss and left. Claire concluded that he was a predatory animal, and that to his mind a birthday party would probably not be the ideal place to try and seduce the object of everyone's attention. The birthday girl was everyone's property tonight. He'd play the game when the odds were more in his favour.

The evening spun onwards, and to her credit Claire did not disgrace herself. She ended up alone in her flat, very drunk, with Angus on her mind. *Soon*, she thought, *on my terms, soon.*

She woke with a massive hangover and washed two aspirin down with a glass of water. She dressed and set off for Hyde Park stables. The morning air was wonderful, crisp and clean by normal London standards, and an hour on horseback cantering through the park in the early morning blew the cobwebs from her mind and took the last of the headache with them. *A shower at work and she'd be ready to face the day*, she thought. She took one final long canter down the sand track, holding her hat by the chinstrap with the wind blowing through her hair. *Should be ready for polo in two weeks' time*, she thought.

She handed back the horse, a lovely bay thoroughbred, and caught a cab to the office.

The basement arrangement was perfect; it had a rear entrance off Seymour Mews that went straight to the shower room, which doubled as a sick room with a daybed. She had a scalding shower, dried her hair and had just finished applying her makeup in front of the mirror when a gentle knock sounded at the door. She was dressed in only her pants, so she grabbed a towel to cover her upper body.

"Who is it?"

"It's me." The door inched open to reveal Angus, grinning. "I thought I'd come and scrub your back," he joked.

"How did you get in? I thought I'd locked it."

"Apparently not," he said, half turning to check the door and then closing the distance between them. They were now only two feet apart and the scent of *Poison* embraced them both.

"Angus, this is not a good idea," she said, but her body language was at odds with the words.

He moved closer and kissed her gently on the lips. She responded, forcefully with pent up passion and the realisation that the chase was over – perhaps a little sooner than she'd planned. Claire's towel slid to the floor, revealing high, heavy breasts with large nipples contracting with arousal. Angus gazed down, admiring the flat stomach, the legs and skin glowing from exercise. He gripped her harder, crushing her lips with his kiss as his tongue joined with hers as they both murmured together. She slid her hand inside his partly undone shirt and wrenched downwards in a sharp motion, causing the buttons to pop off, and pulled at the belt buckle of his trousers, undoing them so they fell to the floor.

He stopped kissing her and moved his lips across her face, down onto her neck and shoulders, cupping her breasts in his hands. She leant back against the daybed on her elbows, thrusting her body forward. Angus took first one breast then the other in his mouth, sucking the nipples hard. She threw back her head and sighed with pleasure as he took one of her breasts and cupped it gently. His mouth moved slowly down her body, over her taught stomach, lower between her spread legs, where he kissed her hard and with one flick of his teeth, removed her flimsy underwear.

He wanted her now, to sate the lust that had built up over the course of the last few months. He moved up over her body, his intent clear, then she whispered; "No, this way."

She turned, rubbing her thighs against him and looking over her shoulder, her eyes half shut with passion, hollowing her back, emphasising her rounded bottom. He entered her from behind and she moaned again and squirmed against him, gripping him tightly inside. It was like nothing he had experienced before. The climax grew quickly within him until he could no longer hold it, thrusting for the last time against her. She continued to move, pleasuring herself as he cried in agony and ecstasy, until she finally let herself go, arching her back for the last time, crying out at the intensity of her own climax.

They sagged forward onto the day bed, panting hard, perspiring where their bodies had touched.

"Wow," he exclaimed. "That was the best." He hugged her, stroking her body gently.

"Mmmm," she murmured turning to face him "Shit! The door's still open. Close it and get some clothes on quickly."

He burst out laughing, realising how embarrassing it could have been. He closed the door quickly and said with more bravado than he probably felt; "Just adds to the zing."

For the first time, Claire realised he was no longer so sure of himself. She decided to make the most of it. Looking over his shoulder and assuming an expression of mixed embarrassment and shock she said, "Oh, God, Tom. Hi."

Angus spun around into the empty room. "You cow, you really had me going."

She burst out laughing.

"And going you had better be. You'll have to buy a new shirt before work."

"What?" he exclaimed, looking down. "Where from, at this time in the morning?"

"Selfridges opens in ten minutes, off you go – oh, and one other thing. If I hear one word of a boast about this in the office, I'll come after these," she said, bouncing his balls gently in the palm of her hand, "with a blunt, rusty, knife, *Capisce*?"

He held his hands up in surrender. "OK, I promise," he said. "But how about dinner tonight and we can do this all over again."

"Lovely idea." A lascivious look on her face. "Call me later, and thank goodness I'm not in your room anymore." Claire had been promoted to Senior Surveyor and moved up to the newly formed Development Department. She watched Angus run up the stairs from the basement with a huge grin on his face, looking down at the battle honours of his torn shirt. She was grinning too, smiling in deep satisfaction. It had been good, and she'd felt totally in control. It might be different tonight, but for now she could at least glow in the reflected glory of sexual emancipation.

God, what a fuck, Angus thought. Then he stopped. He realised that somehow, she had contrived to stay in control, as if she had planned both the act and the actions, and that she had had him, not the other way around. *Well, tonight would be different*, he thought, *after dinner, yes. Many thanks!*

Rupert was at his desk bright and early, if a little bleary eyed and struggling with the alterations to the figures he had faxed across last night, to find a reply by return waiting on his desk this morning. He sent off a second set in a matter of minutes, and received a call half an hour later.

"Rupert Brett."

"Simions. The figures are fine, we just need to put them into presentation format, then send the letter with the lower figures across to Carpenter. He'll expect a bit of give and take, so we'll have to go higher, but protest strongly and try to convince him it's our best shot, OK?"

"Fine, but I still think it's a cracking figure anyway. It'll surprise him."

"Maybe, we'll see. Oh, one other thing, with regard to the shoot. You have received the licence I sent you for Gavin Knott, the council's chief planning officer?"

"Yes."

"I want you to take it down to Purdey's in South Audley Street and collect a gun for me. The gun is to go on my account, but use Knott's licence, not yours or mine, understood?"

"Yes, but if it's a new registration, I doubt they'll allow it out of the shop unless the licence holder is present, will they? I'll give it a try and let you know."

"Do. If there is a problem, call me on my mobile number. I'm having lunch with Knott today in the West End."

The call cut off. *And a jolly good morning to you too*, Rupert thought to himself. Now why would Simions need a gun put onto Knott's licence? Was it a threat or a bribe? Maybe a little of each. Is this how Simions gets his planning deals through? Had to be, which is why he'd been so certain of getting consent. Clever, untraceable, easily deniable, providing Simions with a future blackmail lever if necessary. Simple but clever; no cash, just a very expensive present. *What did a Purdey cost these days?* he wondered, *fifteen, sixteen thousand? Plus all the accessories. Knott must love his shooting.*

He got a cab down to South Audley Street and stepped into the hallowed halls of England's leading gunmaker, if not the world's. The smell of gun oil assailed his nostrils, along with an unhurried aura of class and tranquillity, a haven of calm in the centre of mad London. *Tiffany's for men*, he thought to himself with a smile. The wooden floors echoed as he walked across the shop and down the few steps to the gunroom, which was lined with glass cases holding shotguns of various shapes and sizes. He turned to the counter and addressed a bespectacled man wearing a black full length apron over his shirtsleeves.

"Morning, I've come to pick up a shotgun for Paul Simions of MAS investments. I believe you are expecting me."

"Good morning, sir. Yes, Mr. Simions telephoned earlier. Now, here we are," he said, unlocking one the cases and removing a shotgun, which he placed on the padded viewing table in the centre of the room. "Side by side, single trigger. I'll just get the form, sir, to check that everything is in order."

The man returned with a standard green Purdey order book and flicked back through the pages to the appropriate place.

"Ah, here we are, sir. Rather unusual, this. We didn't actually measure the gentleman himself. We took the measurements from a gun that was not one of ours – which, if I may say so, is not good practice at all," he frowned in frustration and apparent horror at such a breach of protocol.

Rupert kept a straight face and nodded in agreement, saying nothing.

The man proceeded to go through the list of specifications: chokes, engraving to the side plates, safe automatic, each item lovingly described and demonstrated. Finally, he handed the gun over to Rupert, who took it, feeling its beautiful balance and weight. At less than seven pounds, it felt incredible. He broke the gun, even though he knew it would be empty, looked down the barrels and closed the breech. He raised it to his shoulder. The Prince of Wales pistol grip fitted his hand beautifully. He could not help smiling in pleasure. It was a thing of beauty and there was no other way to describe it. He turned the gun over and there in the magic Purdey gold oval, were the letters GRK. Obviously, Mr. Knott had a middle name.

"That is beautiful," was all that Rupert could say, realising why such a gift might hold such influence over Knott.

They went over to the counter, and the man packed the gun in a car case, along with accessories and cartridges. Rupert produced the licence without uttering a word. The details were checked and the assistant looked up to check the photo. He looked puzzled.

"Is this your licence sir?"

"I'm afraid not. I'm picking it up for Mr Simions, the man who telephoned you earlier."

"I'm sorry sir, I can't let it go without the licence holder being here for first registration."

"Oh, I see." *Damn*, he thought, *I knew it*. He had no choice but to call Simions.

Ten minutes later they appeared, Simions and another man. Simions crossed the sales floor with his customary arrogance, as though he owned the shop, but when he spoke it was with a softer tone.

"Morning to you, Masters, sorry about the confusion. Rupert here must have misunderstood my intention. Still, no harm done. Here is the owner of the licence."

Rupert fumed. Simions had planned it all, knowing that it would not be possible to take a new gun once they had checked the licence photograph. Simions indicated his companion; a short, stocky man of about forty-five with mousey coloured hair parted to the side, shrewd brown eyes, lined skin and a careworn look that went beyond his years.

He was dressed in what Rupert would call a typical local authority suit: grey, shiny material with pinstripes of dark, muted colours, set off by a white shirt and red tie.

Rupert forced a smile.

"How do you do. Rupert Brett," he said, shaking hands.

The handshake was limp, the greeting not effusive. Knott only had eyes for the gun. Like a rabbit caught in the headlights, he stared at it the way some men ogle a beautiful woman. He picked up the offered gun, broke it, closed it, held it to his shoulder and pointed it to the ceiling. Rupert had some sympathy for how he was feeling, but the look of rapture on Knott's face was something to behold.

"I wanted to surprise you with it on the day of the shoot so you could...um...borrow it," Simions interjected suavely. "Trouble is we need to put it on your licence as it's the first issue and mine's a bit full. Would you mind?" he asked plaintively as though Knott was really doing him a favour. It was beautifully done, and Knott was hooked. Their eyes met, each understanding the other without a word needing to be spoken

"Of course," he said. "I'd be happy to help, especially as I will be able to try out the gun."

So the deal was done, thought Rupert. He was looking forward to the events of the day's shoot to see how exactly the handover would be completed. The certificate was signed and the gun packed away in the car case. The account was signed for the sum of £18,700 for the basic gun, Rupert noticed, plus extras that took the total up to over £25,000. *Some planning notice,* he thought, *probably more than Knott made in a year with the VAT added on.*

The private shoot took place on the Hertfordshire estate the following week. A resident expert was on hand to give beginners a helping hand and to effectively coach the more advanced participants, many of whom were veterans of driven shoots across the shires of England. A few of those present were genuine sportsmen, lured by the draw of the countryside and the love of the sport for its own sake. However, the majority were there to be seen as enthusiasts, loving the act rather than action, with little affinity for the sport in its rawest form.

Their outfits caused Rupert some amusement. They had obviously gone to their tailor and said, "Dress me for shoot-ing" – to which the hapless man had obliged, making them look like extras from *Toad of Toad Hall*. Others were obvious townies who were not prepared to change their jumper-and-jeans approach for anyone. A few got it right and it was into this category that Gavin Knott fell. This group had their own guns, handled them professionally and looked the part.

The setting was delightful, rolling countryside with the woods providing a dramatic backdrop. The day consisted of clay shooting in the morning from normal traps, across a small hillside. They followed realistic and difficult targets, released from behind cover to emulate birds more accurately.

When they broke for lunch, they gathered around trestle tables, where food was laid out with a conspicuous absence of alcohol, which for obvious reasons was not permitted.

One of the other parties noticed Knott's gun.

"Fine looking gun you've got there, Gavin. Mind if I have a look?"

"Of course not, be my guest."

The shotgun was handed over for inspection. The man broke the gun, checked it and closed the breech, admiring the balance. He then looked at it more closely and exclaimed.

"My God, a Purdey! No wonder the balance is superb. You must be doing alright, Gavin," he remarked pointedly.

"I was fortunate. A legacy, it was a holiday or a second-hand Purdey. The wife wasn't very happy though," he joked. Rupert looked across first at Knott and then Simions, who had a slight grin etched into the corners of his mouth as he gave Rupert a small, almost imperceptible nod. The thirty pieces of silver had been taken, Rupert thought. Planning would no longer be a gamble; of that he was certain.

The next few days were very tense for Rupert and Simions. As predicted, Carpenter rejected the initial bid, forcing them to increase the offer by over £250,000. But it was still nowhere near the "hope value" that would be achieved if planning were to be granted for retail consent. It also gave Rupert the opportunity to get one last condition accepted; that the contract be signed within two weeks, before the publication of the new Structure Plan.

It was a gamble. The lawyers would have to work around the clock, but Rupert had no doubt that the area would be zoned for retail in the new plan, paving the way for full blown consent.

The next two weeks were frantic, and Rupert received the letter of support from Carpenter prior to seeing the planning application and the revised Structure Plan. The lawyers were for once very good. They were thorough and pragmatic in their approach. *Whatever he's paying them*, Rupert thought, *they are worth every penny.* All searches and due diligence were completed in time and they exchanged contracts the day before the plan came out, with completion scheduled for a week later, allowing time for all monies to cleared.

The following day Rupert was at the council offices to see the first public display copy of the new Structure Plan. Just as he suspected, the area to the front of the industrial estate, including other frontages, had been zoned for future use as retail. He scanned down to the small print and muttered the words out loud: "To help build integrity and synergise the area, to alleviate traffic congestion from neighbouring town centres and to provide... blah blah..." *Bullshit. Typical Local Authority bullshit,* Rupert thought. *Well at least this time it's to our advantage, so what the hell.* But he was not feeling quite so calm and collected at the end of the week when he took a call from Graham Carpenter of Cauldron Domestics. Unsurprisingly, he'd been unable to get hold of Simions. He wanted to vent his spleen on someone – and that someone was Rupert.

"What the hell is going on?" he demanded.

"I'm sorry, Mr Carpenter, I don't understand. What do you mean?" Rupert replied in his most vague and pompous manner.

"Don't play games with me, young man You know bloody well what I mean. The site you paid for was zoned for Industrial, and now the plan comes out its re-zoned for retail. How did he do it, eh? Simions? Bribe a planner or three? I will raise hell over this. It's corruption, that's what it is. Corruption!"

"I should be very careful if I were you, Mr Carpenter. The slander laws are very actionable on such statements."

"Only, when they're proved false."

The line went dead and Rupert grinned. He called Simions, and explained what had happened word for word.

"Let him say what he wants. Hold your stance on legal action. It will go no further, and what's more there is no evidence. In the meantime, we shall be offering Section 52 agreements to pay for road improvements, more car parking and the usual legitimate planning hoo-ha."

"OK, but in the meantime do we press on with formal planning for the site?"

"Yes, and I want a full list of potential tenants, with expected rents and premiums payable, also funding. Speak to Hugo Curtiss and liaise with David Shingler on both matters; he must be kept informed."

"Of course," Rupert replied.

"Good. I'll wait to hear from you – and well done," Simions finished.

"Thank you, will do." *My God*, thought Rupert, *Praise from Simions. I've made it.*

The next few weeks proved Simions right: rumpus in the local paper, allegations and counter allegations, and finally the threat of legal action for slander, with a heavy duty writ served on Carpenter with Simions and the Council as joint appellants. Carpenter backed down and made a begrudging public apology. Formal planning applications were lodged, with the council's backing to approve. *It did not pay a man to fight Simions,* Rupert realised.

Chapter Five

London: Autumn 1987

The markets were becoming more and more heated. The Big Bang had taken place in the city just as everyone had said it would, revolutionising share dealing. More importantly to the individuals concerned, it doubled and even tripled individual bonuses in the City. London's business district teemed with Porsches and designer suits, and even the pessimists were feeling like the good times would never end. Yuppies endorsed the growth of consumerism, the trend towards owning things just for the sake of having them. Hedonistic days of champagne, parties, long lunches and ordering the most expensive wines on the menu because at those prices they were bound to be good. In the new film *Wall Street*, Gordon Gekko summarised the zeitgeist with two famous lines "Greed is good" and "Lunch is for wimps". It was a doctrine that everyone seemed to embody; power breakfasts were becoming the norm, with the constant striving to obtain inside information on trades, exchanges and futures. Anything to outrun the competition.

Prices for land and buildings were increasing at unprecedented rates, to the extent where it became possible to "turn" a site or buildings having only just exchanged contracts on a deal, often before completion, making a ten or twenty percent profit.

In this atmosphere of runaway inflation, it was easy for the unwary to get caught out and for the ruthless to exploit any loophole they could.

In the investment department, Mike Ringham was at the sharp end, learning new tricks every day, it seemed. His reputation as a deal junkie meant that he was enjoying himself immensely, and had come to love the cut and thrust of investment as the fastest moving of all the sectors.

Monday morning, after a particularly heavy weekend, he was having an early morning coffee with Rupert before meeting his friend Julian Charteris, who would be arriving in the next ten minutes or so along with a colleague.

"It's incredible," Mike said. "We're on a deal treadmill, with harder yields pushing the prices up, yet the stock just keeps on walking out the door. But what's worrying is that some of the old rules are falling by the wayside. I offered a deal, a forward funding, to United Assurance to buy a retail warehouse park. It's just got planning, but the developer only has an option on it; he doesn't actually own it, d'you see?"

"Yes," Rupert replied.

"So, once I'd passed them all the information, they went straight to the owners direct – without even referring to me

– offered them more money than the developer, bought the contract and broke the bloody option agreement!"

"UA did that? Bastards. I thought they were a respectable fund. I bet you were Mr Popular with the agents," Rupert laughed.

"Don't even go there. It was Julian and he went apeshit. But guess who the fund used to broker the deal? David Shingler. Watch that bugger," Mike warned. "That man has a lot of fingers in a lot of pies."

"Did you get your fee?"

"Surprisingly yes, but it took a call from Hugo Curtiss and old man Cowell himself to make them see the light. So what about you? Dealing?" Mike asked the time-honoured question.

"Yeah, I'm dealing," Rupert replied. It had become the mantra of the agents in this uncontrolled maelstrom of deals. Rupert felt it as much as Ringo did; the suits he wore were louder and his confidence was sky high. Nothing could stop them in this crazy bull market. "Luckily there's no danger of that happening on our scheme. We completed last week and now it's straight into planning and tenant demand, hence the meeting with Julian's colleague this morning. He won't broadcast it around the market, will he? Bearing in mind that he will have a lot of the funding information?" Rupert said, alarmed.

"A man from Halpern and Beams blasting something around the market? Perish the thought. There are still some standards you know," Mike mocked in his foppish way.

"Just be a little wary, is all. I hear his colleague from

Retail Warehousing has been seen with Ricky Barston on more than one occasion, and he *will* blast it around."

"Ricky Barston? Bugger gets everywhere. What do think? Reckon he's on a backhander to supply tenant information to get an introduction in?"

"It doesn't take much," Rupert said. "All they need is a good tenant line-up with a few rents thrown in," he finished cynically.

At that moment Julian Charteris arrived with his colleague in tow, who proved to be a man of about twenty five, medium height dressed in a grey, Spivvy-looking double breasted suit with wide lapels. *Like its owner*, Rupert mused to himself.

"This is Richard Lloyd, from our Retail Warehouse Department," Charteris said. "Should be able to help you with your tenant demand for the new scheme."

They shook hands, sat down and ordered more coffee. Rupert studied Lloyd more closely; he had fair skin with old pockmarks, sandy hair and sharp eyes.

"Where is the delightful Claire? I thought she was your retail warehouse specialist," Lloyd said in jest, but with an undertone that Rupert didn't like.

"Signing new tenants for the scheme. Just now she's in a legal meeting," he explained. "She's dealing, and at what a rate."

"Yeah, I hear she's been promoted on the back of her latest scheme."

Mike confirmed it, and they chatted about market developments and exchanged bits of gossip – particularly the recent events regarding UA, which they decided was a sign of the times.

"Well if they pull stunts like that, they can't expect agents to honour the one introduction at a time rule, and we'll all start pushing to multiple parties," Charteris concluded.

He was referring to the common practice that agents should only introduce one property to one party at a time. But as the clients became more devious, taking longer to return calls and trying to avoid paying introduction fees, the need to back up introductions with a second runner was becoming more and more pressing, despite being strictly against RICS rules. But as they all knew, the clients brought it upon themselves.

Their coffee finished, Lloyd invited Rupert back to his office to go over specifications for his client's retail operation and to look at some artists' impressions of other schemes where they were represented.

They walked into the reception area of Halpern and Beams – a rather clinical affair of sterile tiles, stainless steel furniture and white walls. *Looks like an Italian brothel,* Rupert thought. The lift took them to the second floor where there was an open plan area filled with padded dividers in bright primary colours that were becoming all the rage, sectioning off secretaries and agents into different compart-mentalised offices.

He walked through the notional corridors with Lloyd and gazing at the various people along the way; ever the agent trying to glean knowledge as he went and trying to read letters upside down on desks as he passed. His eyes rested on a secretary who seemed familiar for some reason. *Of course,* he thought, *Nana Mouskouri*. Straight black hair, thick-rimmed black glasses and those same three gold bangles. She half turned and their eyes met. He stopped, smiled and realised that she was wondering where she recognised him from, although she didn't return the smile.

"Hi. You were at CR weren't you, in retail?" he said.

"Um, yah, possibly on the temp round. Different week, different company, you know how it is." She shrugged her shoulders, gave him a half smile and went back to her computer. Rupert carried on following Lloyd to the glass box at the end of the floor reserved for meetings.

"Why her? She looks too much like Nana Mouskouri to me. See if you want some action," he nodded, "try Tracey over there. Great tits, fabulous arse, and she's just a girl who can't say no."

Prick, Rupert thought. But he played the game. "Yeah? Well if you put it like that...." he left the words hanging, "But there's something about Nana back there," he nodded in the temp's direction. "Can't figure it out, what's her name?"

"Liz Carmichael, works for that temping agency, started about two years ago with the catchy title. What is it now? Something about sex, no doubt..."

"Secs in the City?" Rupert guessed.

"Yes, great wordplay, yah?"

"Clever, but you still didn't remember it. Can't be that good." *Much like yourself.*

Lloyd shrugged and proceeded to talk about plans, specifications and deals, as if to cover his embarrassment. They talked for the next half an hour, getting closer to a mutually agreeable rental for the Hertfordshire retail warehouse development which had been tentatively named the Golden Triangle Park, marking its significance as the premier park for the area. *Sounds like far eastern brothel this time*, Rupert thought. Provisional terms thrashed out, Rupert shook hands with Lloyd, liking him no more than when they had met. He refused Lloyd's offer to show him out and made his way back through the divided workspaces to the lift. On his way, he made sure he passed Nana Mouskouri's desk, but she wasn't there. He got to the lift and found to his surprise that she too was on her way out and waiting by the doors.

"We'll have to stop meeting like this," Rupert said.

Her half-smile said 'God is that the best you can do'. At that moment the doors opened and they both stepped into the empty lift. The silence was embarrassing and he was desperately trying for a line.

"OK, not the most original line under the sun," he said, deciding to throw himself on her mercy. "But I keep seeing you around the West End, which I find tantalising and deeply frustrating."

She raised an eyebrow, amused at his embarrassment, inviting him to continue.

"Oh come on," he pleaded. "Don't make it so hard. Say something, even if it's only piss off!"

At that point she giggled. It was a lovely, mellifluous sound, which allowed Rupert to smile and relax.

"There. That's better, at least I made you laugh. So, presuming upon the acquaintance of two whole minutes, can I ask you to dinner?"

"You sound like a character from a Georgette Heyer

novel. It marks you out from all the other braying animals around here – and for that alone, I'll accept," she replied in a mocking tone. When she smiled her face changed, the beauty behind the façade shone through.

"Excellent. How about Friday? Say 7.30, I'll pick you up from wherever you live?"

"Alright, but let's meet in town. Here's my number," she produced a pen and scribbled her number on a piece of paper which she found in her handbag. "Call me first, yah?" her insecurity shone through for a brief moment.

"After all this effort?" he mocked, "Damn right I will."

The lift discharged them at reception and they walked out into the street. Rupert waved farewell and walked jauntily back to CR's offices. *Way to go, Rupes*, he thought. He felt good. A rocky start but a good finish. Hopefully the number was correct.

The next few days moved slowly, but the lettings for Golden Triangle Park continued unabated, much to Claire's satisfaction. The scheme was oversubscribed, and she told Rupert that it allowed her to set premiums over the base rents, which the funders loved. The Triangle was becoming a potentially hot property for investors and tenants alike.

Friday night came around and Rupert found himself anticipating it eagerly, all thoughts of Kate dismissed from his mind. They had drifted further apart during the course of the year, and in that peculiarly British way they had broken up without ever really talking about it.

He had arranged to meet Liz in Covent Garden. She was a North London girl from Hampstead, and Covent Garden was easy for both of them. They had arranged to meet at the western end of the galleried open area. With numerous restaurants and speciality shops, it was frequently used by budding opera singers who were either resting or waiting for their big break. Such was the case now. A pretty buxom blonde with a round and jolly face was singing beautifully and encouraging the early evening crowd to join her for the chorus of *Carmen*. She had a tape machine by her side and an assistant moving through the crowd soliciting offerings and selling cassettes of her work, which, Rupert thought, would be brilliant if her live singing was anything to go by.

It was a beautiful, balmy evening. He had arrived ten minutes early to pick up the ambience and because he genuinely liked Covent Garden. Despite being touristy and rather passé, he loved its vibrancy and found it more genuine than most other popular haunts.

He had managed to shoot home and change into a more casual attire – a jacket, an open-necked shirt, trousers and tasselled loafers. He gazed at his reflection in a shop window and was satisfied with what he saw. Rupert became so engrossed in the singing that he forgot the time until at ten past eight, when an arm snaked in front of him, complete with three gold bangles. He inhaled a hint of Chanel No. 5 and turned to smile at her.

"Sorry I'm late," she said lightly, "the tube was hell."

Neither she nor Rupert were worried. It was all part of the game as far as they were concerned – the rules unspoken but understood. When he saw her, his jaw dropped and for a moment he forgot to breathe. His face must have been a picture because she erupted into laughter at his expression.

Gone were the Nana Mouskouri glasses. Her cheek

bones were heightened and sharp, but the most dramatic change was her hair. It was no longer straight and black. It was short and cropped in a funky, highlighted style that accentuated her eyes. Shocking pink lipstick drew his eyes down to a turquoise sheath of shot silk that set off her slender figure to brilliant effect.

"Wow!" was all he could manage. "But the glasses, your hair...?" He left the statement hanging.

"Contacts and a wig," she laughed. "I got fed up with being chatted up by all the wide boys, so I toned myself down a bit. I knew it would put them off. It's the first test," she chided.

"Well, I obviously passed with flying colours, and thank God I did," he said, still taken aback by the chameleon-like transformation.

They walked through the crowded piazza with its street performers, throngs of tourists and theatre goers. Looking in the windows of the small boutique shops as they passed, they made their way in the direction of the opera house and a small restaurant where Rupert had booked a table. They arrived outside a glass fronted building on two levels. The upper level opened out onto a partially covered decking area, which allowed the gentle autumn breeze to waft through, cooling the humid evening.

They were shown to a table bathed in sunlight over-looking the old Covent Garden market below; it was a delightful setting.

"This is sublime," Liz remarked. "I love Covent Garden with all its bustle and hum. Just to sit and people-watch is enough, but up here you're away from it all and yet still a part of it. It's truly lovely, thank you."

"My pleasure. It is my favourite part of London, especially with the opera house so close. Do you like opera?"

"Oh yah, very much. Not the terribly heavy stuff – I mean, I couldn't sit through twelve hours of Wagner, but I love *Rigoletto*. I could watch it again and again," she enthused.

Their drinks arrived; gin and tonic and a glass of Chardonnay, which they sipped appreciatively and carried on an easy conversation over the next ten minutes while making their choices from the menu that offered a fine eclectic mix of seafood with an oriental bias for the main courses.

"I would love the tiger prawns, but I'm not brave enough to eat them in front of someone I've only just met," she laughed.

"Don't worry, I'll send you the dry cleaning bill once I've shaken the worst of it off."

They both laughed as they made their choices and settled into an easy and relaxed conversation that seemed to flow without either of them having to try too hard. They had a lot in common and the evening went well. They finished their final course and Liz flicked open a packet of Marlborough Lights, offering one to Rupert.

"I don't as rule. Trying to keep off them, but tonight I think I'll join you."

He took a cigarette from the proffered packet and proceeded to light them both before handing the lighter back to Liz. They relaxed back in their seats.

"So," Liz began. "My wig didn't put you off, so why did you ask me out?" she fished, with a self-mocking smile.

"I thought you were a secret agent stealing industrial secrets, and I rather fancied becoming involved in high espionage," he finished with a grin.

For a brief moment her face clouded over with a frown, but it vanished before Rupert could comment.

"So what did you call me; what was your name for me I mean? Was I Moneypenny or 007?" she laughed the moment off.

"Nothing so exotic I'm afraid. Nana Mouskouri or Gold Bangles."

She glanced down at her wrist and giggled.

"I think I prefer that to Nana Mouskouri. Evidently I remind everyone of her."

They drifted around backgrounds and found they had something else in common. "You were at Dean Close? Amazing! I was at Cheltenham Ladies, just across the other side of town. You never know, we may have passed each other on The Prom or Montpellier."

The declaration somehow brought them closer together and they compared notes on Cheltenham.

Rupert paid the bill and they sauntered back through the Piazza in the warm evening air. As they walked to the Strand he reached out and took her hand. She smiled and tucked her arm into his as they walked. The evening finished well; he kissed her lightly on the cheek as they arrived at the taxi rank.

"Thank you for a lovely evening. The meal was delicious."

"And the company?" he queried.

"Stop fishing," she chided him. "But not bad, not bad."

She smiled at him. A broad and genuine smile this time, not the insipid half-smile she'd offered him at the office. She slipped into the taxi and waved goodbye. Rupert grinned to himself and lifted a hand as the taxi moved off.

Chapter Six

October 1987 brought some of the worst storms in living memory. The hurricane force winds that swept through the capital caused havoc. Roofs were pulled off houses, office blocks had their windows shattered, cars were thrown aside and trees were uprooted. London had never experienced weather like it. There were many fatalities and everyone suffered. But while insurance claims were high, it only served to fuel the bottomless greed of the property markets. After the recovery, in the aftermath of the storm, renewed confidence pulled the capital together, ever onwards and upwards, with inflation raging and capital values rising.

Everyone wanted to buy a slice of the cake and own property – particularly commercial property.

MAS developments was no exception. The company made some extraordinarily good purchases, and it seemed that Paul Simions could do no wrong. He was the new golden boy, buying well and consistently.

Rupert picked up a copy of the Estates Gazette, and

there in the news section was a picture of a grinning Simions standing next to a scale model of the Golden Triangle retail park above a headline claiming that that the scheme was three times oversubscribed by prospective tenants. It was an incredible piece of marketing which was attracting all kinds of speculative bids from funding sources. Rupert realised that they were all keen to acquire a foothold the jewel of retail parks.

Mike Ringham called, interrupting Rupert's thoughts.

"Rupes, see your scheme's hit the big time. Simions'll be offering you a job next. You'll be leaving us poor agents behind," he mocked.

"Hah, how about you? Dealing?"

"Yah, three in lawyers, one to follow."

"Investment surveyors get an easy life," Rupert joked.

When they'd finished speaking, he thought more about Mike's opening shot. Jump the fence? Become a principal? Would he like that? He had never considered it before. It would be a powerful move, but working for Simions? He shook his head.

The following day he took a call from David Shingler inviting him to a meeting at his offices to discuss the Triangle scheme and associated issues.

"Shall I bring Hugo Curtiss along for the funding?" Rupert asked.

"No, I don't think that will be necessary. Just peripheral issues really," Shingler added enigmatically. They set the meeting up for the following day, and Rupert, while heeding Tom Lovich's advice, failed to see how he could have manipulated the location and prevented the meeting from taking place at CR's offices.

Rupert took the Underground to midtown, that no-man's land between the City and the West End which housed a variety of different businesses and could possibly only be called home to Fleet Street, the buzzing hive of the press. He came off the tube at Holborn, walked north towards the offices of Shingler Cariss in accordance with the directions he had been given.

When he arrived, he was surprised and shocked at how entirely unprepossessing the building was. It was neither Old Money, as so many west end offices were, or smart contemporary. Instead it was a drab concrete affair that looked like it had been constructed in the sixties. It was, in short, grimy and depressing.

Rupert entered the building through glass doors to a reception area that was perfunctory in style and was directed to the second floor by a security guard.

The offices upstairs were a little better; very minimalist and still lacking in atmosphere, although the receptionist was pleasant enough and offered him coffee, inviting him to sit and wait for Shingler who was just finishing a telephone call. *Here we go*, Rupert thought, *the games have started. Let's see how long he keeps me waiting.* Ten minutes was his guess. The door opened fifteen minutes later and Shingler walked out.

"Sorry about that," he said without even pretending to sound sincere. "Just had to finish a call to a very expensive QC. David Shingler."

Rupert shook hands, noticing that Shingler had that annoying little habit of people who always try to gain the upper hand. He offered his hand almost palm down as if he was half expecting its recipient to bow and kiss the back of it. The idea was obviously to put the other person at a disadvantage, and Rupert countered the manoeuvre by taking Shingler's hand firmly, twisting the wrist to the vertical and pumping Shingler's hand in an unnecessarily hard grip. He was rewarded by a slight wince of pain in Shingler's face.

"Come on through to the office," Shingler gestured towards the open door.

Rupert followed him into a comfortably furnished and immaculately tidy office, which was at odds with the rest of the building and décor. *Always be wary of a man with a tidy desk,* he thought. Rupert studied the man before him. Shingler was in his thirties, about six feet tall, medium built, with blond hair framing a good looking face that was well preserved, tanned by the elements and perhaps topped off by a sunbed.

That explained the pictures of yachts on the walls and the golfing photos, Rupert thought. *New money hobbies of a social climber who wanted everyone to know how much he was earning. It went rather well with the gold Rolex on the left wrist and the chunky gold identity bracelet on the right.* When he spoke, his voice was over-modulated. Like someone who was pretending to be something he was not, or running from a past he'd sooner forget about. He was a good match for Simions, Rupert thought.

Shingler sat himself down behind his over-large desk and faced Rupert across the expanse of polished leather and wood.

"Down to business." There were no perfunctory

niceties, no 'thanks for coming over', just straight to it. Rupert took an instant dislike to the man and his arrogant attitude. "We need to progress this scheme so that we're in a better position to fund it. What's the rent roll to date and the full tenant line up? I just need these to see if we're batting from the same hymn sheet," he finished.

Rupert winced at the mixed metaphor, but he still felt disadvantaged, as Lovich had warned he would. Shingler was a bully. There was a sense that he was being made to feel small, with no ground given to move in and no option but to obey. Shingler was a man with shortcomings to make up for, be they class, education or something deeper, more pathological. The desk was a useful prop for his ego. Rupert produced the papers from the open brief case on his lap and prepared to present them. Shingler held up a hand to stop him.

"That won't be necessary. Just let me look for myself." He extended his hand palm upwards, beckoning with his fingers. Rupert leaned forward and prepared to hand the papers over, but as he did so his finger and thumb slipped together in a seemingly accidental gesture and the papers fell, scattering themselves at his feet.

"Damn, stupidly clumsy of me," he said.

The look on Shingler's face was one of smug superiority. He tutted and sighed. Rupert bent over, putting the open briefcase on the floor in front of the desk, and proceeded to collect the papers. As he did so he shuffled them, dropping two sheets into the back pocket of the lid with a clever sleight of hand. He passed the remaining papers across to Shingler with a muttered apology, his eyes downcast in apparent embarrassment. Shingler skimmed through the summaries to the core of the information and frowned, looking back and forth from one page to the next.

"There are two pages missing on rents and areas for the second phase. Where are they?" he demanded. He got up and came around his desk to look on the floor with Rupert, who was making a good show of scrabbling around in a futile search.

"They don't appear to be here, I'm afraid."

"Check in your briefcase again," Shingler ordered, pointing at it.

A change came over Rupert. He stood, shot his cuffs and gave Shingler a level stare before resuming his seat, crossing one leg over the opposite knee and leaning back. "Right, *Mister* Shingler," he said. "Let's get a few things straight right from the start, shall we? This meeting was supposed to be a meeting of minds, not a clash of personalities. I don't like your tone and I don't like your attitude. The missing pages are probably with Claire. She will have had them when I copied the file."

Shingler was unabashed. "Call her, then. Get them faxed over," he retorted. He leaned forwards, "Please," he added sarcastically. Rupert dug himself in, determined not to pushed around by this little shit. He was about to lose his temper and tell Shingler to go fuck himself, but then he realised that a mild and diffident attitude would probably annoy him more. It was the route he chose.

"No can do. She is out at a tenant meeting until after lunch. I'll get them sent over then and–"

"That's all very well," Shingler interrupted. "But we need them now, not later."

"Why, what's the hurry?"

Shingler scowled and shrugged.

"Well, it can't be helped either way," Rupert said jauntily. "What else did you want to discuss? What about the funding?"

"It's too soon to talk about that yet. In any case, Mr Simions may have other ideas," he commented cryptically.

The meeting was clearly at an end, and Rupert felt he had scored some small triumph, in the power contest that had been played out across Shingler's desk. More worrying was the last remark. *What was he alluding to*? he thought. They shook hands with tight lipped smiles that didn't reach their eyes, both realising that each of them, in his own way, had conceded points to the other. This time, Rupert noticed, the hand proffered for shaking was vertical not held at some obscure angle.

As he left the office, he continued to mull over the last words uttered and saw them as a veiled threat – but a threat of what, exactly?

After the door closed, Shingler steepled his fingers, a deep frown creasing his forehead. *We shall have to do something about that arrogant little bastard*, he thought to himself. *Who does he think he is?* He considered how else he could obtain the necessary information to carry out his plans. After a few seconds, he smiled. It was not a pleasant smile. It was the kind of smile a shark offers at it rolls onto its back in those last few moments before pulling its victim beneath the surface. Shingler picked up the telephone and dialled.

"Simions."

"It's David. I think we may have a problem developing. At this stage we can obtain information by other means, but Mr Brett may need a reminder about the pecking order around here. He may need sorting out with more extreme prejudice at some stage," he finished.

"Maybe so, but he is doing good work, and I can't give you the information without causing suspicion. It has to come from him directly. You're both big boys. If you want to squabble, fuck off outside and do it the playground. In the meantime, come to some kind of accommodation with the man. We might well bring him onside in due course: he is a dealer and he's learning fast."

Shingler heard the connection terminate. He put the telephone down carefully and picked up a glass paperweight from his desk, a sphere of transparent glass with a delicate strand of red coral at its core. He weighed it in his hand, then grimaced and hurled it at the painted brickwork of his office wall, where it shattered into a thousand pieces. *Mr Brett, you have no idea just who the fuck you're dealing with*, he thought to himself. He toggled the intercom. "Alice? Get in here. Bring a dustpan and brush."

When Rupert returned to CR, he discovered that Claire was indeed out, and that her secretary had left her a note asking her to call David Shingler on her return. Rupert wrote a note to the effect that she was not to speak to Shingler under any circumstances until she'd spoken to him first.

Later that afternoon Claire appeared at his door.

"Rupert? what's with all the cloak and dagger stuff? What gives?"

"Shingler. I met him at his office earlier; jumped up little arsehole!"

Rupert proceeded to give Claire a detailed account of the meeting.

"What's he up to?" she mused, amazed at Rupert's attitude and realising just how much he had changed since he had been at CR. The West End dealer was taking over.

"I don't know, but I think we ought to alert Hugo, especially as it might affect the funding."

They went down to the investment department and once again Rupert relayed the events of the morning.

"I know exactly what he's up to," Hugo Curtiss commented. "He wants to – what's your phrase? – whang it around the market as a funding opportunity, cut us out and keep control of the investment – with or without Simions' permission. Do not, under any circumstances, give him this last piece of information. Stall him, give him any excuse, but stall it for at least a week. Threaten to talk to Simions if you have to. If Shingler's got any sense, he'll be wary of crossing him, at least."

They discussed various aspects of the deal for the next few minutes before leaving to consider their delaying tactics.

Two days later, Rupert and Claire met up for coffee at the end of Grosvenor Street. Claire was in a foul mood.

"Why so glum?" he asked.

"Bloody secretaries. Tracey was fine yesterday, now she's called in sick and I've got a damn temp. Who is useless. I have to explain everything twice. At least she's bright enough to ask questions, but just when I need this letting report typed."

"It's not Nana Mouskouri, is it?" he asked.

"Ah, the elusive Nana Mouskouri. When are we going to meet her?"

"When I finally do," he replied.

"What do you mean?"

"Oh, I don't know. We've had a handful of dates. All great. Good conversation, but I'm getting nowhere."

"What, you're not getting your leg over?" she interrupted, grinning.

"No. Well, yes, but not so much in the physical sense. I can't seem to get close to her at a personal level. It's like a wall comes down just when I've got the winning post in sight."

"Well we've all been there on both sides of the fence, but too much baggage is a real problem. You can't keep bashing your head against a brick wall, God alone knows you're sensitive enough to be sympathetic to the right overtures." She looked at him meaningfully. Rupert smiled across at her and met the concerned gaze of someone who genuinely cared for him.

"Oh stuff it," he finished. "So if it's not Liz you've got working for you, who is it?"

"Some dizzy blonde called Sophie. Same agency, though. Secs in the City. Clever. I like that name, it sticks in your head."

"Yes, though Richard Lloyd didn't remember it. Strange, that."

"That guy's an idiot. He's always undressing me with his eyes. Ugh, he's revolting." She gave a little shrug.

"Come on, let's away to the office and see how your report is getting on."

They paid for the coffee and left, walking along Grosvenor Street, watching Christmas lights and decorations being put up in windows.

"Soon be that time of the year again. What are you up to over the break?"

"Gloucestershire for Christmas with the wrinklies, then back for a New Year's bash with Angus at some club or other. You?"

"Depends on the next forty-eight hours really, and how things pan out with Liz this weekend. We've got dinner this Saturday and I'm going to take your advice: make or break."

She looked across at him quizzically.

"Don't get hurt, Rupes," she said with compassion, putting a tentative hand on his shoulder. He smiled back at her.

"I'll try not to," he replied, although his mind was elsewhere, not wanting to consider the possibility that it could all go wrong. He liked the ladies, but was not a womaniser like Angus. He was not immune to the pull of the heart.

When they returned to the office, Claire found to her surprise that given the break of a couple of hours the temp had, despite being very slow and having hardly achieved anything of substance, finally got the message and understood fully what was required. Better still, Tracey had telephoned to say she was making a recovery and would be back in the office by the end of the week.

The following day saw the final compilation of the report, and Claire left the office in good spirits on Friday, safe in the knowledge that everything would be ready for the meeting at MAS's offices the following week.

She was looking forward to a good weekend, starting with a dinner party at Mike's with Jemma. As she walked to the tube station, she mused over the idea that it wouldn't be long before an engagement was announced. Despite looking upon Mike with the almost proprietorial concern of an elder sister, she approved of Jemma, who was no gold digger and appeared to have a genuine affection for him. Mike, for his part, appeared smitten for the first time in his life. After many romances and affairs and a trail of broken-hearted Sloane Rangers abandoned in his wake, things finally looked like they were falling into place for Ringo. In contrast, Claire considered her position with Angus. There were few parallels. Theirs was a relationship based upon the chase, the ego, mutual satisfaction and pleasure, and they both knew it. For all that, they both enjoyed exploring those hollow virtues to the full, and the attraction was becoming much more than a passing fling.

Claire was beginning to form a much stronger attachment to Angus than she had first anticipated, and her general policy of letting no one too close was being tested to the limit. A sometimes selfish girl, who realised and was comfortable with her attraction to the opposite sex, Claire had always – with the possible exception of Rupert – been able to walk away intact and fall back upon her driving ambition and love of sports. She was equally at home in male and female company, a rare attribute for one so attractive to the opposite sex, and this helped her to emerge gracefully from all manner of potentially tempestuous relationships.

Leaving the office some time earlier, Rupert was looking forward to the weekend with some trepidation, and was only sorry that he would not be able to attend Mike's dinner party, to which he too had been invited. He also sensed an auspicious occasion in Mike's life, but was too intent on making a success of his relationship with Liz to risk jeopardising it for an invitation to dinner, much to Mike's chagrin.

The following evening Rupert had arranged to pick Liz up at her apartment somewhere in Hampstead. She had given him the address, but only being used to the environs of Knightsbridge and the West End he got lost and was consequently late. When he arrived, he saw a large mansion block of typical 1930s Art Deco design, divided up into a large number of flats, their lights blazing like the Marie Celeste. The spacious enclosed gardens and car parking areas were clearly lit and he pulled up in an area marked VISITORS, locked the car and approached the main entrance.

He buzzed the intercom and awaited a response.

"Yes?" Liz's voice emerged from the intercom.

"It's Rupert. Sorry I'm late."

"I'll forgive you, just this once. I'll be straight down."

The intercom clicked off. So, thought Rupert, I still don't get to see her lair. Five minutes later she appeared through the glass doors.

"Wow, you look gorgeous!" he exclaimed. She was dressed in a simple but extremely elegant black dress that only the best designer of *haute couture* could create. A single string of pearls was strung around her neck, her mascara was heavy and her hair was elegant, her lashes dark and long. She twirled for him in mock elegance, smiling and striking a model pose with one leg extended.

He grinned in response and moved forward to kiss her, enveloping himself in a cloud of perfume that seduced his senses still further. He motioned her towards his company car, a benefit that came with his recent promotion to Senior Surveyor. It was a VW Scirocco GTX hatchback, with clean, racy lines.

"How is the new beast going?" she asked, mocking him slightly with her head inclined on one side in an endearing manner, at the same time running her hand gently and sexily along the bodywork. He was seduced by both her smile and her attitude.

"Wonderful, goes like a dream and the acceleration is incredible."

"Boys' toys," she said as he opened the door for her.

They accelerated off at a pace to a smart part of Hampstead and a Chinese restaurant of her choosing, where she had reserved a table. The restaurant was a far cry from the usual run of the mill standard fare. The décor was stark white, with modern black furniture and an atmosphere of frenetic activity, with waiters bustling around busily, showing off their art. They were shown to a corner table with a good view of the restaurant, and Liz was clearly a well-recognised regular, enjoying a welcoming smile from the head waiter.

"Miss Lizzy, it is good to see you again." The man bowed and gestured to the seats.

"Thank you, Ying, it's good to be back." She smiled.

They ordered, and the food was excellent and beautifully presented. In a relaxed atmosphere they flirted, and Rupert studiously avoided talking about work or related matters which normally caused her to clam up and become tense.

Over coffee, she lit her first cigarette of the evening, having subconsciously cut down since she had known Rupert. Blowing the smoke in a gentle stream through pursed lips, she toyed with her coffee cup and smiled gently across at him, half preoccupied, as though considering something yet not giving the subject her full attention.

"Penny for them?" he said. "No, I don't want to know. My sister always said it was the kiss of death to ask any girl what she was thinking, and that I'd never get a truthful answer anyway." He grinned.

"I like your sister already, and I haven't even met her yet," she laughed. "Is she in Town? Don't tell me she's a surveyor too?"

"No way. She wants to be a marine biologist. Saving the planet is the up and coming thing, evidently. Soon we're all going to want to be doing it, so she says. She is on her gap year at the moment out in the Florida Keys, taking samples of the lesser spotted great crested tiger plankton or something, I don't know. Sounds like a euphemism for a skive to me, but there we are."

"We all need saving in one form or another," she said enigmatically.

Determined not to let the conversation take on a morbid note, Rupert immediately responded flippantly.

"Ah yes, let's all hug a whale and save a tree – or is it the other way round? Anyway if I promise to do my best Flipper impersonation will you hug me later?"

"You're crazy, but yes, hugging a dolphin is definitely a possibility."

They finished their coffee, Rupert paid the bill and they sauntered, relaxed, arm in arm to his car. He drove slowly to her apartment block and pulled up outside, a question mark hanging in the air between them.

"Nightcap?" she said finally, breaking the tension.

"That would be lovely," he said.

They left the car, moved into the glazed communal entrance where they were greeted with a blast of warm air. They entered the lift holding hands and he kissed her gently on the lips as the doors closed. She smiled back at him, her eyes filled with warmth. The lift stopped at the third floor and they stepped out into a T-shaped landing with the flats feeding off the communal areas. She moved forward and opened the front door to her flat, which led into a small hallway and some internal stairs that went up to the main area. It was tastefully furnished, mostly from Habitat, he guessed. Bright pastel colours and bold prints on the curtains, oriental rugs hanging from two walls and laid haphazardly on the carpets. It was a flat of contrasts, aptly reflecting the personality of its owner. She went into the kitchen and filled the kettle.

"Coffee?" she asked.

"Please."

"What else would you like? No, not that," she chided lasciviously from under half closed lids.

"I have no idea what you mean," he responded innocently. "Single Malt, if you have it."

"Smooth idea. In the cupboard above, to your left."

Rupert reached up and removed two glasses and the bottle of scotch, from which he poured two generous measures.

They left the kitchen and moved to the living room. He sat on the sofa while she put on an LP on the turntable and lifted the stylus arm to the record. Sade's melodious voice floated into the room. Liz lit a cigarette and blew the smoke gently from her lips. The light from the table lamps caught her profile, casting half her face into gentle shadow.

"You have to be the sexiest person ever to smoke a cigarette," he said.

She laughed huskily and turned to face him. He kissed her gently. Her mouth opened in response, tongue probing gently at first and then more aggressively. They broke apart briefly.

"I'll be back in a minute," she whispered, laying the cigarette down and rising from the sofa.

She left the room and returned minutes later appearing in the doorway, half backlit by the landing light. Rupert could not see her properly until she entered the room and when she did his throat went dry. She had shed the black dress and stood only in a black silk teddy and stockings, looking demure and irresistibly provocative at the same time.

"Well?" she said.

Rupert stood and stepped in front of her, smelling her scent and cupping a hard-nippled breast with his right hand while kissing her hard on the lips. She responded in kind, running her hand into his hair and forcing herself against him. He felt the heat of her body through the silk as she thrust herself forward, rotating her hips against his groin. She virtually ripped his shirt off, while he struggled out of the rest of his clothes and she sank to the floor, kissing him all the way down his body and making him moan in ecstasy. Her lips played with him until finally he could stand it no longer and he too dropped to the floor. She pushed him gently onto his back, sat astride him and pinned his arms to the floor, kissing him hard on the mouth, moaning as her actions became ever more frenetic and aggressive.

She reached down between her legs, pulling aside the crotch of her silk teddy and used her fingers to position him so that she could slide down onto him, causing them both to gasp. She pinned his arms and rode him hard, her face an almost manic mask of intent, as though she were trying to exorcise something. She became more frenzied, writhing and panting, and suddenly Rupert knew that something was wrong.

"No," he cried. "Not like this, no!" He held her still and moved from under her, catching her as she fell sideways. She looked at him as if in a trance and then crumpled, sagging into his arms.

"What's wrong?" she mumbled.

"Everything," he said gently. "Be yourself. You've nothing to prove to me."

He scooped her up in his arms and carried her through to the bedroom, laying her gently onto the bed. They lay together in each other's arms in the half light. Rupert kissed her gently, running his fingers through her hair. When they were ready, they made love, guiding each other like experienced lovers with pleasure and warmth until they climaxed together in harmony, pleasing themselves as much as each other. Rupert went to stroke her face, and when he realised it was wet, he pulled her to him and stroked her hair. She relaxed in his arms, her breathing gradually subsiding into a gentle rhythm.

He pondered her reaction and the events of the last few weeks, which seemed to be as big a mystery as ever. His last conscious thought before he finally succumbed to sleep was that she must have been deeply hurt in the past, but in what way, shape or form was unclear.

Chapter Seven

The New Year came in, and the positive vibe from the old year prevailed. Optimism in 1988 was still the premise by which everyone was living. The chattering classes talked of nothing more than how much their properties had risen in value over the last few months, sometimes even weeks, without realising that property values were a dangerous barometer of overconfidence.

Into this maelstrom of financial volatility, the Chancellor slipped the final ingredient necessary to tip the balance into economic meltdown. He declared in advance that from October of that year, dual tax relief on mortgages relating to property owned by two or more people would be abolished, but that all mortgages (and therefore properties) bought before the October cut-off date would continue to benefit from the existing provisions. This incredible piece of legislation gave everyone a few months' notice to benefit from what in real terms amounted to a continued 25% tax benefit.

The property markets, already fuelled by the Big Bang

and huge City bonuses, went berserk, with people clamouring to get themselves onto the already highly inflated property ladder before the tax benefits of doing so disappeared forever.

The commercial markets, always sensitive to the economy as a whole, benefited from this further injection of energy and surged forwards, with more development being carried out and new sites sought more desperately than ever.

At the forefront, as always, was MAS, with Simions leading a charmed life in his quest for new opportunities. The Estates Gazette was always featuring a news item on his latest bid or acquisition, along with the breathless declaration that once more he had beaten his rivals to the spoils.

Rupert's relationship with Simions continued to grow, despite Rupert's personal misgivings regarding the man's morals and his way of doing business. He and Claire had succeeded in completing the letting of the Golden Triangle retail development to various tenants, and the scheme was about to be put out for funding by the institutions at a total cost of some twenty million pounds, representing a huge profit once the funding had come in. But not everything always runs true to plan, even for Simions, and on Tuesday morning Rupert received the sort of call that every agent dreads.

"Rupert? What the bloody hell's happening to my site?" Simions demanded. He wasn't shouting; he never did. He just emphasised the latent menace in his voice.

"What do you mean?" Rupert asked.

"You're my agent, you should know. What am I paying

you for?" Simions almost whispered. "I have just been asked if I'd be interested in buying my own fucking site."

"What? Who the hell by?" Rupert asked. *This could not be happening,* he thought, *what a bloody nightmare.*

"Some runner on the phone this morning. It'll be all over the West End by lunchtime. Find out who's punting it and end the bastard. I don't need to tell you what a mockery this will make of the funding package." The line went dead.

Oh great, Rupert thought, *fan-fucking-tastic, just what we need, to lose control of it at this stage.* He telephoned Claire straight away, who was annoyed and amazed in equal doses. His next calls were to Tom Lovich and Hugo Curtiss in the Investment Department, who were equally pissed off, but more sanguine. Age and experience gave them the advantage, having encountered this sort of situation before. By lunchtime they had found the source of the information leak and the identity of the runner who was offering the site for sale around the market without any instructions, relying on a spurious price tag and the hope of a fee. An internal meeting took place in CR's offices at midday between Rupert, Claire, Lovich and Hugo Curtiss.

"Ricky bloody Barston, it would have to be him," Curtiss fumed.

"But what I don't see," Rupert queried, "Is how he got enough information on rents and tenants to run it around the market."

"Simple really. The bugger picks up a letting brochure and a site plan, gets the lowdown on two or three tenants who may have been reported as interested in the scheme. All he's got to do then is guess the rest of the rents, assume 25 year FRI leases and estimate a price from there. Not rocket science," Curtiss finished angrily.

"But this covering letter of introduction has more detail than that," Rupert said, waving the round robin letter. "Look, it details too many specifics for guesstimation alone. My money says Shingler had a hand in this."

"Shingler?" The other three cried in unison with puzzled expressions on their faces.

"Why him? What motive could he have for screwing up the deal?" Claire demanded.

"When I met with him at his offices, he was more than keen to get a full tenant line up with rents and all the information, to the extent that he was furious when I refused to give them to him." Rupert related the full events of that meeting, and they all remembered the sketchy details from the time it happened.

"Hugo thought Shingler was after the funding, but I think he's gone a stage further. He wants to sell the site through the back door, get all the letting fees *and* the funding when the purchaser buys it."

"No, he would never get away with it. Simions would have his bollocks for breakfast."

"One, Shingler would deny it and inveigle his way back in, and two, have you ever known Simions turn down a deal when there was a huge profit involved? No, exactly. I think this was his plan all along – and I think he maybe has some kind of hold over Simions."

"Possibly his plan, yes," Lovich conceded, "But I don't buy that he has some hold over him. But the rest stacks up, so we have got to put the lid on this before Barston flogs the lot and laughs in our faces on his way to the bank."

Rupert remained to be convinced, but he was learning all the devious tricks and getting to know how to think like his enemy. The meeting ended and they all went back to their separate offices to carry out a damage limitation exercise. But for the rest of the day, Simions remained incommunicado, boding ill for Rupert and his colleagues. By close of business they had still not heard from him.

The next day they were summoned to a meeting at MAS's offices, and all four arrived at the front door on Manchester Square at the appointed hour. They were shown through to the meeting room on the first floor, where not unsurprisingly they found Shingler in attendance. Curt greetings were exchanged and they got down to business straight away, with Simions opening the proceedings.

"What we have here is a cock up," he opined. "I feel badly exposed by all this. Not to mention foolish – and more importantly I stand to lose a great deal of credibility."

Rupert noted that at no time did Simions mention financial loss, which in a perverse sort of way boded ill for what was to happen next. He waved down the proposed response from Rupert with a dismissive hand movement.

"It doesn't matter what has happened. What is more important is how I salvage my position and reputation from the ruins of this exposure."

Rupert was aware of Simions' use of the personal pronoun, and prepared himself for the worst.

"The only positive benefit I can see from this farce is that it has shown me just how valuable my site is. I have been offered, albeit spuriously, roughly three times what I paid for the site through the dubious channels of Ricky Barston and the saving graces of David Shingler here." He gestured in Shingler's direction, and Shingler smirked at Rupert and his colleagues. "Therefore, in order to save face and secure a large profit, I have decided to accept the offer."

The words hit the CR team hard and confirmed Rupert's worst fears. He realised that Shingler had set them all up, but everyone except Rupert refused to consider that Shingler might have forced Simions' hand in the matter.

"That is all very well and good," Hugo Curtiss responded. "And I'm sorry this particular initiative has to end in this way, but where does it leave us with regard to the funding and letting fees? Claire especially has put in a lot of work into this with agreements to lease for all the parties tied up and the whole scheme let."

"*Provisionally* let," Simions corrected him. "Those agreements to lease will be worthless once the scheme has been sold and the new owners take over the lettings. However, I do of course appreciate all your efforts. and you will be looked after in terms of some form of abortive fee structure," he offered with a magnanimous gesture of his hand.

All four of them knew immediately that "looked after" meant they were going to be screwed. And there was not a thing they could do about it, except to accept the offer in good grace or never work with Simions again. He was too powerful for that, and they all knew it. The meeting came to an end with Simions refusing to reveal the name of the purchaser, except to say that it was a fund.

They aired their frustrations as they left the building.

"What really pisses me off is Shingler. That smug, odious little shit is going to get all the fees while we pick up the crumbs from his table," Rupert said.

"I know, especially all the letting fees," Claire agreed. "Is there no way we can do anything about that, Hugo?"

"We can fight it in court, in which case, win or lose we'll never do business with Simions again, or we can appeal to his better nature, which would be pissing in the wind because the bastard doesn't have one."

"Do you know the best thing we can do?" Tom Lovich commented. "And don't shout me down before you hear me out. I think the best thing we can do is to find him a new deal and quickly; while the subtle discussions over fees are still open to debate."

"What?" Claire said. "But why, when he's just shafted us? What's to stop the devious bastard doing exactly the same thing all over again?"

"Tell us what you really think, Claire," Tom retorted sarcastically, earning him a grimace from Claire. "Suing him is counterproductive and futile, if we want to do business with him again. So let's find him a new deal and get on his good side. We might have a bit more leverage on the fees for this fiasco, however much it goes against the grain. Business is business," he remarked pragmatically. *My fadda taught me, keep your friends close and your enemies closer.*" Lovich quoted the line from *the Godfather* in a Brando mumble, earning him a laugh that helped dissolve the tension.

"Ok, I'll find him another site," Rupert said bitterly.

"No, *we* will find him another site – and this time, *we* will make sure we control it." Lovich finished for him.

The rebuke was stinging, and Rupert realised he had a lot to learn.

The following days saw Rupert listing areas that he proposed to canvass with a view to finding a site. South of the river was becoming one of the latest hotspots for occupiers, and it was they who drove the market. Rupert's experience of canvassing was telling. It was one of the many skills he had acquired and it now stood him in good stead. After two weeks of hard work, he found a site and more importantly someone who was willing to sell. The bad news was that it was already let to a tenant, a firm called Moorcroft Industries which specialised in supplying oil rigs and drilling equipment all around the world. In these inflationary times, their business was booming as the price of crude was high and rising higher. They occupied a site on the corner of Castle Road and River Street with extensive frontage, close to a junction controlled by traffic lights in what was about the most perfect location for that part of London. Following a letter of approach to the MD, Rupert received a call in response.

"Mr. Brett?" asked the deep voice, "Michaels here, from Moorcroft Industries. You wrote to me concerning our property on Castle Street."

"I did, yes. Thank you for getting back to me. Is our proposal something that might, in principle, be of interest to you?"

"Well, the tone of your letter implies that you are only interested in the freehold. If that is the case, we won't be able to help you, as we are only leaseholders here ourselves."

"OK. Well yes, I guess that's really the case I'm afraid.

But...umm..." Rupert hesitated, carefully feigning slight ingenuousness. "Do you know who the freeholders are, by any chance? I don't want to put you to any trouble, of course."

"I do actually. It happens that we only have a matter of months to go on our lease, and we are in renewal negotiations with them at the moment."

Rupert held his breath. The information would either save him time, trouble and money, or provide him with an opening to take things further.

"It is United Assurance. Do you know them? Would you like the address?"

Rupert feigned ignorance, took the address and finished the call, thanking Michaels for his help. UA! Of all the funds they would be perfect to steal the site from, without them realising. They appeared sharp enough in individual deals, but notoriously lax when it came to seeing the bigger picture within their own portfolio. *Like a lot of other funds*, Rupert thought cynically.

He weighed his next steps carefully. Approach the fund directly or go to Halpern and Beams? They'd almost certainly have all the information as they acted for UA on the professional work. He phoned the Honey Monster, who grunted in his usual way but as ever seemed ready to help, particularly with a bit of clandestine work rather than the usual boring lease reading. Half an hour later the Honey Monster called back with the information. It was more than Rupert could have hoped for. He had chapter and verse on the lease, with all the terms, including the rents and values.

More particularly, UA's Development Department was not involved, and were unlikely to be.

"So," he finished, "you owe me a serious lunch for all this. And I know what you all call me, so we are not talking a bowl of fucking cereal. Let's put something in the diary now."

It was done, and Rupert was more than happy to oblige. Better than sharing any fees, he thought, and cheaper by a long shot. His next call was to Mike Ringham.

"Ringo? Rupert. How are you doing? Got the date set for the wedding yet?"

The dinner party he had missed was indeed to announce the engagement to Jemma.

"Yah. On top form actually. This autumn, so keep it free. Now, cut the bullshit, Rupes. Whenever you're being this nice to me, it usually means you're after something. Skip to the good part, old chap."

"Oh, Ringo. So harsh. I don't know what you mean, I only have your best interests at heart."

"Right, so what do you want?" Mike continued.

"UA. You remember that conversation we had a while back, just before we met with Richard Lloyd? I'm after a contact there; someone who deals with the Industrial Fund. Do we know anyone?"

"Yah, actually we do. We're buying something off them at the moment and they're on this week's Lunch List. Why?"

Regularly distributed among the surveyors, the Lunch List was always the most up to date information on current target clients CR wanted to establish a special relationship with. Rupert rummaged in his tray before pulling the list out and scanning through the list of names, until he came to Clive Roberts of UA.

"I've got the potential makings of a deal."

"Do tell." Mike was interested. Rupert heard the change in his tone, so he laid out the whole story, right up to the details of the lease terms.

"Sounds as if it's got potential, but make sure you get your full fees this time," Mike responded sarcastically.

"For those kind words, I thank you," Rupert responded. "But listen, can we make an approach, sound him out and see if he'll sell. We need to get this off-market, without anyone else realising the development potential of the site."

The lunch was on Thursday of that week and Mike ensured that he would be sat next to Clive Roberts, who turned out to be a short, pugnacious man with a bad taste in suits, slightly greasy hair and an attitude that spoke of a class-related chip on his shoulder.

"We're looking for short leased properties at the moment," Mike murmured. "A specific client can get tax breaks from short leases and will pay top dollar accordingly."

"What sector? Where?" Roberts responded curtly, stuffing his perspiring face with dessert as if someone would steal it from him if he didn't eat it fast. *The youngest child*, Mike thought. The man had *South London Council Estate* written through him like letters on a stick of rock.

"For this particular client, we'd be looking primarily at industrial. Got anything that might suit?" Mike asked languidly, as though this was all a bore and was the last thing on his mind. Like many people, Roberts made the mistake of taking him for an upper class twit, a bleating sheep ready for the shearing. His response was exactly what Mike had wanted.

"Yeah, we've got some industrial tat in sarf-east London. Problems with a lease renewal, months left on the lease and the tenant's shapin' up tricky. If that helps," he said, sprawling back on his chair and rinsing his mouth with a gulp of wine, "I always thought you lot was like taxi drivers, didn't like it sarf of the river, but I could let you have some info."

"Might well be the ticket. Where is it exactly?"

"Corner of Castle Street and River Street. Shabby stuff. But if your man wants some short leased crap it would be ideal. It'll cost you, mind." Roberts grinned unpleasantly, revealing crooked, nicotine-stained teeth.

Gotcha Mike thought. "Sounds like a reasonable scheme. Fax the information across and we'll run it past our man, see what he says." Mike sounded as nonchalant as ever.

The next few days dragged for Rupert. He knew that he couldn't hurry Roberts without arousing his suspicions. Roberts faxed the information across to Mike Ringham the following Tuesday. It was just as they had hoped. The next call was to Simions, and a meeting was arranged for the following day. Rupert and Mike deliberately arranged the meeting on home turf, gaining the psychological upper hand and ensuring Shingler would not be present for some bogus reason or other of Simions' invention. The pleasantries were quickly dispensed with, and as ever Simions cut straight to the chase.

"Well, what have you got for me?"

"A deal," Rupert said. "A deal as good, if not better, than

the Golden Triangle." He used the analogy deliberately to inspire guilt and goodwill simultaneously.

"Really? Tell me more, but I won't believe it till I see it."

Rupert laid out the details to Simions up to the point of receiving the information from Roberts, including the price they had been quoted, which seemed high, even in the present circumstances. Simions considered everything they told him. He looked again at the site plan from the OS sheet, studied the lease details and his face became totally unreadable to Mike and Rupert. He ran his hand through his grey mane in a reflex gesture, the only sign of the tension in his body, and scratched his fingers backwards up his cheek in an effete gesture that may or may not have been an affectation

"I like it. Run some numbers, get me tenant demand for the area–"

"Already done, and its superb. A *Who's Who* of DIY anchors and the usual subsidiary retailers."

Unused to being interrupted, Simions visibly fought to keep himself calm and not respond aggressively.

"Well done," he said quietly. "And I'd also like details of the planning for the area, zoning etc."

Rupert, having learned his lesson, quietly handed over a planning brief. "It's all in there, and it looks positive. From the initial chat we've had with the planners, they'd be more than happy to see the site turned into sparkly retail sheds – well, as far as any planners are ever happy about anything," he added as a caveat. They went on to discuss a few more aspects of the site, including the possibility of getting vacant possession.

"I need a copy of the existing lease," Simions said "I also

need to know what action has been taken about getting shot of the current tenants. I do not need to tell you how important this is. Who's acting for Moorcroft?"

"Halpern and Beams, their Professional Department. No involvement from the agency boys at all, and we want it to stay like that."

"Good. Right I'll look at all the information. If it stacks up, we will make an offer subject only to contract. No planning, no vacant possession, just get control of the site ASAP. Tell UA that if and when we make an offer, they're not to take any more steps on terminating the lease. We don't want the waters muddied." They all smiled and Simions prepared to leave.

"Oh, one final matter," Rupert contrived to make it sound like an afterthought. "Your man Shingler. If you bring him on board at a later stage, I want to avoid any repetition of the problems that occurred last time. I think you owe us that much."

Simions considered Rupert for a few tense seconds before replying. "You have my assurance that this will not be sold without instruction," he said eventually. "You also have my assurance that either you will be involved in the sale of the investment or I will pay you a fee in any case. You may draw up a letter to that effect. That particular subject is now closed."

After Simions left, Mike turned to Rupert.

"You believe in living dangerously, I'll say that for you," he commented. "But you were pushing your luck there."

"It had to be said, and he knows it's a good deal. Besides, it was fun." He slapped Mike on the shoulder and laughed softly. The cockiness and confidence of a deal maker were manifesting themselves in the new Rupert.

They went to their separate offices, Mike to work on an offer and Rupert to do more research.

Rupert reflected that whatever other faults Simions might have, lack of speed was not one of them. Once Simions made up his mind he launched himself into action with alacrity, much faster than any pedantic fund manager who would prevaricate, go through numerous board approvals and then decide not to buy on some spurious excuse after wasting everyone's time. *Maybe*, Rupert thought, *maybe I could work for him: it would certainly be exciting.*

The full documentation came through from UA, and as luck would have it, despite having opened negotiations on the lease renewal, no formal notices had been served as they were still slightly in advance of the timescale set out in the lease. Surprisingly, the tenant had instigated the discussions rather than the Landlord, probably in an effort to come to some less than formal arrangement without having to involve the courts. The legal system for lease renewals was a nightmare and conflict was to be avoided at all costs. Simions called Rupert as soon as he received the information.

"I have several files relating to the deal. I will read them in the next hour or so and come back to you as soon as I can. From what I have seen so far this has got to be put under offer as soon as possible. There are so many ways it could leak into the market, and I will be very unhappy if I find myself bidding against all and sundry. One more thing, I see that

Moorcroft are listed. Can you get me a full company search? Creditors, so forth?"

"I have already asked our Research Department for the information," Rupert lied, making a mental note to do it after the call. "Should be with me tomorrow at the latest."

"Good. Sooner if possible. Speak later."

The line went dead. *Never one to waste words, is our Simions*, Rupert thought, shaking his head and smiling to himself. He wondered why Simions was after a company search if he wanted them out anyway.

Rupert would have the answer to his question if he'd heard the subsequent telephone conversation between Simions and Shingler.

"The boy Brett has done it again. He's found a great site. He has a talent for it, I'll give him that."

"What? Where?" Shingler demanded. "And why wasn't I in on it?"

"He's getting wise. Don't worry, we'll split it as usual. Stop being greedy. You got the lion's share last time, but if I cut him out this time, he won't offer us another deal. And like I say, he's getting good. I might have to poach him. Tell Pauline we might need someone in Halpern and Beams soon. I take it she's still connected with the head of personnel there."

"Thick as thieves," Shingler responded. "And why wouldn't she be, with a retainer from Secs and the City? Money talks, Paul, money talks."

"Doesn't it just? Right, I'll let you know when we have more information." He finished the call.

Rupert telephoned research and spoke to the one of the

girls; a pretty thing called Jessica, he remembered her from one of the office parties. He flirted with her for a couple of minutes and then begged a favour. She demanded a drink after work in payment, a promise that Rupert had no intention of keeping. He thought suddenly of Liz and had an urge to speak with her. He called Secs in the City, the West End branch just off Oxford Street.

"Liz? No, she's not been in today, but we have an assignment for her towards the end of the week, so if you speak to her, ask her to get in touch, will you? Smashing. Take care." The girl finished in her professional sing song voice. Rupert wondered why everyone said "Take care" when the last thing in the world they really cared about was the person they said it to? *It ranks up there with "have a nice day,"* he thought. The age of professional insincerity was upon them. He wondered where Liz was, but only for a moment. There was business to be done.

Mike continued to pursue Clive Roberts at UA to try and settle on a firm figure at which they felt a deal could be struck. So far, the response had been only that he needed to be "higher than book value." As luck would have it, an acquaintance from university worked in the Valuation Department, and might be persuaded to part with the information. Mike called him, praying that he would help. A languid voice answered the telephone.

"Charlton."

"Morning Chaz. Mike Ringham here, how the devil?"

"Ringo, old chap. Yah, splendid, thanks. Your good self? How's it hanging, as they say on Wall Street?"

Mike grinned to himself at Charlton's clipped tones and

insouciant manner; a façade that hid an agile, if rather formulaic attitude. After the initial pleasantries, Mike turned the conversation to valuations, claiming that he was buying something and needed some information on value.

"Shouldn't really of course, but give me the figure you're at and I'll nod at the appropriate moment. How's that sound?"

"Yeah, Chaz, that'll work well on the phone, you daft sod. Just stay silent when I hit ballpark, 'kay? I'm at two and three quarter nil. Are we on the same hymn sheet?"

"Sharpen your pencil and head north, Ringo."

"Do me a favour. It's a fag end of the lease. I thought values were supposed to go down at this point, not up," Mike said.

"Yeah, but we've had orders to push up the performance as the figures are lagging behind at the moment. Totally independently, of course," Charlton said cynically.

"OK. Three mil?"

There were a few seconds of silence on the other end of the phone

"Chaz, you're a star," Mike commented.

"It has been said, it has been said. You owe me lunch."

They fixed a day for the following week, and Mike thought he would drag Rupert and Claire along to alleviate the boredom. He went to Rupert's office to discuss his discovery. The firm had decided that Rupert would continue to progress the investment purchase, partly to get his share of the fees, but more importantly to maintain the illusion that they were only looking at it as an investment, without exposing the massive potential for redevelopment. Rupert phoned Simions for instructions and was pleased to find him in a benign mood and open to persuasion on the level of offer.

The offer was put forward at just under £3m, subject to contract only and with no other conditions. It was, as they all expected, summarily rejected. They increased the offer to £3.1m, enough to tip the balance in their favour. UA agreed to sell.

They were all euphoric at the acceptance of the offer, none more so than Rupert, who was determined not to have it sold from under him this time. The lawyers were instructed to prepare a contract as soon as possible. Every moment that the deal went unsigned presented an opportunity for news of it to leak into the open market. A week later, the lawyers were ready for exchange. Five working days, a new company record. Rupert thought how good it would be to be in charge and work at this frenetic pace.

Mike took a call from the lawyers confirming that contracts had been exchanged on the Friday morning, much to everyone's relief. Rupert took a call from Simions just before lunch.

"Rupert?"

"Yes. Heard the good news?"

"Deal done, I hear? Good, now the real work starts. On Monday we start to turn the screw and find a way to get the tenant off the site. Have you found out who at Halpern and Beams is dealing with the lease renewal?"

"Yes, a chap called Steve Jackson, head of their review team. He's just been formerly instructed to liaise with us on the matter."

"Also, I need to know his secretary's name, just for completeness."

"Secretary? Sure, I'll find out for you," Rupert said, a little puzzled.

"Do that, please. Have a good weekend. Speak Monday."

"You too." As he put the telephone down, Rupert thought that Simions must be having a funny turn, asking for a secretary's name and wishing him a pleasant weekend.

Chapter Eight

After the storms of 1987, the following spring brought warm sunshine and high April temperatures, and many Londoners opted to vacate the city at the weekends to get away from the smog and bustle. Claire was no exception. She and Angus continued with their intense relationship, and as Friday came they planned their leisure time over a rowdy lunchtime session in *The Guinea*.

"We haven't made any plans for this weekend yet," Claire said.

"No. Haven't got that far yet. But I've got a lad's night with some of my Scottish friends on Saturday before they fly out to go skiing on Sunday afternoon," he answered.

"Really? You didn't mention it earlier." She looked at him, studying his face carefully.

"Yeah, I did. I told you last week. You were probably too wrapped up in this new deal of yours to take any notice," he replied glibly. Claire's career was flying and in the short time she had been at CR, she had begun to make non-retained deals in her own right.

"I'm sure I'd have remembered. Never mind, come round for dinner tonight, I'll cook for you." She smiled winningly at him. Their relationship had lasted a few months now and although at times tempestuous, Claire was sure that it was becoming something more than a casual affair, and there was a growing sense of commitment on both sides. With a typical women's intuition, she knew when to back off and not appear too clingy, giving Angus enough space to keep him interested.

"That would be good, but we're off to the dry slope first tonight so I can show them how it's done before they leave for the real slopes."

Angus, she knew, was a superb skier and could not resist showing off to the boys. The last time they went on the dry slope he had been asked to leave after jumping off the lift while it was still in motion.

"So how about dinner afterwards? Nine o'clock? Dinner and me, in that order." She gave him her sexiest smile. He responded in kind.

"Make it 9.30, that gives me time to get back," he replied.

"Yah, deal." she responded, hiding her disappointment. *Stop it Claire. Half and hour's nothing,* she thought.

Later that evening she prepared dinner in her flat. At 9.30 she lit the candles, everything ready, wine chilled, last minute preparations ready to go. She sat back with a glass of wine and relaxed to the sound of Everything but the Girl playing softly in the background. She lay back on the sofa, sheathed in a black velvet dress with her hair drawn back, accentuating her high cheekbones. She looked stunning and she knew it.

But for some unknown reason, Claire was nervous and unable to relax. She flicked through the television channels, unable to find anything that held her interest. This was the second time something like this had happened. The first time was at the start of their relationship and she'd thought nothing of it, but this was a different matter. The telephone gave a shrill ring, breaking into her reverie and jarring on her nerves.

"Angus?" she said, regretting her obvious need.

"Hi, babe. Sorry, I'm running late. Things got out of hand, I –"

"Angus, don't give me that crap. Where are you? It's way past 9.30."

"Calm down. I just had one too many with the lads. I'm getting a taxi now, I'll be there in half an hour, OK?"

"Do what the fuck you like," she responded and put the phone down. *Stuff him, the little shit*, she thought. Friday night and nowhere to go. Her mood darkened, but she snapped out of it quickly. *No way*, she thought *I'm twenty-five, not fifty-five.* She looked up at the clock. The West End bars would not have even begun to hum yet. On an impulse she rang a friend.

"Caroline? Hi, it's Claire. How are you?"

"Oh fab, doll. Absolutely. You?"

"Well, actually I'm pretty pissed off and I could do with a night on the town."

"Brill. We're off to Smollensky's for about 10.30, come along. We'll see you there, yah?"

"Caz, you're a star, love to. See you in half an hour, byeeee!"

She put the telephone down, suddenly uplifted. *Sod Angus*, she thought, *he can have a curry with the boys*. She changed into something more obvious, a short skirt with a slit at the side and a low-cut white blouse. She put on more makeup and some chunky jewellery and looked approvingly at the result in the mirror. She left the flat and caught a cab to Smollensky's.

It was in full swing when she arrived just after 10.30. She met Caroline and they embraced and kissed the air next to each other's cheek.

"Tell me what the bastard has done now," Caroline demanded. Claire told her over the loud music and a few drinks.

"Oh he's just being a typical pig. You won't change him. Either ditch him or get used to it. At least he is being faithful!"

"Caz, you're such a cow! But you're probably right. Come on, let's dance."

They hit the dance floor, and half an hour later adjourned to the bar. As they leant on the bar, a small commotion started on the opposite side of the room, and sure enough there was Angus, with a familiar girl on his arm. It was the girl from the bar from a few months back. The one he sang to. She was certainly more than friends with Angus; she was draped all over him as she sashayed backwards onto the dance floor swaying her hips in his direction.

Claire's first instinct was to go over and slap him. Then

she stopped and ducked out of sight, leaving with Caroline hot on her tail.

"Don't say I was here, alright? Not a word," she begged. "I'll deal with him later."

"OK Claire, but will you be alright?" Caroline asked, putting an arm around her.

"Yah, fine. I'll get a cab," she turned on her heel. "Not a word, not a fucking word, OK?" she pleaded.

When she got home, she flung herself on the bed and wept. She told herself that night to be harder and stronger, starting from the next day.

Only one thought was uppermost in her mind – vengeance!

The next day she got up and rode early in Hyde Park: the feel of a good horse putting her in a better frame of mind. She was too late to leave for polo this weekend, but perhaps she'd go next weekend as the season had started again in earnest. A plan began to form in her mind.

Oh yes, she thought, *just perfect*.

She returned home and showered. She was sitting down with a freshly brewed coffee when the phone rang.

"Babe, I'm sorry, really I am. Couldn't get taxi for love or money. I tried to ring but it just rang out, I –"

"Stop!" she cried, steeling herself to appear natural and calm, laughing down the phone. "Forget it. I gave up waiting for my Scottish hooligan to appear, pulled out the phone and went to bed with a good book. I must be getting old. Now, are you still on the town with the boys tonight, or are they all off on the piste?"

He was obviously taken aback by her calm attitude, and Claire drew him in exactly as she had planned it.

"Aye, but Sunday would be good, are you around?"

"What, to nurse your hangover? In your dreams. Maybe for lunch but I'm out on Sunday night with the girls. So you can take me out somewhere near Richmond Park and we can walk off the beer."

She knew he would not be able to take the rejection, and sure enough he responded positively. She put the telephone down and clenched her hands. Looking furiously at the telephone, she said to herself; "You wait, you Scottish git, just you wait. I'll have my revenge."

Sunday afternoon saw them walking in the pale spring sunshine through the park. The buds on the hawthorns were coming through early, the daffodils were on their way out and the sweet, heavy smell of freshly cut grass wafted on the air. It was warm, and they meandered arm in arm in shirt sleeves and in Claire's case a light linen jacket. Two horses cantered past, carrying their riders gently through the park before disappearing into the avenue of shrubs.

"That's what we should be doing," Claire remarked casually. "Except that you can't ride, can you?"

"Can't ride?" he howled as she knew he would. "I've been riding since I was yay high," he held a hand palm down at knee-level. 'I can ride just as well as you – not poncing around a park, mind you. I'm talking the wide open spaces of the Scottish countryside."

"Och, away the noo," she mocked. "Really, Angus, you never cease to amaze me. But they all ride back to front and facing backwards up there don't they? Not proper riding at all."

She ducked as he made a lunge for her and they ran chasing in and out of the trees, to all the world like two carefree lovers. Angus would have been surprised to have read her mind at that moment, as she sprang the final part of the trap.

"So then, Monarch of the bloody Glen," she continued when he finally caught her in a laughing embrace, "come to Gloucestershire with me next weekend and we can ride the polo ponies, do a bit of stick and balling. If you're good enough," she taunted, "we might let you play a few practice chukkas. Providing they can understand your accent."

The last was a reference to the fact that like most Scots, Angus reverted to a strong Scottish accent when he was with his countrymen, which always took a few days to wear off.

"Well if you're talking English, what are practice chukkas and stick and balling?"

"Heathen. Stick and balling is just polo practice, passing the ball, hitting it more gently to get your eye in. And practice chukkas are low level polo, not a full blown game. Just a couple of chukkas, of seven minutes or so. It's great fun, unless of course you're frightened of falling off," she taunted "So are we on? Come up and stay at my parents' house."

At this he span round, aghast, Angus had an aversion to meeting parents.

"Um...let me see...this weekend... I might be busy..."

"Don't worry," she interrupted. "They won't be there. Anyway, we can take a car each, so you can escape whenever you want. The look on your face was a picture, classic case of parent evasion."

They laughed together and finalised arrangements for the following weekend.

"So, a whole weekend together. What on earth are we going to do for all that time?" Angus asked with wide-eyed innocence.

"Well, if you don't know, you're not the man I thought you were," she retorted.

They finished their walk and drove back to Chelsea. Claire was delighted with how it had all slipped into place so smoothly. Her revenge was in sight.

Meanwhile, clandestine plans of a different nature were being put into place at the MAS offices. Shingler called into see Simions.

"Do we have good news?" he queried.

"Yes all arranged. A very bad case of spring flu is about to hit H & B."

"Who do we have going in? Liz?"

"Trying for her, but I think it is another girl. Liz is busy on a legitimate assignment apparently."

"Really? How odd."

They hatched their plans and Shingler left.

Chapter Nine

Monday morning began expectantly for Rupert. Now was the chance for him to shine on this deal and start putting the screws on towards gaining vacant possession of the site. Rupert and his colleagues decided to avoid any face to face meetings with the MD, Mr. Michaels, and to do their best to keep everything clinical and at arm's length.

Before any further action was taken, however, Simions called a council of war to co-ordinate the deal. They met at MAS's offices later that morning.

"Right, Rupert, instruct your PSD to serve the relevant notice for termination of the lease. I believe we are still in time to do that."

Rupert nodded. "Unfortunately, there doesn't seem to be anything to our advantage in the lease terms. Notice to be served no later than three months before termination and counter notice no later than three months thereafter."

"No 'Time is of the essence clause' I suppose?" Simions asked.

"No. The lawyers said that was all pretty straightforward as well."

"Very well," Simions continued. "Mike, carry on with the investment purchase – and no press release. If anyone asks, we bought it as part of our short term, high yield income strategy. Feed them some meaningless nonsense or other." He gave Rupert and Mike a cynical smile. "Who knows, we might get offered more of the same stuff. Could turn interesting."

"Claire," he said, turning his full charm upon her. "I would like you, very discreetly, to start putting together a list of possible tenants and the rents they would be prepared to pay. Only in general terms, nothing too specific, understood?"

"Of course. I know the form."

"Good. In the meantime I've been looking at the company itself. It appears to be in good shape financially, and most of the shares are owned by family members, so we've no way in there. But they do have some large debts to suppliers, notably Diamond Drilling Services, a small quoted company that's doing rather well after the Big Bang. Maybe we could bring a bit of pressure to bear there?" he mused. "Yes... Rupert, could you go and look at their premises for me. Just a general view. Value, location, this kind of thing."

"Sure," Rupert said accepting a piece of paper with the address on it.

"Right, that's it. Let's crack on and find a way to get VP."

The meeting ended and Rupert, Mike and Claire left MAS's offices. Out on the street Mike mused; "I wonder what pressure he is going to try and bring through Diamond Drills or whatever they are called?"

"Whatever it is, it will be barely on the right side of ethical, I'm sure," Rupert retorted.

"Simions can be a nasty piece of work. I wouldn't want to get on the wrong side of him, that's for sure," Claire commented.

They returned to the office and Rupert went to see Chris Hughes in PSD.

"Ah, so the mountain has come to Mohammed. What's the problem this time?"

"And a fine good morning to you too, Chris. Actually I want to give you some work. I've brought a lease with me: we need a notice serving for termination of a tenancy."

Rupert explained the situation in full, omitting nothing. When he was done, Hughes leant back in his chair, pulled out a cigarette and lit it. He drew hard, blew smoke into the air and squinted in his customary manner through the haze. "You've read the lease?" he asked. "Nothing special, no time of the essence?"

Rupert shook his head. "No. I went through that particular clause twice, and so have the lawyers."

"So what do you need me to serve the notice for, then?"

"Two reasons. Firstly you're the best, and secondly I need a bit of distance so no one sees exactly what we're trying to do."

"Fine by me, but I'll take a fee. 7.5 percent of the rent passing?"

"Yeah, I agreed that with Simions. Don't forget to send

him a letter confirming the terms though. Pin him down, he's a shifty bugger."

"Stop trying to teach your granny to suck eggs, old chap," Hughes chided. "I was doing this when you were running round the playground still thinking girls were soppy."

Rupert pulled a face and left. He drove to the address Simions had given him, an industrial location at the front of a 1970s estate south of the river. The estate was typical of its kind. A few neat rows of uniform sheds painted the ubiquitous brown and yellow, with lines of large refuse bins on wheels marking the boundary of each business's territory. *What the hell did he want me to look at this for?* Rupert thought. *He can't want to buy it, surely?* He drove back, disgusted at the waste of a day. Stuck in a traffic jam at the south end of Tower bridge, he reached down to play with his new toy – a car phone.

The company would only pay for one if the employee was a partner or above, so he had agreed a deal whereby he had installed it and all business calls would be paid for by the firm. This one was personal, though. He had been trying to get hold of Liz for a while. She had been at her parents for the weekend and he was keen to see her tonight. He dialled the number of her new mobile.

"Liz?"

"Good afternoon, Mr Brett, how are you?" The formal response indicated that she could not talk. They'd agreed upon the system as she often worked for agents and property related firms, so discretion was the best policy.

"Can't talk huh?"

"That's right."

"Where are you?"

"Halpern and Beams, on Grosvenor Street."

"There again? They must have a permanent flu bug," he joked.

"Of course, yes, something like that."

"OK, I understand. Can we meet up tonight, 7.30 at your flat?"

"Yes, that would be fine, Mr Brett. I look forward to meeting you." She rang off.

It wasn't her fault, but he still found it frustrating that she couldn't talk openly to him. She didn't want to draw attention to herself, he supposed, especially as their relationship was not public knowledge yet, even among CR staff.

Rupert decided that by the time he'd fought his way through the traffic there was no point in returning to the office, so he went directly to his flat, where he changed and went for a run to relax himself in preparation for the evening ahead. His usual four mile route led him through backstreets and a few small parks. He needed to keep fit, not only for work but because he'd been a member of the TA since his teens, and he felt it was necessary to continue with the fitness regime he had always followed. He returned from the run hot and sweating, but feeling good. He did a few stretching exercises, showered and got himself ready for the evening.

When he arrived at Liz's flat, she was ready by the door and clearly delighted to see him. They kissed and hugged as if they'd been apart for weeks, not days. Their relationship had become deeper since the night they had first slept together, and although he sensed that there were still aspects of her past which Rupert felt he could not ask her about, his feelings for her were strong enough for it not to matter.

They settled down with their drinks in a quiet corner of the Flask, a local pub that was unusually busy for a Monday night.

"I don't know what happens in deepest, darkest Sussex, but whatever it is, it suits you. You look gorgeous." She blushed slightly at the compliment, enhancing her fading tan.

"Well, if you're a good boy, you might be invited next time, if you faaancy a weekennd in the cunnn'ry." She laughed.

"That has to be the worst country accent I've ever heard." He rolled his eyes "But yes, that would be good – and a bit scary, meeting parents and things..." he let the words tail off.

"Oh don't worry, I only let them out of their coffins at night. Just carry a crucifix and a bulb of garlic, you'll be fine."

They chatted easily for the rest of the evening, easy and comfortable in each other's company. It was only when the conversation turned to work that things became a little tense.

"I'm thinking of taking a full time job. The agency has put me forward for a permanent post," she said.

"Really? I thought you liked the freedom of temping?"

"I do – or at least I did, but I feel like having a bit more security. The post is for a PA, a chance to work with the business."

"What company?" he asked.

"Crispin and Howell, the quantity surveyors. They specifically asked for me."

"Quantity surveyors?" he gasped. "My God, you'll be bored out of your mind."

"Don't be like that. It's a great job and I've got good potential to grow with the firm. We can't all be whiz kids, you know," she smiled to take the sting out of her words.

"Sorry. I'm being an arsehole, ignore me. It sounds great, it's just my natural agent's prejudice showing."

"I know," she said putting her hand on his knee. "All you deal junkies think about is buy, sell and whatever the latest angle is."

"Well, it's not quite all we think about." She read the look in his eye, smiled and finished her drink.

"Come on then lover boy, let's go."

They left arm in arm, the moment forgotten, and returned to her flat where they made love and fell asleep in each other's arms.

Chapter Ten

The next day Rupert received a call from Chris Hughes to go up to his office for a chat. Hughes would not be any more forthcoming on the telephone. He ran up the two flights of stairs and arrived breathing heavily.

"I don't know why you keep fit fanatics bother. A fag is much better for you, you know."

Rupert grinned. "Come on, give. Have you found anything exciting?"

"Dunno, really. Depends what you call exciting," Hughes commented. "You said that you'd read the notice clauses and found nothing, yes?"

"Yes." Rupert felt his mouth go dry. *What had he missed?* he thought to himself. The idea of making a howler and screwing up the deal filled him with dread.

"But what you didn't look at is the Definitions section, setting out all the minutiae, did you?"

"Oh shit, what have you found?" he asked.

"Well, it states, and I quote. '*for the avoidance of doubt, all timescales contained herein with regard to service of notices in all clauses* ... blah, blah... *will be taken to mean that time will be considered to be strictly of the essence in every case* ... blah blah.'"

"Wow, so if they don't respond within that one-month timescale to us contesting the application to terminate the lease, we get vacant possession and can kick them off?"

"Well done, Sherlock! Bloody agency surveyors couldn't read a lease if their lives depended on it." he said scathingly.

"Yea, well even the lawyers didn't pick it up."

"No surprises there then."

"Chris, you're a star, wait 'til I tell Simions."

"Don't count your chickens, they probably will respond in time. Remember they have Halpern and Beams acting for them, and no deal's done 'til it's done."

"Yeah, yeah, but at least it gives us hope."

He left in a hurry, made a quick call to get an appointment with Simions and arrived at his offices within half an hour. He was shown straight up to Simions' room.

"Rupert, you sounded excited on the phone. It must be good news to necessitate a visit. I have literally twenty minutes."

"We've been going through this lease again – or rather Chris Hughes in PSD has – and he's found a time of the essence clause that works in our favour," Rupert finished.

"Really," Simions responded calmly. "Why didn't we find this sooner?"

Rupert shrugged and explained the whole situation. When he had finished, Simions smiled to himself and turned to look out of the window. Rupert had a feeling of déjà vu, but he couldn't place it.

"Good work. I'll speak to the lawyers, give them a bollocking and get a definitive answer as to our position. Of course it all depends upon whether their agents spot this in time or not and respond accordingly."

"Of course," admitted Rupert. "But it gives us a possible loophole."

"Indeed it does. Right, if you don't mind, David Shingler will be here anytime now, and although he will be brought in if the scheme proceeds, I don't want him involved at this stage."

"Yes, understood."

Rupert left feeling a little deflated at the response, and slightly unnerved by the constant spectre of Shingler looming on the horizon. Still, at least Simions had guaranteed him control this time. Back at the office, he bumped into Claire and relayed the events to her. While she was pleased with the possibility of a loophole, she did not share his unbridled enthusiasm.

"What's up?" Rupert asked. "You seem terribly preoccupied."

"Yah, well, we've been here before and it's a long way from cut and dried. Besides, I've got a lot on my mind with letting this new scheme up in the West Midlands."

"Fair enough, but it seems more than that. You sure you're alright?"

"Yah, just leave it Rupes, OK? I'm fine."

"OK, OK, but if you want to talk you know where I am."

"Sorry. Yes, of course I know. I didn't mean to be that sharp."

They left the corridor and went their separate ways.

For Rupert the next few days was a waiting time as the deal progressed, For Claire, the strain of appearing normal for Angus and other colleagues was getting to her, and she couldn't wait for the weekend to arrive.

Chapter Eleven

When Friday finally came, Claire made an excuse not go the pub at lunchtime and met Angus at her flat. She had to fight him off as he had other things on his mind than just leaving for the country.

"No Angus. We've got all weekend. I want to get on the road before we hit the rush hour traffic and get all snarled up in it. God, you're like a bloody octopus." She forced herself to laugh lightly.

"Mmm, can't we just have a quickie before we go?" he begged, kissing her and fondling a breast. She nearly gave in, despite herself.

"No, you sex maniac. We can spend all weekend together in bed if you want, but for now let's get going. Build up your passion on the journey and we'll go straight to bed when we get there."

He pulled a sulky face, but finally agreed. They got into their separate cars; Claire's a Golf GTI, her first company car, of which she was very proud. Angus followed in his BMW

2.5i, and a race would have ensued if the traffic had been light enough. They were both recorded members of the Park Lane 100 club. To become a member, one had to start at one end of Park Lane and reach 100 miles per hour before hitting the brakes at the other end, a particularly difficult challenge that required nerve and skill to avoid slower vehicles.

They followed the steady queue of traffic along the M4, but as they neared Swindon the traffic finally thinned and they turned off towards Cirencester. Claire's family home lay some ten minutes outside the town near Edgeworth, a small hamlet with a pub, a village shop and a church. It was a lovely setting among rolling hills leading down to a valley and up to Cirencester Park on the other side. Claire's parents' house was set high up on the side of one of the many valleys that cut through the Cotswold countryside, creating beautiful, undulating landscapes.

Angus drove impatiently through a maze of small country lanes until he saw Claire turn through an open set of gates. He followed her across a cattle grid and along a stone driveway.

In front of them stood a large stone house in classic vernacular architecture. Constructed in an H-shape like many Cotswold houses, it had green painted woodwork and Wisteria covering most of the frontage. It was imposing, in the afternoon light, and Angus was impressed despite being used to the granite monoliths of his Scottish homeland. A large group of outbuildings stood off to the left, including a small barn, a stable block and open garaging, and it was to this that his eye was drawn.

A security light had flicked on as soon as they neared the

house, highlighting the cars parked in the garage. He looked at them with a sense of unease as Claire got out of her car and went to stand beside him. "Whose are they?" he asked. "I thought you said your parents were away?"

She laughed gently. "Don't worry. Josh will have run them to the airport. They've gone off for a long weekend to the opera in Venice. And before you ask, Josh will be off bonking his new girlfriend, and he couldn't give a damn about who I bring home anyway. Now, come in and meet him if he's in. The lights might be Mrs. Crawford, Mummy's housekeeper." she pointed at a glow emanating from the house.

His nervousness was temporarily abated. The last thing he wanted was to come away with no sex after a weekend of having to put up with being polite to Claire's parents. A brother would be bad enough.

As Claire turned away, she grinned to herself. *Part one completed,* she thought. The main light to the covered porch was switched on and as soon as the door opened slightly, a large Springer Spaniel bounded out to meet her.

"Jess!" she cried and crouched down to be licked and pawed. The dog rolled over on to his back to let Claire rub her tummy.

"Jess, meet Angus, Angus meet Jess. Beautiful girl," she said rubbing her tummy. "Where's Boot?"

A limping Jack Russell of ancient vintage wobbled into view, wagging his stump of a tail.

"Hello Boot, how are you?" She rubbed his ears and tugged them playfully, looking at Angus's glum expression He was obviously dreading a weekend of dogs, horses and trying to cook things on an Aga. He was probably looking forward to a parent-free weekend of shagging. But this illusion was soon shattered. A deep, well-modulated woman's voice hailed from the house.

"Hello, darling! what a lovely surprise."

"Mummy, what on earth are you doing here?" Claire said in well-practiced tone. "I thought you were in Venice or something?"

"Oh darling, that's next weekend," Claire's mother said coming, over to embrace her daughter and kiss her on both cheeks. "But never mind, it's lovely to see you. Now who is this fine young gentleman? Do introduce me."

"Mummy, this is Angus. Angus, my mother."

She was laughing with glee on the inside. *He couldn't escape now*, she thought. She watched his shoulders slump as he was presented to her mother, who was a tall, handsome woman in her fifties, slightly more rounded than Claire, with a lovely smile and twinkly blue eyes. She wore a dark blue twin set, pearls and a tweed skirt, her clothes well-fitted and not the usual frumpy county style. Good legs showed from beneath the skirt. They shook hands.

"How do you do, Mrs. Sewell?"

"How do you do Angus? But please call me Jane. I hope you both had a good journey. Claire, your Father is getting logs in for the fire. We find it still gets chilly in the evenings. Now come on in, bring your bags, I'll air the beds. Angus you can go in the Yellow room; it has lovely views in the morning," she finished, as mother and daughter walked arm in arm towards the front door.

To Angus, it appeared that Claire had taken on a new

persona, one which he couldn't fathom, and a hard exterior that he could not pierce. He had previously thought that she was a city type, at home in an urban environment, but now he was seeing another side to her. One with which he was not altogether comfortable, he decided.

The door opened onto a flagstone floor with warm light spilling onto the hallway from all angles. Various white painted doors opened off the hall, one of which led to the snug, which was painted a dark, warm green. Pictures adorned the walls; family photos and homely *objets d'art*. Rugs were strewn randomly over the tiled floor, creating a cosy atmosphere. A log burner in the fireplace was already alight and starting to give off heat.

A door opened to the right and a slightly stooped figure appeared carrying a log basket laden with logs. The man dropped it by the fireplace and stood erect, opening his arms for an embrace from Claire.

"Darling, how lovely to see you," he greeted Claire.

"Daddy, how's you?" she asked, a familiar greeting from childhood days.

"I'm very well. Mint condition," he responded.

He was a tall, lean, cadaverous man in his late fifties. To Angus he looked capable and fit, although his dark hair was streaked with grey. He was dressed in moleskins and a check shirt with a pullover across his back, the knotted arms at his chest. He shook hands with Angus, introducing himself as John, and they exchanged pleasantries. "So, you've come up to see us, how lovely," he said.

"Yes, Daddy, but I got the dates wrong," she said looking at Angus, who gave her a thin smile in return. "I thought you were going away this weekend, not next, although it is great to see you both."

Her father smiled ruefully and looked hard at his daughter, never one to be taken in. Angus knew he'd be in for a long and tedious weekend. Claire's father poured drinks and the conversation turned to London and work, with Rupert's latest deal coming to the forefront of the conversation.

"I knew that boy would do well," Claire's mother said. Angus tried to keep a straight face.

"He should pull it off if he can get the planning," she explained.

"Yeah, and pigs might fly. It's such a long shot; although with Simions' dirty tricks brigade on side, he might do it," Angus said scornfully.

"Oooh. That sounds suspiciously like sour grapes to me, young man," Jane retorted. "But what do you mean, dirty tricks?"

"Well he has a certain reputation for getting things done, no matter what the cost. We'll see," he finished cryptically.

"It sounds like you're both talking a foreign language to me," Claire's father joked. Claire laughed and explained some of the more esoteric points and the evening continued in good humour until they went to retire to bed.

"I've put Angus in the Yellow Room," her mother said, a perfect smile in place. "It's all aired. Anything you want, just shout, Angus. Good night."

They said their goodnights and Claire and Angus went upstairs together. When they were alone on the first floor landing Angus turned to her and said: "Can I sneak down later? This cannot be for real, sleeping apart?"

"Look, I'm really sorry, but there's nothing we can do – and no, you can't come down later. These stairs creak like a trumpet voluntary, you'll wake the whole house. Come on, just one weekend, you'll have fun tomorrow and they'll probably go out; we'll have the house to ourselves."

Angus pouted and sulked, retiring ungracefully, giving Claire a perfunctory goodnight kiss.

As Claire turned and opened her door, she made an excuse to return downstairs for a glass of water. When she entered the kitchen, her parents were tidying up.

"Now then, young lady," her father said, grinning and shaking his head with mock severity. "What is all this about?"

"I knew I'd never fool you, Daddy. But I was hoping you would both play along." She proceeded to outline her scheme, giving her reasons and telling them how upset she felt.

"You're playing with fire with that one. I wouldn't trust him further than I could throw him!" he commented sagaciously.

She kissed both her parents goodnight and returned to her room with a glass of water.

The following morning was bright and warm; with spring sunshine banishing the night's chill from the air. Even Angus was in good spirits. Claire found him tucking into bacon and eggs at breakfast.

"I feel really good this morning," he said. "No hangover and ready to face these polo ponies."

"Good, we'll finish breakfast, walk the dogs and get there for the second string, about 10.30."

"What's a string?" he queried.

"Oh, it's just the name we use for each group of horses the grooms exercise," she explained.

Twenty minutes later they were ready to leave.

"Let's go in your car. It will be fun turning up in a smart BMW for a change."

They packed the car with all the gear and drove about a mile along the lane, pulling up where Claire indicated in front of a large pair of wooden gates, so high that it was impossible to see over. A painted sign bore the legend *Edgeworth Polo Club.*

She got out, opened the gates wide and beckoned Angus through, closing the gates quickly behind him. The enclosed yard was bordered on two sides by rows of stables, with various equine heads protruding from the open upper doors. To the right stood a large Cotswold stone house, opening out via a back door to the parking area.

Angus got out of the car and was immediately assailed by the smell of horseflesh, creosote, shavings and sweaty leather.

"So, this is where you hide away," he said.

She smiled, "Yes, isn't it wonderful?" she breathed deeply. Again, Angus noticed that she was a different person to the one he knew in London.

Looking around, he saw that the yard was a hive of activity; grooms were leading horses, washing them, tacking up or grooming. Hails of greetings were directed in Claire's direction.

"Is there anyone English here or are they all colonials?"

She grinned. "I know. I think John P deliberately recruits them from all over the world, except England."

At that point a tall figure appeared, walking over with a horseman's rolling gait. He was slim with grey blue eyes, greying hair and a knowing smile.

"Morning John P, how are you?" Claire greeted. He smiled with genuine warmth, kissed her cheek and was introduced to Angus.

"How you doing?" he asked, an Australian twang overlaying his English accent.

"Well, thought I'd come up and see how it was done polo style," Angus replied. John P assessed humans in the way he did horses, with an innate intuition that was rarely wrong. Angus felt the other man's eyes boring into him and finding him wanting. He didn't say anything or give anything away by his manner, but it was there for those to see who knew him.

"Good. We can always do with people to help exercise and I gather that you're playing chukkas later?" he said, his voice rising slightly at the end of the sentence in time-honoured Australian fashion.

"Yes, if that's OK."

"Fine, fine, I'll see you later," John P said. He walked off to correct a groom who was clipping a horse.

"He's a man of few words," Angus commented.

"But what he does say usually matters," Claire said.

Angus was beginning to feel more out of place with each introduction, and was pleased to be finally mounted and leading two horses, one in each hand, heading out to the exercise track. The track lay some three hundred yards away from the buildings and comprised a sanded, oval exercise run, around which strings of horses were already walking.

"How do you feel?" Claire asked, obviously enjoying his obvious discomfort at having to control three horses at once.

"Fine, just fine. But I didn't realise I would be leading two as well as riding one."

"Well, you said you could ride, didn't you?" At which she increased the pace to a trot and moved onto the track into a gap between two of the existing strings. Angus followed. After ten minutes he was told that he now had to canter with the two horses in tow for a further twenty minutes. He was aghast.

"What! Twenty minutes? You must be joking."

"What's the matter, scared or too tired?" she mocked, laughing at him as she moved forward into a canter.

He responded by kicking up hard into a canter, but unused to the sharp response of a polo pony, the fast change of pace unbalanced him. He managed one lap with the pony, discouraged by his increased movement in the saddle and the two horses he was leading, which by now were almost beyond his control. This extra movements caused Angus to grab the pommel in order to try and regain his balance. At this point every groom's nightmare happened; the outside horse he was leading stopped dead. Instinctive reaction took over and Angus tried to hang on to the lead rope and his own horse simultaneously. Something had to give, and it was him. He sailed backwards out of the saddle, appearing for an instant to hover in mid-air before finally measuring his length on the compacted sand. He hit the ground hard, the air was expelled from his lungs and he narrowly missed being trodden on by the oncoming horses. He moaned, rolled over and tried to stand.

"You OK?" called Claire, still cantering easily round the exercise ring, trying not laugh along with the other grooms who considered this an occupational hazard, one which usually called for a case of beer to be bought by the unlucky individual.

"No I am fucking well not!" he shouted back.

"Get off the track," John P yelled. Angus gave him the finger and moved off, limping and without his horses, all of which were caught expertly by the grooms who added them to their strings and continued four-up as though nothing had happened.

"That'll cost you a case of beer," Claire laughed as she passed. "I can't stop, see you back at the yard." She carried on cantering around the track. Angus was furious when Claire finally appeared – happy, smiling and chatting to one of the grooms.

"How are you, darling?" she cooed.

"How do you think? You might have stopped, for fuck's sake."

"I know, it hurts doesn't it? But the ego probably came off worst, I should imagine," she answered calmly, refusing to be drawn into a quarrel.

"Oh, ha bloody ha. Look at the grazing I've got here," he said lifting his shirt to show friction burns.

"I'll be with you in a minute."

She un-tacked the horses and talked to them softly as she showered them with one of the hosepipes and scraped the water from each horse.

"OK, OK, I couldn't stop," she said to Angus. "I've told you why. Now let's forget it. Besides, you did look funny. So, a game next, you on for that?" she asked innocently.

"No, I'm bloody not, can't we just go?"

"What? You must be joking. This is what I came for," she said ambiguously.

At that point, a Porsche 911 Targa purred into the yard with the top down and music playing. The engine stopped and out stepped a suave, classically good looking man in his forties. He looked Mediterranean, from his swept back hair, tanned olive skin and open-necked polo shirt down to his handmade loafers. He saw Claire and smiled.

"Bello!" she rushed across to him and was swept up into his arms as he planted a kiss on her lips. She responded in kind and they talked in quick-fire Spanish for a couple of minutes.

Eventually he released her, but he kept a proprietorial arm around her shoulders. She turned to face a furious Angus.

"What the hell's this?" he demanded.

"What? Surely you're not jealous? That would be a little hypocritical, don't you think? If you are you can fuck off, just like you wanted to," she responded. "Besides, Juan and I are having dinner tonight after he's given me some lessons."

"You fucking bitch! I ought to smack his face in as well."

She smiled wickedly. "Oh, I wouldn't do that. He's an expert in some sort of Brazilian martial art, very nasty."

"OK, Martini. I know when I'm not wanted."

"Martini?" she looked puzzled.

"Yeah. Anytime, anyplace, anywhere..." he sang, a smug grin on his face. She was not to be drawn.

"Well if you want comfort, I suggest you head back into the arms of Suzanne or whatever her name is. I'm sure she'll keep you warm. And next time, Angus, don't even try to cross me, you lying little shit."

He made as if to protest, then it hit him.

"You planned this all along, didn't you? How long have you known?"

"Long enough to start seeing Juan," she lied. "And he's a bloody sight better looking than you, Angus."

He fumed, stormed off to his car and made to drive away.

"My parents will have your bags ready for you. Drive safely," she said with a smile.

As he left in a cloud of dust Juan turned to Claire and said, "You do wind them up, pretty girl. Now, tell me all about it, the full story, so I can stop pretending to be the great Latin lover and get back to my dear wife."

So she told him the full story, filling in the details of the brief explanation she had given him on the telephone. He understood her feelings well, having been a good friend of her family since they were both children.

"Now, tell me more about your work," he said. "I need to set up an offshore fund for my family trust away from the Brazilian tax authorities, and the UK market may well suit."

They talked at length about all aspects of her work and the markets. Juan was interested and wanted to explore the opportunities further.

"But," Claire said. "First we have a game of polo to play."

Chapter Twelve

As Rupert walked down the corridor to his office, he thought about the way his Castle Street deal was progressing – not for the first time. He had changed over the last eighteen months, and he would be the first to admit it. The eagerness of youth had disappeared, replaced by a determination to get the deal done at all costs. A hard shell was enveloping him, a carapace that inured him to the world in which he lived. He had become tougher mentally, which was reflected in his working life as well as his personality outside the office. His family had noticed the change – which to them seemed much more obvious – on his rare visits home to Warwickshire.

Lost in his reverie, Rupert almost bumped into Claire, who was coming from the opposite direction.

"Oops! Nearly got you," he said. "How are you doing? Good weekend?"

"Ah, actually yes, in a funny sort of way. Listen, do you

fancy a coffee? I need a break and we can discuss Castle Street."

"Yah, absolutely. Let me just get some papers and I'll be right with you."

They walked along Grosvenor street to the usual coffee bar on the corner. As they went in, they nodded to various other agents and property people who made up most of its clientele at that time in the morning. Hushed conversations over coffee, deals being made or broken, information being exchanged. Not for the first time did Rupert consider the value of having eyes and ears all over the place, sucking up information, being party to all that was being said. *Maybe putting a trained waitress in every coffee bar in the West End would be a good idea,* he mused to himself. They got a coffee and settled down in the corner where they could not be overheard.

"So, tell me all," Rupert said. "You look like the cat that got the cream – and a rather malicious cat, at that."

"Well, I had a rather cathartic experience at the weekend. I lured Angus away and hit him where it hurts – in his ego – before finally dumping the bastard," she added gleefully.

"What? Oh, do tell," he begged, grinning from ear to ear.

So she did. The full story, from catching him cheating to finally taking her revenge on him with the help of Juan. Rupert found her story very appealing, especially the bit where Angus was pulled from his horse. He was secretly pleased for his own reasons, too, about which he kept quiet. His relationship with Liz was going well, but there was still something about her that was closed away, something mysterious that he couldn't define.

"So you just left him? Stuck in deepest, darkest, Gloucestershire? Oh well done you, that's absolutely perfect."

"I must admit I enjoyed it. Every single minute, from the moment he arrived and saw my parents to when he stormed off after meeting Juan. Who, incidentally, might want to start an investment company of his own. So, back to being young, free and single again," she sighed.

"You won't be that for long, darling. Soon as they know you are on the market, half the surveyors in the west end will be wanting to clinch a deal of their own."

She leant across and gave him a kiss on the cheek. "Rupes, you're great for my ego. Do you know that?"

He grinned appreciatively.

"Anyway, on to work. I've lined up all the tenants I can without being too specific, which we cannot be until we're sure that we can get VP. Agreed?" said Claire.

"Yes, and we still haven't had a counter notice back from their agents. They've only got two more weeks to go and that's it. Bang!" He slapped his palm into his fist, making various occupants of the coffee bar looked around.

"Easy, tiger, you'll have the market thinking you've pulled off another coup."

He grinned proudly.

"That will do no harm at all. I actually found another site today after a bit of canvassing. Looks promising, great deal."

"Deal junkie!" she accused.

"Hah, hark whose talking."

They both laughed, fully aware that beneath the banter

the reality they had become Thatcher's Children, out for the kill in a raw, commercial, avaricious world.

Chapter Thirteen

Over the next few days, Rupert was on tenterhooks. The cut-off date for the counter notice was looming, and he was called to a meeting at MAS's offices to discuss how the deal was progressing. Discussions did not go as planned due to the presence of David Shingler, who had once again been brought in as the deal came closer to fruition. Simions was in an ebullient mood, optimistic about the outcome of their chances of obtaining vacant possession. Rupert was more cautious, explaining that even if the notice was not served in time the company could still raise an objection that the clause was unfairly harsh and apply to the courts for justice.

Simions dismissed it out of hand. "Don't worry. The accounts for the company made very interesting reading; they aren't as strong as they would have us believe. If anything, they should be moving to more efficient premises anyway. So who cares, we are just hurrying them along. They'll thank us in the long run," he laughed harshly.

Rupert left the meeting, troubled as ever by the presence

of Shingler. While he was now able to hold his own with the man, and was determined never to be trapped like he'd been before by him, he was unable to fathom the close relationship between him and Simions. *Why did Shingler always get brought in?* he wondered. There would be an extra cost to Simions, as he'd have to pay two lots of fees on letting. Then there was always the danger of leakage, as had happened with the last deal. There must be some strong link with the past that bound them together. Rupert knew that if he could find that link, it would release them both.

He turned his thoughts to the week ahead and thought about Liz. She was becoming a larger part of his life. He missed her when they were apart. Despite his feelings of guilt where Claire was concerned (who he knew would never consider him in that way) Liz's magical, elusive quality intrigued and entranced him like no other woman had before. They were good together; she was great company and they shared the same sense of humour, and she was great in bed and completely uninhibited, a big plus as far as Rupert was concerned. On impulse, he called her when he returned to the office, and for once she could talk, openly flirting with him over the telephone.

"Tomorrow evening sounds good, if you're not too tired of course. You looked a bit shattered after the last weekend," she teased.

"Can anyone hear you?"

"They think I'm talking to my squash partner," she giggled.

"OK, lover, Thursday. I'll pick you up at 8-ish but you'd better be lively."

"Mm, but it wasn't me who fell asleep after the second game, was it?" she teased.

"You'll pay for that!"

"Promises, promises! See you Thursday, bye."

The line went dead. Rupert grinned to himself. The eagerness of the chase now over, he was still on a high, still in the first throes of excitement familiar to all experienced lovers. And their relationship was still at the point where they couldn't keep their hands off each other.

The next morning he caught the tube to work and found himself struggling with the Telegraph crossword, caught up in concentration as he tried to decipher an anagram by doodling the letters in the blank space next to the puzzle.

His mind absently scanned the business news snippets in the column above. *Diamond Life: Mystery Offshore Bid*, he read. The article went on to say that an esoteric, off-shore company called Mission Machines had bought a substantial holding in Diamond Drilling Services.

His mind sprang into focus; Diamond Drilling Services were the company he was looking at for Simions. Simions! *Hah, anagrams*, he thought, realising that MISSION was an anagram of SIMIONS. *Oh, beautiful*, he reflected. Although surely Simions would have to declare an interest under stock market rules? Maybe not if it was offshore, and proving who the directors were would be difficult. No doubt financial pressure would be brought to bear to induce Moorcroft Industries to vacate their site.

Suddenly it looked far more likely that the gamble of getting the site for development was a real possibility. He considered the moral position for a moment, but it was not strictly blackmail, it was just...business. Rupert thought hard about it for the rest of the day in terms of how it impacted on his latest deal. But the day was soon to turn into a nightmare for him, all because of a whim.

The previous day he had dropped his car in for a service at the garage the company used just to the north of Oxford Street. Now he decided to walk to the garage as there were no cabs around. He walked across Oxford Street into Duke Street with a view to cutting across Manchester Square to the garage, which was near Portman Street car park. He turned left into the square, and as he did so he decided to call into MAS's offices on spec to congratulate Simions on his strategy.

Looking ahead, around the central park to the front of their offices, he was at first delighted then horrified to see Liz. The sight of her was a pleasurable surprise; he still couldn't get used to her wearing a wig and glasses to work. What was not pleasant, however, was that she was deep in conversation with Simions! He nearly shouted across to them, but something held him back. It was their attitude; familiar, almost intimate, facing each other making eye contact like old friends or, dare he even think it, lovers? He changed his position and placed himself in a less obvious situation where he would still be able to see them.

They walked slowly around the square, heading for the eastern side and Hinde Street, which in turn led to Boswells. He watched them enter the pub together, and something struck a resonant chord in his memory. It was as the sunlight, which for a brief moment hit Simions' shoulders, highlighting his steel grey hair. Of course, he was the man in

Boswells Rupert had seen Liz talking to all those months ago. At the time he hadn't seen the man's face and was too preoccupied with fitting in with the CR crew, but he knew there was something familiar about Simions ever since he'd turned his back to the light in his office at their first meeting. So, that was it. He was her lover, and had been all this time. Suddenly the hesitation and unexplained absences became clear.

He followed discreetly, bought a drink and thanked God for Boswells' high-walled booth arrangement. At this early hour the pub was not busy and it was possible to catch most of their conversation.

"...I don't want to do this anymore. I'm too close to Rupert now. It just won't work. He will begin to suspect. I want to finish it now."

The response was lost and she said something else, then; "Thank you anyway. But it had to end sometime and now seems right."

Rupert was furious, he nearly burst in on them then and there, but he held back. Realising the conversation was at an end, he left his drink unfinished and walked quickly through the side door. Gulping fresh air as he walked along the pavement, he thought he was going to have a heart attack. He was livid with rage. *All the lies and deceit, how could she? And now she wants to end it. That was big of her, the bitch!*

He walked on, needing to calm down and think. Without conscious pause for thought he headed in the direction of the garage. His mind was a whirlwind of emotion. He couldn't believe what Liz had done, he thought for the thousandth time. At no point did he feel he had done anything to deserve that kind of deception, and he had no idea what had caused it. *Why start a relationship in the first place?* He couldn't fathom it. It hurt all the more because, privately, he admitted to himself that he was in love with her, which made it that much worse.

The journey from the garage to her flat was slow because of the rush hour traffic, and as he approached the block of flats he saw that lights were on in the windows on the second floor. Obviously, the journey by tube had been quicker. He parked his car with precise care, taking his time, anticipating the conflict and yet not wanting to end the relationship, despite everything.

He walked across to the front door and pressed the intercom to be let in. As he pushed the door open, it was caught by a woman who had appeared silently behind him. She nodded her thanks, showing a slightly chipped tooth in her smile. Rupert smiled wanly back and proceeded to the lift, pressing the button for the second floor as the woman headed for the stairs.

Before he could even think about what he was going to say, the lift opened its doors and Rupert was pressing the buzzer on Liz's front door. It opened almost immediately and Liz appeared, smiling. Rupert thought she looked slightly stressed, but still lovely. She came forward and kissed him and although he responded in kind, he felt her stiffen, as if she sensed that something was amiss.

"Come in. You look upset, what's wrong?" she asked, frowning.

He moved forward and up the small flight of stairs to the landing, where he continued the conversation.

"That depends, really."

She tensed. "On what?" The old Liz returned as the tension in him became palpably apparent.

"One's point of view," he continued. "You see, to my way of thinking loyalty is the key, in business, pleasure or love. I value it highly and expect it from others."

"Rupert, what the hell are you talking about? Stop being so damn pompous and obtuse and tell me what this is all about. You're obviously upset, so just tell me." In a way, it was as though she had not spoken, except that he picked up on the insult of pomposity.

"Pompous? Well at least it's a genuine emotion! At least I don't have secret assignations; secret relationships and other lovers."

"Rupert, will you talk sense? Come and have a drink and calm down." She led the way into the kitchen, opened a cupboard and produced a bottle of scotch and two tumblers. She poured two good sized measures and offered one to Rupert, who downed it in one go.

"Now tell me what you mean."

"I saw you with Simions. Simions, of all people! He's old enough to be your father!"

Her facial expression changed from puzzlement to hurt anger.

"You bastard. How dare you?! Have you been spying on me?"

"Spying? No, I merely came across you and your lover when I was on my way to see a client. I couldn't believe what I saw and so I followed you to the pub where I heard everything." He relayed all that he had heard from behind the booth. "You've been seeing him for weeks, even before we got together, haven't you? It's so fucking awful, words just fail me! I loved you, do you know that? You've just thrown it in my face!"

"Oh I see, and that is your conclusion is it? I'm having an affair with Paul Simions. And you are judge, jury and executioner, are you? I must be sleeping with him, there's no other possible explanation. Well I loved you too." She was shouting now. "I let you into my life where no one had been for a long time, and for what? For this?" She parted her arms in exasperation and disgust, emphasising her point.

"I heard your conversation. You can't deny it. You're just his part time whore!"

"You absolute bastard! Get out!" she shouted. "Get the hell out, now!"

"With pleasure." He turned on his heel and made his way down the stairs, ducking as a vase just missed his head and exploded against the wall. One of the flying fragments caught him just behind the ear, cutting him slightly. He raised his hand to find blood and reached for the door lock hurriedly.

"You fucking bitch!" he fumed and left hurriedly, slamming the door behind him. He stormed along the corridor, turned left into the lobby area and took the stairs two at a time. He did not see the figure of the woman for whom he held the door, moving quietly along the corridor from the opposite end of the building. She watched him go, a wry smile on her lips and proceeded towards Liz's flat.

Rupert got into his car, revved the engine and flew out of the car park, wheels skidding, entering the traffic without looking and earning himself an angry rebuke from other drivers. He ignored them and sped off, thoroughly upset.

Half an hour later, as he was entering his flat, a telephone call was made to a house in Stanmore.

"Double five one?"

A woman's voice said: "It's done."

"When?"

A slight pause. "Half an hour ago."

"Any problems?"

"No, it went smoothly. She'd just had a row with her boyfriend. It will be perfect," she chuckled.

"He didn't see you?" the voice asked.

"Do me a favour, of course not."

"Good, thank you for letting me know. We will settle up as usual."

The line at the other end went dead and David Shingler put down the telephone.

Chapter Fourteen

The day started badly for Rupert and went downhill from there. He got to work with a bad hangover. His mouth felt as if a pigeon had shat in it, probably from when he collapsed on the sofa last night after his final glass of whisky. *Never again,* he thought, *never again.* He watched as two Alka Seltzers fizzed in the glass of water in front of him. He waited until they had dissolved then swirled the glass and gulped the contents in two mouthfuls. It tasted awful.

"God you look rough," Tina commented as she entered the room. "Good night?"

"No, bloody awful actually."

"Ah, burning the candle at both ends, and on a weekday too. You boys. I don't know how you do it!" She smiled warmly in sympathy and walked on towards her desk.

The morning dragged on, and just as Rupert was starting to feel slightly better, things became unimaginably worse.

He received a call from Matthews, the company secretary

querying his car type and registration number, which he verified.

"Why what's the problem?" he asked. "Not another bloody speeding ticket?"

"I don't think so, not unless they send detective inspectors round to investigate speeding fines."

"What do you mean?"

"A Detective Inspector Fleming phoned about your car. It's registered to us, obviously. Anyway, he'll be here in about ten minutes and he wants to talk to you, so I should pull yourself together a bit if I were you. You haven't done anything we should know about, have you? You weren't actually driving it last night, surely."

"No, absolutely not!"

"Good. Well let me know, will you?"

He put the telephone down and Rupert felt that cold tingle that any law abiding citizen gets when the police start involving themselves for no apparent reason. He didn't have to wait long. Reception called about fifteen minutes later to say that two police officers were asking to see him. He made his way down to reception with a feeling of trepidation. *What have I done?* he wondered. He thought about all the border line cases of illegality he'd been involved in with Simions. Should he have reported bribing a planning officer? Was there more than just the threat of menace when Cauldron's MD backed away from the court case? And what did any of it have to do with his car?

He walked into reception and the receptionist nodded at the two men reclining on the sofa. They got up together and Rupert would have known straight away that they were policemen. They had a certain manner and cynical way of looking at him, he decided. They were two completely different people to look at, yet they both looked the same. The taller of the two walked forward with no offer to shake hands. A bad sign, Rupert decided.

The Inspector's voice was clipped and hard. "Mr Brett?"

Rupert nodded in acknowledgement.

"I am DI Fleming, this –" he jerked a thumb over his shoulder, "is DS Brooke." They flipped open warrant cards and then snapped them shut.

"Good morning, how can I help you?" Rupert continued, sounding more confident than he felt.

"Is there somewhere we can talk, Mr Brett? Somewhere a little more private."

The insinuation in Fleming's tone that they would need privacy was another turn of the screw to intimidate, to make the recipient more uncomfortable. It was obviously a well-practised technique. Rupert showed them towards one of the meeting rooms leading off from reception. He switched on the lights, offered them coffee – which they both refused – and sat down.

He studied them again, trying to gain some kind of clue as to what this was all about. He saw Fleming's cold eyes looking back at him from a gaunt, lined face that had seen too much and trusted nothing. His hair was prematurely flecked with grey from overwork and long, stressful hours.

The detective sergeant was stocky and square; his broad shoulders hinted at power beneath the grey jacket, which did not match his trousers. An ex-policeman friend of Rupert's had once told him that CID officers always wore mismatched jackets and trousers. They might have matched when new, but after various scuffles, scaling fences and walls and chasing villains they had to buy new pairs of trousers which seldom exactly matched their jackets.

"So, is one of you going to tell me what all this is about?"

"Do you know an Elizabeth Carmichael?" Fleming asked.

"Liz, yes. She is my girlfriend. Why? Has something happened to her?" he asked, concern evident in his voice.

"Why should something have happened to her?" DS Brooke asked, making the question sound like an accusation.

"Well, by the fact that you're here asking questions about her. Look, if something has happened to Liz please tell me what it is, or get to the point." He had not enjoyed the last twenty-four hours, and he was getting to the end of his tether, police or no police.

DI Fleming looked at Rupert, as if reassessing him. "We were called this morning to check on a flat belonging to Miss Carmichael, as one of her neighbours was concerned. You see, she had arranged to look after said neighbour's cat as she was going on holiday today, but Miss Carmichael didn't call round this morning to collect the keys as per their arrangement. She gave us your car registration. Said you were quite a frequent visitor. The neighbour also said that she heard a disturbance the night before, and was understandably a little worried.

"We telephoned Miss Carmichael but there was no answer. In the end, we had to break the door down, and guess what we found?" Rupert began to feel weak. He didn't know what was coming next but something told him it was going to be bad. "We found Miss Carmichael dead, Mr Brett."

"Oh my God. How? Why? Where?" The words came out in a high-pitched squeak, as if they had been torn from him. Shock must have been obvious on his face as the full implication of what Fleming had said hit home.

"Where were you last night, Mr Brett?" Brooke said.

He did not answer immediately. "I was at her flat, but why...I mean...what does that mean? I wasn't there when she died. How did she die?" He stumbled over the last words, the reality hitting him that he would not see her again made worse by their final acrimonious parting. He would never forgive himself.

"We are not sure how she died exactly, but we think it may be drugs related."

"Drugs? But that's ridiculous! She never took drugs."

They ignored his statement. "How well did you know Miss Carmichael?"

"She was my girlfriend. We'd been seeing each other for a few months."

"Were you intimate?"

"What? Did we sleep together? Yes, we did and at no time did I see any needle marks."

"Who said anything about needles?" It was Brooke again, being clever.

"I naturally assumed that as it was drugs that it would involve a needle. Isn't that how you take drugs? The sort that'll kill you, anyway"

"Not necessarily. They could be administered orally."

Rupert shook his head in disbelief. The DI changed tack.

"What time did you leave the flat?"

"Just after seven, I think. I don't know exactly. I came straight from picking up my car from the garage."

"Where was that?"

"Just off Manchester Square, it is the main garage the firm uses."

Rupert did not mention seeing Liz with Simions or the overheard conversation in the pub. He didn't want to incriminate himself any further at this stage.

"So, you went straight from the garage to her flat?" the question was left hanging in the air.

"Yes. We had a date for that evening. I arrived to pick her up, we were going out to dinner."

"And you arrived, then what?" The question was framed in such a way that Rupert suspected that they knew more than was being said and decided to come clean.

"We had a row. After we argued I left the flat and drove home. I probably got home about eight. Maybe eight-thirty."

"What did you argue about?" It was Brooke again. Rupert explained in more specific terms this time, including the events that occurred in Manchester Square and finishing with him leaving the flat.

"That is the whole story, with nothing left out," he finished.

"So now you say another person was involved and you were jealous? Why did you not mention this before? You didn't assault Miss Carmichael in any way?" DS Brooke sneered again.

"What? Are you crazy? Of course I didn't hit her."

Rupert's face hardened in anger and grief at the insinuation. "And I didn't tell you because I didn't think it was relevant, although now it appears it may be. But, no, I did not force her to do anything. Why, was there a sexual assault? And for the last time, I did not know that she took drugs and still find it incredible to believe. How were they taken if there was no injection?"

"We are asking the questions, Mr Brett," Fleming said. "Now who was this other man she saw? What is his name and how do you know him?"

Rupert answered, naming Paul Simions and telling them about his connection with him.

"So let me get this straight. This Mr Simions is your client, and he holds sway over you. You see him having an affair with your girlfriend, you get mad, rush to her flat in a rage and you are the last person to see her alive. Is that correct?"

The silence was shattering. Rupert went red and suddenly found it hard to breathe.

"No, it wasn't like that. We rowed, but I left her alive and well, just upset. This is a nightmare," he said.

"Did you try and contact Miss Carmichael again by telephone after you had left her flat, Mr Brett?"

"No, I didn't"

"Why not?"

"Because like I told you, we argued, and as far as I could tell we broke up. At least it seemed that way at the time." He gazed into the middle distance, his thoughts in tatters.

"Would you mind explaining that cut on your neck, Mr Brett?

He flinched as he touched the newly healed scab on his neck. "Yes. Liz," he paused at saying her name. "The row got a bit heated. She threw a vase at me as I was leaving and –"

"And you just took it without retaliating? You just went on your merry way with a 'thank you very much', did you?" DS Brooke asked.

"Yes. I was nearly out the door. What do you think? That I ran back up and strangled her or something?"

"Who said she was strangled?" Brooke came back at him.

Despite the shock, the surveyor took over. Rupert's wits were his greatest asset: "Precisely. You said it was drugs related. If it was, do you think I went there armed with a syringe or a lethal dose of pills or whatever just in case we might have a row? I was taking her to dinner. I'd booked a table and everything!" he shouted, realising he was close to hysteria. "I had nothing to do with her death," he finished vehemently. "Go and talk to Paul bloody Simions, he's a much more likely..." Rupert forced himself to silence.

The two detectives exchanged a glance and DS Brooke closed his notebook.

"We will have some more questions for you in due course, Mr. Brett, so please remain available," concluded DI Fleming. Brooke asked Rupert to write down his contact details and they both got up, Rupert rising with them, his mind in turmoil. "Right, that's all for now, Fleming said. "Thank you, Mr Brett." They left Rupert with his thoughts.

Rupert's world had collapsed, and it had taken less than a day. He slumped back in the chair in the quiet of the meeting room. He needed a drink, a smoke, something... someone, any–

Claire. He needed to talk to Claire.

Out on the street the two policemen walked in the direction of Manchester Square.

"What do you think, guv?" Brooke asked the inspector.

"I don't know. The grief was genuine, but they had a row. He looked genuinely shocked, not a twitch or anything, just tears and grief."

"Yes, but were they tears of guilt at something that had gone too far?" DS Brooke queried cynically.

"I think you were a bit hard on him mind with that sex comment."

Brooke shrugged. "Got a response, though, didn't it? Anyway we'll see what the autopsy says, I asked for a priority so we should have it tomorrow. He is still the best suspect we have and the last person to see her alive. But he's right about the drugs. They have a row, she hurls the vase at him, what's he gonna do? He'll do what most of the buggers do, he'll bash her over the head with something. Strangle her. Do her in with a kitchen knife. He's not going to sit her down and say 'here, love, why don't you take this lethal cocktail of drugs I just so happen to have about my person.' Is he? It's beginning to look a lot like suicide..." Brooke sang to the tune of a popular Christmas melody, earning himself a frown of censure from his superior. "Sorry, guv. Where to now, the mysterious Mr Simions?"

"Yes, let's pay him a call while everything is still up in the air. You never know if Mr Brett might want to tip him off," Fleming offered.

They arrived at MAS's offices on Manchester Square and announced themselves at the ground floor reception. One of the stunning blonde secretaries called Simions. The two detectives noticed the pause in the conversation despite being able to only hear one side of it.

The receptionist beamed at the two men, who were completely immune: "Mr Simions is on the telephone but will be with you as soon as he can."

Brett! Fleming thought. To the secretary he said. "Would you mind phoning Mr Simions again and telling him to get off the fucking telephone and get his arse down here," The last half of the sentence was spoken is strong contrast to the first, and as Fleming anticipated, the receptionist jumped to it with alacrity.

The detectives nodded, exchanging glances. They judged their lives by a series of rules, one of which was that delaying tactics were more often than not a sign of guilt. The receptionist told them to go up to Simions' office. DI Fleming and DS Brooke left the lift on the top floor. As they were shown into Simions' office by yet another gorgeous blonde. Brooke eyed the movement of her skirt and exchanged an appreciative glance with his superior. Simions watched the farce, smiling to himself as he made a pretence of finishing a call, so that he could assess before being assessed. "Yes, yes, of course," he said into the telephone. "Will do, and please have the papers sent around by this afternoon. Goodbye."

Anyone who knew him well would know he was putting it on; he was rarely polite enough to say goodbye.

He rose from his chair smiling, the picture of urbanity, every inch the captain of industry, extending his hand as he came around the desk.

"Gentlemen, good morning. Paul Simions, but I expect you know that already as you've come to see me," he joked.

They shook hands, intimidated to a level they had not been with Rupert earlier. "DI Fleming and DS Brooke. Thank you for agreeing to see us."

"Please sit down, tea, coffee?"

"Already been offered. One of the blondes is bringing us some," Brooke replied affably.

"Good, good. Now what can I do for you?" Simions' hands were expansive, the gesture open; he was the picture of calm.

Oh he's good, Fleming thought. *He's very good, and if I hadn't been briefed by Rupert Brett first, I'd almost be completely taken in.*

"We are making enquiries about a young woman who we believe you may know."

Simons gave them a benign smile that did not reach his opaque, lupine eyes. "Oh dear, you'll have to be more specific. I employ a number of young ladies, as you can see, both here in and in other offices I run. What is the young woman's name?" he asked.

DI Fleming grinned at this suave show. "Miss Elizabeth Carmichael."

Simions adopted a puzzled expression seeming to theatrically search his memory.

"Elizabeth Carmichael? Oh, *Liz.* Yes, of course I know her. Tall girl, very pretty, but hides it well behind glasses?"

Fleming frowned. "Glasses? We'll come back to that. So how do you know her?"

"As I said, I employ a number of people, she temped for

me through an agency." He shrugged as though that explained it all.

"So you didn't see her outside office hours?"

Simions continued as benignly as ever. "Not in the normal course of events, no. But funnily enough I did bump into her leaving the office yesterday evening. I asked her for a drink and we went to a local pub. She didn't stay long. Told me she was off to meet her boyfriend." He smiled; it was not a nice expression.

"Where did you go afterwards?"

"Detective Inspector, this conversation is taking a distasteful turn, and I would like to know where it is leading. However, I went to my club, The Carlton, where I had dinner with two business associates, whose names I am happy to provide, along with the name of the club secretary, who I spoke to just before leaving at around 10.30. Then my chauffeur drove me home and my housekeeper provided me with a night cap when I got there. Now what is this all about?"

DI Fleming did not blink or show any emotion, he merely thrust straight ahead with the brutal statement, watching for the response on Simions face. "Mr Simions, Elizabeth Carmichael is dead, and you were the last person who knew her to see her alive," he lied.

"Liz? Oh heavens, surely not. What a terrible thing to happen!" Simions' face showed shock and sadness, but then his expression changed through puzzlement to anger. "And what, you think because I had a drink with the poor woman that I might have followed her home and...? Good heavens, that is absurd!" he said.

Fleming and Brooke exchanged glances again. Simions had not done the one thing that all innocent people do, which was to ask how Liz had died. Simions' next statement was predictable enough.

"Well if this the tone and direction this conversation is taking," he continued, "I think I had better have my lawyer present before we continue this discussion any further." He reached for the telephone on his desk and began to dial a number.

DI Fleming held up a hand; "I don't think that will be necessary just yet, Mr Simions," he said. "We're just establishing some preliminary facts at this stage."

Simions replaced the receiver and looked at the two officers in a way that suggested he had won a point. They stood to leave, and Simions rose and began walking them to the door, which he opened for them.

"That won't be necessary, sir. We can find our own way out."

"On the contrary," Simions said. "I shall see you from my premises."

They gave him a flat stare as they went down in the lift, and as they were signing themselves out, he spoke to his receptionists; "If either of these gentlemen call again, the first thing you do is call Andrew Davis, my solicitor, and do not admit them any further until he arrives. Is that clear?" The two women smiled and accepted the order as if such things were an everyday occurrence. They looked haughtily at the two policemen who smiled at the thinly veiled threat. They'd heard it all before.

"Thank you for your help, Mr Simions. We will be in

touch with more questions, rest assured, with or without your lawyer's permission. This may become a murder enquiry in the fullness of time." Fleming retorted, smiling at the double intake of breath from the blondes. He gave Simions a curt nod and the two men left. Fleming had the pleasure of watching Simions' lips narrow in anger as he turned on his heel and walked towards the lift.

As the policemen reached the street, Brooke grinned. "Well that was fun. I want to put that bastard away on general principles. He may not have been there or done the deed directly – if indeed it was a murder – but he has some connection there, a good deal more than he let on."

"Agreed," Fleming said. "The question is, what and how does it tie in with Rupert Brett? I wonder if everything's as straightforward as Mr Brett is making out, or are they colluding somehow and sending us off on a tangent? We need more information. I need the autopsy result ASAP so we know whether or not we're looking at a murder. In the meantime, look into the backgrounds of all three of them; Brett, Simions and Miss Carmichael. We're missing something and I want to know what it is."

"Right you are, guv," Brooke said.

The two detectives would have been very interested to hear the conversation taking place between Shingler and Simions at that moment. Simions explained the events to David Shingler, who was both furious and worried.

"What? You know this is the first time we have ever had any kind of connection with Secs and the City. We need to do something about this, and Mr Brett appears to be the biggest problem. We need to dissuade him," he finished.

"We do, but not in the way you mean. I intend to bring Rupert into the fold. The police will see it as an alliance between us and he will be marked and lose credibility. The market will hear about this and will react negatively. His girl-friend is dead. Murder or suicide, whatever it is, he'll be tainted, and there is no sorrier sight than a tainted, friendless agent, you mark my words."

Shingler was not convinced, and although he agreed in principle, he had other ideas which he put in place as soon as his conversation with Simions had ended. It was on such actions that the game revolved, and this was to prove no exception to that rule.

Chapter Fifteen

Rupert was on autopilot as he walked from the conference room and out into reception.

"You OK, Rupert? You look as if you've seen a ghost," the receptionist commented. Rupert didn't acknowledge her. He turned and rushed to the nearest toilet, where he threw up. He staggered upstairs and called Claire, asking to see her straight away. They met in the street and headed along Grosvenor Street towards Hyde Park. He blurted everything out, eventually stopping at a park bench, where she held him as the tremors of grief and shock rippled though him. She comforted him as best she could, rocking him gently, saying nothing, her mind in a whirl. Finally she said, "Rupes, they can't think you did it. How could they? It was drug related."

"No, but they think I am involved, even if it's only indirectly. No smoke without fire, you know? Also, if this gets into the market, which of course it will, I will be ostracised, just you see if I'm not. It will spread like a fucking virus you know what gossips everyone is in this bloody game. I doubt even Matthews will be discreet."

"No, they'll stand by you. You're well thought of and you've built a great reputation too. You're a dealer! Everyone loves a dealer."

But Claire was to be proved wrong. By late afternoon the rumours were spreading; anything from an unfortunate suicide to Rupert killing her in cold blood while she slept. It quickly spread to other firms, and by the next day some of his calls were not being returned. No one wanted to be associated with a loser, and the brutal reality was that Rupert was only as good as his last deal.

The next twenty four hours were a nightmare for Rupert. He explained the events to the company secretary, who while sympathetic, was also keen to avoid any scandal attaching to the firm – particularly as the police enquiry had not exonerated Rupert. Indeed, from the way Rupert described it, he was a prime suspect. Accordingly, he offered to let Rupert have some time off, more with a view to distancing him from the firm than any sense of benevolence. It was couched as an offer, at least, but Rupert knew that it was a veiled order really.

Rupert was not keen at all, and the thought of sulking at home in his flat or walking aimlessly in the park with more time to think held little appeal. The weekend loomed, a weekend for which he and Liz had great plans. He still could not believe what had happened: first the deceit, then the row, now her death. It was like something from a terrible nightmare which he could not escape.

He tried to concentrate on his work for the rest of the

morning as he pondered his options, looking at the numbers again for the Castle Road project, which in turn brought him back to Simions. He must know, Rupert imagined. The detectives probably went straight to him when they left him. What would be his reaction? Grief, horror, surprise? In a moment of spiteful impetuosity, wanting to lash out at something for the terrible thing that had happened, he arranged a meeting for that morning on a spurious excuse. He was told that Simions could spare him a few minutes late morning. He grasped the opportunity and entered the offices just before 12.30.

He was shown up to Simions' office. Suave as ever, Simions stood backlit against his office window with the sunlight silhouetting his shoulders, bringing back awful memories. He moved away from the light and Rupert could see he was wearing one of his customary handmade navy blue suits; immaculately groomed as ever. The aftershave reached Rupert slightly ahead of the extended hand.

"Rupert, good to see you." He was subdued yet polite.

Something was wrong, Rupert decided. "Morning Paul, how are you?" he said

"Very well, but rather better than you look," he said commenting upon the ashen face and the blue circles around the eyes.

"You'll have heard about Liz Carmichael," Rupert raised his head, finding eye contact difficult but studying Simions' face for any tell-tale emotion. "She was my girlfriend."

"Rupert, my dear boy, I am so sorry. But what are you doing at work? You should be taking some time off. Go home, the deal will look after itself."

"I can't bear it at home. Just thinking about Liz, it all comes back." Rupert paused, gulped a couple of times. "You knew her, I'm sure. Did a lot of work for property people, they seemed to ask for her," he trailed off, part acting, partly genuinely upset. Simions' face appeared to consider the name for a moment, searching his memory.

It was then that Simions realised it would have been Rupert who had seen them together, and that his discussion with the police would have led them straight to him. On a hunch he played a card he was holding close to his chest. "Yes, Rupert, I knew her. She was working for me yesterday and has done so before. We had a drink together after work, at Boswells as a matter of fact, over the road. She left, said she had a date. Of course, that would have been you. But the police were here as well, asking questions because I'd employed her. I expect they're doing the rounds of most surveyors in the West End. They get everywhere, temps. Look, I think you should go and get some rest."

Rupert ignored the offered advice. "What, she was working for you? I thought she was at Halpern and Beams?"

"Oh, she popped over afterwards to pick up some information, to look at a bit of freelance work she was going to do for me next week," Simions responded.

Quite the consummate actor, aren't you? Rupert thought. He decided to change tack too, switching to property. "Master stroke by the way," he said ambiguously.

"What?" Simions suddenly looked more alarmed than Rupert had ever seen him.

"The anagram of your name. I saw it in the paper.

Buying out Diamond Drilling Services. Surely, it was you. Good idea to put some leverage on them.

For a brief, fleeting moment, anger, relief and frustration fought to gain supremacy on Simions' face. Finally, denial won; with a bland, puzzled expression he fixed Rupert with his gaze.

"I'm sorry, I don't know what you mean. I've been looking into Diamond, but for now I'm relying upon the non-service of notice. In any case, you shouldn't concern yourself with details like that now. I really think you should be getting some rest."

The meeting was clearly at an end. *There was no point,* Rupert reflected, *in pushing it further, he'd thrown in enough ambiguities and had seen Simions' reaction.* He would bide his time.

He walked out of the office door and could not help but mull over the events of the past few minutes. *The little shit!* Not a flicker of emotion other than hiding behind his concern for Rupert. Something else was niggling at him, something that was said or not said, which he felt was important. Of course, why didn't he ask how? He didn't ask how she'd died. Surely everyone asks that? It is always the first question on everyone's lips.

He resolved to check upon the details of the Mission company who had just taken over Diamond Drilling Services.

Once Rupert had left the room, Simions turned to look out of the window, gazing into space. He was not pleased at all with the way things were progressing. He turned abruptly and made a call.

"Paul? Yes, Brett's just left. No I am not pleased. He is putting too much together, even called me out on the Diamond Drilling deal. No, it's too risky, I don't like that idea. Mmm, possibly. All right, try it, if not we may have to approach things from a more benign angle."

The call ended and he replaced the receiver. He returned to the window, deep in thought. *What*, he wondered, *was the cut-off date for counter submission?* He checked the file and made another call to the recruitment consultant. They confirmed that a specific secretary would be available on the dates requested.

He made a second call to Shingler, confirming the date and action to be taken.

When Rupert returned to the office, the Mission company was the last thing on his mind. Fleming and Brooke had returned and were waiting for him. They had been there for about half an hour when he walked into reception. With a manner less courteous than before, they asked for a meeting room where they could talk again. As soon as the door closed behind them, the receptionist was on the internal phone, and minutes later the news was flying around the building: Rupert Brett was being questioned again.

The two detectives settled down in the chairs and began asking questions. Rupert confirmed his story.

DS Brooke was as aggressive as before. With the preamble over, they started the same line of questioning again.

"And at no time did this argument take on a physical aspect at all?"

"No. Absolutely not. Apart from Liz throwing the vase. We had a row and we shouted at each other. It was heated, yes, but there was no physical contact at all. She asked me to leave, and I did, pretty much straight away. I was angry. I practically ran from the place."

"When did she throw the vase at you?"

"Just as I was going down the stairs. Luckily I saw it coming and ducked just in time."

"Well that's strange, you see, because we have found traces of blood on a fragment of the vase and it matches blood we found on the lock. Did she cut you with the vase?"

Instinctively he reached up behind his ear and felt the small scab.

"Well yes, she caught me with a fragment, but it was just a scratch, like I said before."

"And you maintain that you your reaction to being hit by a vase was to leave. Did you return to hurt her?" Brooke said.

"No. Look, I was upset, but I wanted to leave quickly. Why all these questions? I thought it was a drug related suicide? Don't you think I feel bad enough? Don't you think I blame myself every second of every waking day? Now it sounds as though you are blaming me for her death too."

"It looked like suicide," Fleming answered. "Drugs – heroin in fact – was the cause of death, ultimately, but prior to that –" he checked his notes. "From the preliminary autopsy report, she suffered bruising around her face and on her upper arms, as though she had been grabbed and held. So we checked again on the contents of the body. She had ingested a lot of whisky, more than you stated, and much of it was not in the blood stream, it was just lying in her stomach. Someone had poured it down her neck after she was dead. But the autopsy also found a tiny quantity of a rare drug which we are still trying to identify. It seems to have the same qualities as gas used by vets, only in ether form. Fast acting, reacts well with alcohol, very hard to trace."

"What are you saying?" Rupert asked, horror written on his face.

"What we're saying, Mr Brett, is that we have ruled out suicide. This is now officially a murder enquiry," Fleming said

"And you think I did it? That's insane!"

"The heroin was administered by injection, and the injection site was between her toes." DI Fleming waited for Rupert's reaction.

Rupert's brain worked quickly. "Hence the question about being intimate. Well, intimacy is one thing, but I don't go around checking for puncture marks in between my girlfriends' toes. Which is why I didn't know that she took drugs." He paused, shaking his head in disbelief "I still can't believe it. What sort of drug was it?"

"We don't know yet, we will have to wait for the full autopsy report. Brooke continued, "But look at it this way. You had access – the door wasn't forced. You had a motive – anger, jealousy or both, and you probably thought you could get away with it."

"I had nothing to do with this. I left Liz alive and well. I think I had better call a lawyer before you make any more ludicrous suggestions."

"There's no need for that at this stage. We haven't

cautioned you, nor do we intend to press any charges as yet, but we will need to speak to you again as our enquiries progress. So please be prepared to make yourself available."

"Well, if you pursue this line of enquiry, I can tell you that I do not intend to speak to you again unless I have a lawyer present, do you understand?" Rupert finished. Fleming and Brooke exchanged glances, a mutual understanding passing between them with no words spoken. They got up to leave.

"We will be in touch, Mr Brett."

As Rupert sat in the meeting room, taking stock of the new information, the door opened and Sheen appeared. He had remained an odd, dichotomous mixture of disciplinarian, mentor and, as in this case, a friendly face. Rupert looked up.

"Rupert, I have heard about what's going on," Sheen began gently. "I know it must be difficult for you and I just wanted to say if you need a friend or anyone to talk to about it, well, please let me know." He attempted humour to lighten the mood, "An old rent review surveyor can often put a different slant on things..."

Rupert smiled at the words. "Thank you. It's much appreciated, but I don't really know what anyone can do at the moment. The secretary advised me to take some time off, but I think it was more of an order than a piece of advice," Rupert gave Sheen a cynical look. "The police are making more enquiries and so far, they aren't charging me or anyone else. It's all in limbo just now," he finished.

Sheen nodded, smiled and left, the master of knowing when to push and when to leave things alone.

Out on the street, the detectives compared notes.

"What do you think?" Brooke said.

"I don't know," Fleming replied. "It looks easy enough – a moment of rage, brought on by being struck by the vase, added to the fact that he was already angry with jealousy. But drugging her...it just doesn't feel right. If it is a liquid form of biometrophoxil that was put on a pad to knock her out, where did he get it? Where did he get the heroin? It was clearly not premeditated. He was on the button the last time we saw him. You don't go armed with a bottle of some weird concoction just in case you have a row with your girlfriend, do you? I've said that before. No, something's not right. I want a full house-to-house done on the whole block and the houses opposite. There's something we're missing, I can feel it."

"Have a heart, guv, it'll take ages!" Brooke complained.

"Get over to uniform, get the plods on it. I want it done, OK?"

"All right, but in the meantime do we keep the pressure on sonny-boy here?" he said, jerking his thumb over his shoulder.

"Leave it for a couple of days, see what the enquiries turn up. This isn't as clear cut as it seems. Brett's tied up in this somehow, and so is that fucking Simions. We know it's drug related and we're sure it's murder now. See if Miss Carmichael had any form, will you? Dig into her background a bit." DS Brooke nodded.

"I hate these types," Fleming finished. "Someone's going to swing for this."

Part Two

Closure

Chapter Sixteen

For Rupert, the weekend began with a series of telephone calls, condolences from friends and drinking to forget. Claire came around more than once to see how he was, together with Mike and Jemma. None of them could believe what had happened; it all seemed so unreal. Mike's attitude was a little more distant, and Rupert caught him looking askance at him once or twice. *If Mike doubted him*, he thought, *what chance did he have of convincing the police?* He had already felt the cold draft of the market: meetings cancelled, a reluctance to be seen in his company, offers of lunch shunned. He was a pariah now, his girlfriend murdered and his reputation further tarnished by his association with suspect number two – Paul Simions.

Saturday passed and he resolved to go into the West End and see a film; anything, he reasoned, just something with a bit of mindless action or adventure that would take his mind off things. He went to see *Out of Africa* hoping to get a little escapism from a depressing London. Driving in, he parked his car in the multi storey with spaces reserved for CR employees and got a cab for the last half mile.

The unhappy ending and the death of the character played by Robert Redford depressed him still more and he wandered back in a fairly morose state. He walked back to the car park, towards the far end where the CR reserved bays were located. As he passed one of the stone pillars, he caught a movement from the corner of his eye. He turned to see a man approaching from some twenty feet away. His manner was positive, almost swaggeringly confident and purposeful. Rupert immediately came alert, sensing that this was a threat. He experienced what fighters everywhere are familiar with – an adrenalin rush – and his limbs refused to obey him.

As the man got closer, his features showed scar tissue above the nose and around his hard eyes. His shoulders were broad and bulky, and they moved easily beneath his open leather jacket. At more than six feet, he seemed to tower over Rupert. but when he was within two feet of him, he spoke and the spell was broken.

"I want a word wiv you," he said, his voice a deep and gravelly East End rasp. "You've been poking around where you shouldn't. It's not healthy, you know."

His left hand moved out to grab Rupert, the other clenching aggressively, his posture perfectly balanced for a blow. The move was fast and practised, having used his words to distract Rupert and close the distance between them. He was supremely confident, assuming that his victim was just some yuppie city type.

In his time with the TA, one of the courses Rupert had

been on was Unarmed Combat. The instructor was an SAS man who came down from Hereford twice a year to reassess them all and sharpen their skills. At the start of the first course, they all imagined that they would be fighting like Bruce Lee within the week, and were swiftly disillusioned. The instructor told them that any martial arts discipline takes a long time to learn and perfect, far too long for the battlefield. Instead he had taught them dirty fighting, how to deal with the first punch and how do as much damage as possible in the first few seconds. The technique still needed practice, but this was something they all did regularly, and now it came into play.

The words of the instructor came back to him again and again. *"Whatever happens, throw something forward. Whatever it is, just throw something forward!"*

As the arm came forward to grab him, Rupert thrust his right arm straight at the man, fingers extended, aiming for the eyes. The other man was fast, although surprised, and tried to avoid the fingers, jerking his head back. Rupert lashed his arm downwards, grabbing the man's sleeve more by luck than judgement. The assailant was caught slightly off balance and turned his head to avoid a blow, exposing his ear. Rupert struck him as hard as he could with the flat of his hand over his exposed ear, driven by fear and adrenalin.

There was a pop as the man's eardrum burst and the result was spectacular. Deprived of his balance, the thug span around, and for good measure Rupert launched a lucky kick that caught him on the kneecap. He howled with anger and pain, but unable to stand, he crashed to the floor. Rupert ran for his car, flicked the lock system, jumped in and turned the key, praying it would start first time. He pumped the accelerator. *Wrong thing to do,* he thought in panic and tried again. It caught on the second try and he sent the car flying forward towards the exit of the car park, wheels spinning on the shiny concrete, desperate to get out. He knew he'd been lucky, that he would ultimately come off second best against a man like his assailant, who looked like he'd grown up on the streets, despite the burst eardrum and the knee.

As if to confirm the thought, Rupert saw the large figure lurch from a supporting pillar into the path of his car. His brain told him not to stop for anything. He thrust his foot hard on the accelerator and at the last minute the man lunged out of the way. He was too late, taking a glancing blow to the hip from the wing of the car. Even above the noise of the engine Rupert heard an ominous cracking sound. It was either Rupert's wing mirror or the man's hip. He saw the man spin round, clutching his side, and expression of agony on his face. Rupert realised he was looking at the man in his wing mirror. *The hip, then.* The man tried to rise and follow the car, but finally crashed to the floor, his face twisted in hatred and pain, grasping at thin air with his free hand. Rupert did not stop until he reached the barrier, where he screeched to a halt, pressed the button and waited for it to rise. *Fine time to worry about your paintwork*, Rupert thought as the barrier rose and he shot out of the car park, narrowly missing an oncoming car in the street. He was breathing hard, shaking with the adrenalin at the sudden violence and his narrow escape. His mouth felt dry and there were beads of sweat on his forehead. *Nothing*, he thought, *can prepare you for the real thing, no amount of practice.* One thing was for sure, the next time he met the instructor from Hereford he was going to buy him a very big drink! Feeling flustered, Rupert drove in the vague direction of home.

What was that? he thought. *A mugging?* The words before the attack were, he assumed, irrelevant, said merely to throw him off balance. Or were they? Surely there could be no connection between speaking to Simions and the attack. He had been blatant in referring to Simions' activities, certainly, but would that have warranted such a drastic response? His brain raced as he considered all the possibilities, but there were still parts of the puzzle that were not yet clear. He drove past Paddington Green police station, and on impulse turned off the main road and parked in one of the sidestreets. He was still badly shaken and sat for a moment considering his actions, listening to the tick of hot metal as the car cooled down, his mind gradually cooling along with it.

He opened the car door, got out and stood up, feeling unsteady as the cool night air hit him. He needed to report the assault. He didn't want another visit from the police after someone else had taken his number as he screeched out of the car park. He imagined the flat gaze of the sergeant – Brown? *Brooke*, that was it. *Your girlfriend is dead, Mr Brett, and now you're involved in an altercation in which a man has been crippled for life. Not looking too good for you, Mr Brett, is it?*

The doors opened to the reception area, security glass everywhere, buzzers sounding as the doors clicked open and closed. The sound of angry voices and shouted commands from behind the glass and heads turning in the grubby reception area in front of the desk. Another Saturday night in London. There were two scruffy people sitting in chairs by reception, looking the worse for drink. The girl had a black eye that was swelling into a nice purple bruise as the man next to her flexed the fist of his right hand, looking vacantly into the middle distance. Rupert avoided his gaze; he'd had enough trouble for one night.

He walked to the main desk. A sergeant was on duty, her blond hair pulled back in a bun, dark eyes that were hard and knowing. They had seen too much and become world weary and tired. Her expression reminded him of Fleming and Brooke, and Rupert wondered briefly what her smile had looked like back in the days before she joined the force.

She was tall, and made level eye contact with him, not aggressive but strong. Already she was assessing him, putting him in a box for consideration. *Not that different to any other receptionist*, he decided.

"Yes, sir, may I help?"

"I hope so," Rupert said. "I've just been attacked in a car park. I think it was a mugging. I managed to escape, but there was an accident as I drove out. I think I injured the man who was trying to attack me. Can I talk to someone about it?" he finished shakily, realising that his voice was still a little high pitched and shaky.

She took out a form, asked for his name and address, looked at him intently again and asked him to take a seat. He turned to go and then a thought occurred to him.

"I don't suppose Detective Inspector Fleming is on duty, is he?"

"I'll ask, Mr Brett. Do you know him?"

"Well, in a manner of speaking. He is investigating the death of...of my girlfriend." His face clouded with pain at the thought, and he realised he had probably said the wrong thing, but it was too late now. "I mean, there might be a connection, I don't..." Rupert's words tailed off and the sergeant looked at him again, the hardened expression returning to her face.

"OK, I'll be back in a minute."

Me and my big mouth, he thought. *When will I learn? 'Just investigating the death of my girlfriend.' Idiot.*

He sat down and waited, avoiding the eye of the couple opposite. He jumped as the electronic locks shot open and two constables left through the glass doors, preparing for a night shift. Five minutes passed by and the door went again. Standing there was DI Fleming.

"Well, well, Mr Brett, this is a surprise. Would you like to come this way?" He motioned with his hand through the glass doors towards the corridor beyond.

"Thank you."

They walked down the corridor to a door marked *Interview Room*. DI Fleming slid the door sign to *Occupied* and indicated the table and chairs, offering Rupert a seat. The room was stark, lit by a single harsh fluorescent light, and smelled of disinfectant and polish. They were followed into the room by a uniformed constable who stood quietly at the back wall.

They sat down on opposite sides of the table. Rupert was relieved to see that DS Brooke was not present. *Small mercies*, he thought.

"So, what can we do for you? I understand that you've

been attacked and fetched up running someone over." He raised his eyebrows at the last statement, as if only mildly surprised at such an occurrence.

"Yes, but it's not quite as bad as you make it sound." Rupert related the events of the evening, leaving nothing out, while the DI made a few notes and asked some questions to clarify certain points. Otherwise he let Rupert talk until he was finished.

"Now, you think that this was more than just an ordinary mugging, because of the words used by your assailant?" Fleming asked once Rupert had finished.

"Yes, I do."

"What exactly, did he say again?"

Rupert repeated the words, exactly as he remembered them.

"OK. Can you think of anyone you might have upset, who would want you to back off? Something related to the death of Miss Carmichael perhaps?"

"Well if it is, it could be any one of dozens of people. Your lot did a pretty good job of making me look guilty," Rupert said. If he expected an apology from Fleming he was in for a long wait, he realised.

"Yes," Rupert said after the silence had stretched out for a few long seconds. "I think that it may be linked to Liz's death." Fleming frowned and started to pay more attention. "You see, I went to see Paul Simions on Friday afternoon on some spurious excuse –"

"This is the man whom you were supposedly jealous of. Your client? Is that correct?" Fleming asked.

"Yes. Simions mentioned that the police had been to see

him. In the course of the conversation, I let Liz's name drop and asked if he knew her through work. He denied it initially and then remembered that he did and that he had been for a drink with her earlier the previous evening. Selective memory, of course. Didn't even blink, the cold-blooded bastard. I knew that he had met her, I saw them together, like I told you and DS Brooke."

"Go on. Anything else?"

"He said that he'd met her for a drink after she came round to go over some work for next week. But then I caught him out. He said she had worked for him this week, but I knew she was at Halpern and Beams. He covered it up, said something about freelance work, but I know he is hiding something.

"Well, I wanted to rock his boat. I made a comment which could have been taken two ways, but when I said it his face changed, and he looked...he looked alarmed. Yes, for a split second he actually looked alarmed, as though it had followed on from our previous conversation. But in fact I was alluding to something else entirely." He proceeded to explain his thoughts on the takeover. Fleming stopped him once or twice when he slipped into jargon, but he picked up the main gist of the deal.

"So you think that he interpreted your comment to relate to the death of Miss Carmichael? It still doesn't put you in a very good light, Mr Brett. This could have been a falling out of thieves. What was this agency Miss Carmichael worked for again?"

"Secs in the City," said Rupert. "Secs as in short for secretaries."

It was quiet for a few seconds.

"Look, would I really have come here now offering all this if that was the case?"

Fleming gave him a cynical look.

"Also, the deal I was talking about seemed to get him pretty upset as well, more particularly the fact that I'd found out about his little takeover scam."

The DI considered the information carefully, as if weighing up what to tell Rupert next. Eventually, he carried on.

"After we left you on Friday, we continued with our enquiries at the block of flats where Miss Carmichael lived. Took us a while, but we think we may have something more to go on."

"Really, what?" Rupert asked, coming alert.

"Well, no matter where you go, there's always a nosy neighbour. Whatever you may think, there's always someone somewhere that sees something. Particularly somewhere as busy as a mansion block, and especially when there's a noisy row and the angry boyfriend screeches off out of the car park in his lovely new car."

Rupert looked abashed.

"There's an old lady on the ground floor. Says she sees everything and everybody who leaves and enters the place. People like her make our lives easier, it has to be said. On the night in question, she spotted a woman leaving the place about half an hour after you. Now because of the series of bays that stick out along the front of the block, it was possible for her to see this woman leave and walk across the car park to the road and out of sight. As far as we are aware, no one in the block had such a visitor, so we need to find out who she is and what she was doing there. In short, we would like her to help is with our enquiries."

"What did she look like?"

Fleming referred to his notes, flicking the pages of the notebook open.

"Five-three to five-five, late twenties, maybe early thirties, wearing a smart suit, dark hair, carrying a large handbag and gloves."

"When I entered the block that night, I held the door open for a woman. I didn't think anything of it at the time, I had other things on my mind." His face clouded at this point as he recalled the events of that evening.

"And you mention this now? That's very convenient, now that I've just told you about the woman and described her. I give you something and you conveniently remember something else."

"Well, here's something you didn't mention, DI Fleming," Rupert took a moment to catch his breath and quash the anger that was rising in him again. "Did this woman have a slight scar on her cheek and a chipped front tooth?"

Fleming stiffened. "You sure about this?" he was suddenly very serious.

"Absolutely. Why?"

The DI ignored the question. "What did the man who attacked you tonight look like again? Describe him carefully."

Rupert thought back and described the man again.

"Right, I'm going to get a mug shot book. I'll get

someone to take a statement of tonight's events and we will put it on record."

He left the room quickly and five minutes later another officer arrived to take Rupert's statement. The DI returned after they had finished with a book of photographs. He opened it at a given page and turned the album round so that Rupert could see it properly.

Rupert looked down at the photographs on the page, then stabbed his finger at the central photograph on the right hand page.

"That's him."

"You're sure?"

"Definitely, I'm not going to forget his face for a long while."

"And it was him you took out before you ran him over?"

"Yes, I got lucky. He'll have a burst eardrum, a bruised kneecap and possibly a broken hip. What? Why are you looking at me like that?"

"He happens to be one of the hardest men I know. Loan sharks use him as an enforcer when people don't pay up. He visits people if they don't pay their protection money. He's a piece of work. Either you were very lucky or there's more to you than meets the eye."

Rupert looked again at the photograph and a chill went down his spine at the thought of what might have happened.

"One bit of good news is that I doubt very much he'll press charges. Not his style, and he would have too many questions to answer himself. Now look at these photos for me," he said, producing another album. Once again Rupert scanned the page and picked out a picture of the woman he thought he remembered from the flats.

"I'm pretty sure that's her, but I only saw her for a few seconds."

"I think you're right. That," Fleming said dramatically, "is your assailant's little sister."

"What?"

"Her name is Maria Rico. He's Claudio Rico. She specialises in murder and professional hits. You are moving in some pretty exclusive circles, Mr Brett."

Rupert could not believe it. "What the hell is going on?" he said. "Liz was killed by a professional hit-man? Hit-woman...hit-person?" He was forced to subdue a hysterical laugh. "She was a temp, for fuck's sake. She worked for a secretarial agency with a stupid name. Why did this happen? Did they even get the right person? I don't get it..."

Fleming explained that the pair of them had a record for petty crime stretching way back. Sometimes they worked together, sometimes alone. Since they'd started offering their services to the highest bidder, it all became rumour. Smoke and mirrors. The criminal fraternity was tight-lipped, and Fleming said they'd had nothing on the pair of them for many years, not since the petty crimes of their youth. She was suspected of various killings and he provided muscles and extortion, but none of it could be proved. He went over Rupert's statement and asked for a few more details about the events. Finally he said that he would call Rupert on Monday to talk to him further.

The interview was over, and Rupert rose to go.

"One final thing," Fleming said. "Be a bit careful for the

rest of the weekend. Stay with friends, don't go anywhere by yourself, and here's my card. Any problems, or if you think of anything else, call me."

Rupert wished him goodnight and was shown from the building and out onto the street. *What a night*, he thought to himself, *and what a nightmare.* The journey home passed uneventfully; no cars followed him, no large thugs or petite women with chipped teeth were waiting on his doorstep. Everything was quiet. He checked the street, looked beneath the stairwell to the basement flat, nothing. *Too many spy movies*, he told himself.

After Rupert had left the station, DI Fleming sat alone in the interview room, tapping a cheap biro onto the photo of Claudio Rico. Maria was the bigger fish, suspected of being involved in a few killings – political, commercial or just for the hell of it, who knew? Rico was out of the picture after all these years, taken down by a yuppie ponce in a tailored suit. Fleming laughed to himself. *Bet you didn't see that one coming, did you, Claudio?* He scribbled some notes on his pad, looked at the picture of the smiling assassin with the chipped tooth and said, "We might just get you this time. We might at that." He picked up the telephone and called DS Brooke. He relayed the evening's events to his colleague who responded with his usual cynicism.

"Brett? Rupert fucking Brett took out Claudio Rico? Bloody hell, guv, pigs might fly yet. Do you think he's still tied up in it? Even white collar crime can turn nasty."

"I don't know," Fleming replied. "There's still something that doesn't sit right. There's a connection we're missing and we haven't got all the pieces of the puzzle. Did you find anything?"

"Well, yes actually, I just thought it could wait until Monday and –"

"Tell me," Fleming interrupted.

Brooke sighed. "Well it seems that Miss Carmichael had a record for drugs. Not just taking them, but dealing as well. Nothing recent, but it's there."

"She was a naughty girl then, not the innocent our Mr Brett thought. Anything else?"

"Yeah, actually. An odd thing. There's a note on her file that if she is apprehended or has any dealings with us, Detective Superintendent Webster is to be contacted immediately."

"Webster?" Fleming exclaimed. "Bloody hell, this gets more interesting by the minute."

"You know him?"

"I do, and I'm going to have a very interesting conversation with him. Listen, as soon as you get anything from the coroner identifying that drug, let me know."

"Will do."

He put the phone down and dialled another number immediately. "Detective Superintendent Webster, please." In less than a minute the line was connected. "Adrian. Steve Fleming, how are you?"

Rank was no object; the two men had known each other since cadet school.

"Steve. I'm well. Long-time no speak, how's things?" They caught up for a couple of minutes, then Fleming cut to the chase.

"I think I've just got something for you; a note on file to contact you." He relayed the events, starting with the murder. He was interrupted sharply.

"What! What did you say her name was?"

"Elizabeth Carmichael, Flat 6..."

Webster finished the address for him and there was silence on the line for a few seconds.

"So she is dead," Webster said. His voice was flat and emotionless, and it was a statement, not a question. Silence again. "Tell me everything again, from the beginning," Webster demanded.

Chapter Seventeen

The rest of the weekend passed uneventfully for Rupert. He called Claire, who invited him over for Sunday lunch at her flat, where they were joined by Mike and Jemma. The conversation revolved around the events of the last twenty-four hours. Everyone was shocked to hear Rupert's news of the attack, but Mike still appeared sceptical of Rupert's theory of Simions' involvement, and continued with his rather reserved demeanour.

"I still can't believe that someone in his position would order such an attack – I mean, what would he stand to gain from it?" Mike commented.

"The fact that he's a developer doesn't give him exclusive rights to sainthood," Rupert snapped. He was getting pissed off with Mike's holier-than-thou attitude. "In fact, quite the reverse. My experience is that the higher you get and the faster you get there, the more likely you are to have a few skeletons in the cupboard. Look at his methods: bribing planning officers, putting pressure on owners, using offshore companies to lever factory closures. How much more suspiciously does the man have to behave?"

"Just an average day in the life of a property developer, I'd say," Claire joked, trying to lighten the mood.

"Precisely. I rest my case. But I keep feeling that there's something missing, something that's tied in with Liz's death. It's staring me in the face, I'm sure, but I can't see it for looking too hard."

"I still think you're reading too much into it. It would be ludicrous to implicate Simions," Mike said.

Rupert was too exhausted to argue and conceded the point. The lunch broke up late, with everyone leaving at about five o'clock. After the goodbyes were said, Rupert lingered on the doorstep of Claire's flat.

"You can stay, you know."

"I know, and it's really kind, but I need some time and..." his voice tailed off and he wasn't sure how to continue. The kindness of the offer held promise, that much was unmistakeable, but he knew that he needed to be alone. She hugged him, kissed him on the cheek and said, "Anytime. You know I mean it. Just call, OK? And ignore Mike, he gets a bit prissy sometimes, you know that."

"I do, and I really appreciate it. 'Night."

Rupert walked the short distance to his flat. He was glad of the support given by Claire and more than a little hurt by Mike. He felt terribly guilty, all of a sudden. A girl he had loved, by his own admission, was dead. Her body was barely cold and he was already thinking about possibilities with Claire.

Was he really that shallow? But then he considered that

Liz had been seeing Simions, probably sleeping with him. They'd had a blazing row and any relationship they'd had would have probably been dead in the water anyway. Wouldn't it? Simions, of all people. His mind turned the facts over for the thousandth time. When he reached home, he once again made the provisional checks on the outside of his flat before entering, all rather self-consciously and to no avail; no one was lying in wait for him. He went in, poured himself a drink and fell asleep in a chair, mentally and physically exhausted.

Early Monday morning, a call came through to him in his office from reception.

"There's a Detective Superintendent Webster on the line for you." The inflection in the receptionist's voice held a tone of mockery, judgemental and unkind.

"Thank you." The call was transferred. "Good morning, DS Webster. How can I help?" Webster wanted to meet somewhere outside the office, and asked him to come to the police station where he worked. Rupert took down the address, and half an hour later he presented himself at a rather nondescript building in Westminster.

He buzzed the intercom system, announced himself and was let in. The reception area was austere, but it didn't have the grubby appearance and the air of menace of a police station. Plain painted walls divided into two colours by a dado rail and a reception desk which was manned by what Rupert assumed was a civilian receptionist in her early thirties. She gazed up at him, unsmiling, and directed him up the stairs to the first floor. The stairs were carpeted and he made no sound as he ascended to the next level.

He was met on the landing by a plainclothes officer and shown into a comfy office with a large desk graced by a computer, two telephones and a table lamp. The walls were lined with bookshelves. The original Georgian fireplace was still there, but a gas fire stood in its hearth. It was not, to Rupert's admittedly limited experience, a typical policeman's office.

A second door opened to the right of the office and Detective Superintendent Webster walked in. He offered Rupert a cold smile.

"Detective Superintendent Webster. Thank you for coming across so promptly. Sit down, please." He gestured to a chair on the opposite side of his desk.

"Thank you."

Rupert studied Webster, and saw a man of just under six foot with a round head and deep set, sharp eyes of indifferent colour. One would, he reflected, be hard put to describe exactly their hue, but whatever colour they were, they were hard and shrewd. Webster's face was becoming a little jowly with age and his midriff was expanding. His skin had a polish, a soft sheen of good living and maybe a few too many lunches. His suit, unlike those of his colleagues, was well made and the trousers matched the jacket. Rupert smiled to himself.

"I will come straight to the point," Webster said in a crisp, mannered tone that was more typical of a politician than a policeman. "I have been appraised of your situation by DI Fleming who, given the circumstances, has passed the case over to me – particularly as I knew the victim." He studied Rupert's face for a reaction and was not disappointed.

"You knew Liz. How?"

Webster ignored the direct question and began obtusely. "I will go back to the beginning. Some time ago the Home Office began to realise that a certain type of crime was falling between two stools, so to speak. For example, fraud and murder, drugs and tax evasion. The details are not important, but what is important is that in an effort to combat this hybrid crime, they decided to set up a number of special units, of which mine is one. We specialise in the London area and specifically we tackle various combinations of fraud and murder. We are called in when the usual police units consider that normal lines of demarcation have been crossed. This is one of those instances."

"But how does all this involve Liz?"

Again Webster ignored the question. "Did you ever get close to Liz? Meet her family, for example?"

"No, She never let me get that close to her. There was a part of her life I couldn't touch, somehow."

He snorted, almost to himself. "That doesn't surprise me in the slightest. About two years ago we started looking into money laundering connected to property, and this coincided with a resurgence of London's drug problems. The two were, we thought, somehow linked, and then a third element was introduced: fraud. The drug squad had been looking closely at a number of clubs; one was Maxine's just off Sloane Square. Do you know it?"

"Yes, I've been there a couple of times. I'd heard rumours that the drugs scene was quite big, and quite a few of my friends go there, mainly the girls." He shrugged, seeing a pattern beginning to emerge.

"It's a major hang out for the Sloane Ranger set; they've got lots of money to spend, and they offer easy access. It's a perfect combination for the dealers, but we've never been able to prove anything, and we've only made a few minor arrests. But the place is also a one way ticket from soft to hard drugs such as heroin, and one of those victims was Liz. She was mainlining, got caught a few times and started dealing."

Rupert shook his head in disbelief. Webster raised his hand to silence him. "Didn't last long, but it was enough to cause her serious problems at the time, and she became an addict. We gave her a choice: she could clean herself up, we would drop the charges and she would start feeding us information. Or she would be charged. She chose to get out of the drugs scene and help us. Simple."

"But I still don't see how this links in with commercial property?"

"Let me ask you something. What is the most important commodity to you in your world?"

Rupert thought for barely a second and shrugged. "Information, I guess. Preferably early and exclusive."

"Precisely. It's the same with us, and now the two are linked. Your Mr Simions is getting early information on the deals he makes. He's using the proceeds to transfer the money into hard currency without paying taxes and then he's using drug addicts to act as couriers and as others to participate in the scam."

"But how is he getting the early information?"

"He uses such an obvious route that it is brilliantly simple. Who has access to all the information? Who is never questioned or noticed? Who can come and go as they please with no accountability?" He paused, letting the answer hang in the air for dramatic effect. "The temporary secretary. How many times have you heard *'Oh she's just the temp.'* Completely ignored in the corner, sitting there reading all the letters she files, supplying information to Simions and others like him.

"From the information Miss Carmichael fed us, we know he has a manager at each branch of Secs in the City working for him. We are trying to find the true ownership base of the agency, but it's tied up in a complicated trust. We're pretty sure we'll get there eventually. Most of them are in his pocket; he pays cash to for them to put a specific girl in to temp for various clients. The girl goes into the given situation and either passes the information on or alters the letters. It is simple and very effective. Simions has a whole network of temps all over the place – all specialising in commercial property, as far as we know."

Rupert was astounded. "Incredible. But how does he get them into position in the first place?"

"As far as we can ascertain, he finds out who the permanent placement is. That person is approached to, say, go sick for a couple of days for a cash payment. The company phones the agency for a replacement. Simions' girl is put in place, information is leaked or used to his advantage and no one suspects. It costs Simons a few grand, but what does he make? You tell me – millions? And the beauty of it is that everyone is paid in cash and it's completely untraceable.

Somehow – and this is the bit we don't yet know – he gets the money from legitimate property deals and converts it into cash for payments to branch managers, temps and the permanent staff, and so on.

"The amounts involved are in the order of tens or hundreds of thousands of pounds. Not huge amounts in terms of the profits involved, but difficult to disguise in terms of cash.

"Now Miss Carmichael, was getting very close to the centre of this. Too close in fact, which is why we think she was killed, and I'm afraid to say ..." and here he hesitated, looking pained, "it was because of her involvement with you."

It fell like a bombshell to Rupert. Suddenly the words in the pub he overheard between Simions and Liz made sense to him. She wasn't having an affair. She was finishing their business relationship; telling Simions she couldn't spy for him anymore. *Oh God no,* he thought, *oh please God, no.*

It all started to fall into place – the way the deals had been exposed on the investment sale when Claire's secretary had gone off sick two days before the release of the information onto the market. Liz's constant attitude of secrecy; her strange, unexplained disappearances. It all fitted together now. At their last meeting he'd blamed her, accused her, insulted her. And then she died horribly, because of him. He stared at Webster in horror.

"I'm sorry I had to tell you, but you deserved to know." Webster looked and sounded compassionate, genuinely sorry for Rupert's plight. He continued, "We also believe that an earlier suicide by Simions' former partner wasn't in fact suicide. Are you familiar with the story?"

"What? Oh yes, vaguely." Rupert stumbled back to reality. "The chap jumped off the Clifton Suspension Bridge in Bristol, didn't he?"

"That's the story, yes. But a woman walking her dog just afterwards said she saw two people. And there was a car parked at one end of the bridge, which we never traced. And we found the dead man's car parked near the spot. He was a tall man, but the seat was forward in a position close to the wheel. The sort of position a short man or a woman would use. Some of the bruising found on his body may or may not have been consistent with his fall and hitting the water. The evidence is circumstantial, but when you add it up it leads us to believe that he was murdered and it was made to look like suicide."

He paused, letting the information sink in.

"Just like Liz," Rupert muttered. "So you believe me, about me not having murdered her or being responsible for her death?"

"Just like Liz, yes. I am very sorry, Mr Brett. And I do believe you, although again a good deal of circumstantial evidence has been placed to make it look as though you were involved more directly than you were." He hesitated, like an actor playing the part and using the pause for effect. He continued at just the right moment, "But there is a way you can help us and help put Simions away."

"How?"

"We think the attack on you was related. A frightener, if you like. Ill-advised and not Mr Simions usual style, but..."

again he paused, letting the sentence hang in the air before continuing. "I think that when he reflects on all this, he will reconsider and try to get you onside by offering you a job. Not unusual in your line of work anyway, is it, that sort of thing?" he asked.

"No. In fact he has hinted at it already. Before...before Liz died. He was impressed, so he said, with my performance. Thought I would make a good developer."

"Good. We want you to take it," Webster stated decisively. "He will want to keep you close, and we want you on the inside to get whatever evidence you can to try and find out how he is laundering the money.

"Now, tell me all you can. Right from the beginning, leaving nothing out. Any tiny bit of information you may have, however seemingly insignificant you might think it is, may help add to the file that Liz had already put together."

Rupert told Webster everything that had happened from his first meeting with Simions, including the bribing of the planning officer and his suspicions about David Shingler. Webster pricked up his ears at the name. It seemed that Shingler was a potential suspect, and possibly the man behind the hiring of the muscle who attacked Rupert.

As he related the facts, other minor points fell into place: like the disguise Liz wore, and the reason why she appeared so out of place for a Sloane in Hampstead. She was avoiding her previous friends and haunts. It all suddenly became understandable.

Webster brought the discussion to a close. "So, what we are really looking for is the link to the money laundering. That will be the key to convicting him. The rest is just circumstantial; yes there are bribes, corrupt managers, but really, so what? It's a grubby little business you're involved in, Mr Brett, and mostly we don't care what you all get up to. We'd never get enough evidence, and we'd wind up breaking our backs just to catch a few sprats and lose the big fish. So you must, at all costs, not show your true feelings and knuckle under. Act like you never have before."

Rupert's irritation showed. "Look, he hasn't even offered me a job yet," he snapped. "It might not work out at all, but if it does I'll do anything I can, if only for Liz's memory and to get revenge on Simions and Shingler. If Simions head-hunts me, my current employers will be glad to see me go. I'm tainted now, things are beginning to slip, so it won't feel that strange if I suddenly shoot off somewhere else."

Rupert was angry and upset at the turn of events, and he felt that he'd heard just about all he wanted to for the moment. He was going over so many incidents from the past few months in his mind, analysing every aspect of his rela-tionship with Liz, his work and all facets of his conversations with Simions, looking at them all in a new light.

Webster asked him not to speak with anyone else about what he had been told. It was imperative that no one else should be party to the information, and nobody should be told what Rupert was doing. Any leaks would endanger Rupert's life. The thought chilled him to the bone. He had never really considered before what he was getting into. The attack could be repeated with more successful results. In the meantime he was in effect being blackballed by the market, which was less than keen to do business with a potential murderer or someone who was mixed up in such activities.

He left the interview with instructions on how to contact Webster and what he should be looking for.

When he walked out of the building, he went into the nearest coffee bar, unable to think straight. It was all too much for him. He was torn between thoughts of guilt, fear and revenge. He hated Simions for what he had done and wondered how much Shingler was involved in all of this. Maybe he was just another of Simions' puppets, just one more corrupt agent bending the rules.

In his office, Webster thought for a moment and made a call to DI Fleming.

"No, I don't think he's guilty. He was completely shocked at what I told him. What worries me is how he will get through this, if indeed he does. He is strung pretty tight now. To work side by side with the man who murdered his girlfriend will need exceptional courage and skill. We'll see."

"I think you may be surprised," Fleming replies. "There's a lot of steel in that boy. He's stronger than you think."

"I hope you're right – for his sake," said Fleming.

The next two weeks went by in a blur for Rupert. He carried on working, chasing deals and following up various aspects of the Castle Road scheme, but it was getting harder. His calls were not returned. Whispers and rumours swirled around, and the market gradually turned against him.

The deadline for the counter notice was looming, and everyone on the Cowell Rubens team was getting tense. Halpern & Beams had given no indication that they were aware that time was of the essence, or that if they missed the response time all might be lost for their client. The last day of the month arrived and neither CR nor MAS Investments received a counter response. Everyone was jubilant, although Simions, when Rupert called him, appeared unsurprised.

"I think we can conclude that they failed to spot the clause, and that their legal position is now non-existent. We can now apply for VP and planning," Simions commented.

"I really thought they would spot it. They must have been over that lease with a fine tooth comb. It's great news, but very strange," Rupert said.

"I wouldn't speculate upon it too much, if I were you. Just accept it and be grateful." It was a veiled threat, menace giving an edge to Simions' voice.

Rupert recoiled at the implied threat, then resumed his passive role. "No, I think it's excellent. Can't wait to see the look on their faces when they realise," he finished.

"Neither can I, but I think they might still put up some spurious legal argument. Delaying tactics, we'll see. But it is a successful conclusion, and a great deal on your behalf. Rupert, I need to see you about another matter, something a bit more personal and to your advantage. When can we meet up?"

"What about later today – say 3.00 this afternoon?"

Chapter Eighteen

The meeting with Simions took place as planned. As Rupert suspected, Simions offered him a job, and Rupert realised that it was for no other reason than to get him onside and move him away from the dangerous position of whistle-blower. Simions was involving him in his own personal game of chess, moving him like a pawn that was threatened by higher forces, putting him into a position of responsibility and – more importantly – complicity. In making the offer, Simions was compromising him just as surely as if he'd offered him an outright bribe. The practice of poaching agents to client side was becoming more commonplace, but for Rupert to be offered such a position so early in his career was exceptional. Rupert listened calmly to the offer, and Simions took it as a sign of the kind of egotistical arrogance he was used to, seeming to recognise a kindred spirit in Rupert, assuming that everyone was as driven as him. Rupert's reaction only helped to confirm that he had made a good choice.

The money Rupert was offered was astonishing: twice his current salary, working with one of the most successful emerging property companies in the market. *What could be easier to accept?* he thought. But his heart was cold with anger as he thought of the deceit and murder committed by the man before him.

He left Simions' office without committing himself, promising to consider the offer carefully, knowing full well that he had to accept in order to feed Webster information. His first call when he returned to the office, after he'd calmed down and dealt with the adrenaline and anger that were coursing through him in equal measure, was to Webster.

"You're right, he offered me a job. Excellent terms too." He went on to outline the salary, company car, bonuses and profit share benefits.

"I'm working for the wrong side, Mr Brett," Webster commented wryly. "Crime is paying well these days." Rupert grinned for the first time that day and continued with the details. "You'll take it of course?" Webster urged, more of a statement than a question.

"I'll let him stew overnight, take it and work my notice. It'll give the market a bit of time to find something else to talk about," Rupert finished, "I'll be yesterday's news and tomorrow's chip wrappings soon enough."

"Good. We'll start working together as soon as you get your feet under the table. I look forward to it." The line went dead and Rupert reflected that the powerful all had the same arrogance, regardless of what side they were on.

On the other side of Grosvenor Street, in Halpern and Beams, others on the right side of the law were having a much worse day. Steve Jackson, the partner in charge of rent reviews, was trying to explain to his exasperated client how he had failed to serve the requisite notice within the timescale.

"Look, it's impossible that it didn't arrive on time. I signed the letter two days before the due date. It was to go by registered mail, guaranteed to arrive and be signed for the following day. I distinctly remember handing it to my secretary – or rather the temp as my regular secretary was taken sick last week – which is why I specifically remember the date of posting. The temp was very efficient."

"In everything except this matter," his client interjected. "you will be hearing from our lawyers directly."

What Steve Jackson didn't know was that the temp had deliberately post-dated the letter by two days so that it appeared to have been written after the deadline had passed. She held it back and it was not delivered until the due date had passed. The girl reflected on her work with Secs in the City, and how easy it had been to make an extra £1,000 on top of her agency fee. It was surprising just how many times bosses didn't check the dates on their letters when handed a sheaf of papers to sign. Jackson had just assumed all his post would be correctly dated as shown on the first letter. She smiled to herself. They were all so predictable. Money for old rope, really.

Pauline from Secs in The City phoned Shingler, who confirmed that all had gone well and that the letter had not been received until the deadline had passed.

"Well done. Usual payment," he replied curtly.

"Perfect. I'll book the flights for two weeks' time, will that do?"

"I'll make the arrangements."

Pauline smiled. *Another warm summer break*, she thought.

Chapter Nineteen

The following week saw an interesting exchange between Simions and Michaels, the MD of Moorcroft Industries. After finding that time was of the essence and that the timescale had not been adhered to, Michaels had applied to the courts on the grounds that the clause was unreasonable. His case had some merit, and throwing himself upon the mercy of the courts offered a possible solution to Michaels' problem – especially as he had nothing to lose and the strategy would buy him more time.

But in the meantime, he had received a communication to the effect that his main suppliers and creditors, Diamond Drilling Services, were calling in their debts and making other financial demands. He was being squeezed and he knew it. More frustrating still, he couldn't find out exactly who was squeezing him – although he did have a pretty good idea.

He called Simions in person, hoping that they could resolve matters amicably, as any major break in production would ruin the company and destroy all chances of keeping the site or recovering. The conversation began well, but deteriorated when Simions alluded to the possible financial problems.

"Now how the hell would you know about that?" Michaels demanded.

"In the financial world, Mr Michaels, there are very few secrets, and listed companies are not one of them."

"Don't patronise me, Mr Simions. I am well aware of how stock market rumours work."

"I am sure you are," Simions replied smoothly. "However, I might be in a position to help resolve your problems. I have, shall we say, some influence in this particular matter which may be of assistance to you."

"What are you saying? That if I agree to drop all court proceedings, you'll get Diamond Drilling to call off their dogs, is that it?"

"Well, rather crudely put, but in a nutshell, yes."

"You bastard!"

"It's business," Simions responded coldly, "simple as that."

"How did you swing it? Eh? How did you influence the late service of the counter notice?"

"I have absolutely no idea what you are talking about, Mr Michaels. Now, do we have a deal? If I help you, will you vacate your site?"

There was a long pause at the other end of the line.

"Like you say, business is business. So be it. But we want full compensation. We will need to agree terms but in principle we have a deal. Get your secretary to call mine and arrange some dates to thrash this out with the lawyers. Goodbye."

Michaels had the satisfaction of putting the telephone down first. It was a small victory. A battle won in a war that he'd lost. He was furious but knew he was beaten.

The deal was signed a few weeks later. Rupert was present, this time representing MAS, not Cowell Rubens, having left CR some few days earlier. The transition had been difficult, particularly in view of his previously vociferous condemnation of Simions' morals and business methods. Many CR personnel, as well as others outside the firm, harboured thoughts that Rupert was not entirely innocent when it came to the death of his girlfriend. Rupert couldn't tell anyone about the larger plan or his involvement with Webster. One word in the wrong ear, one temporary secretary listening in on a conversation could report back and blow the whole thing out of the water – and very likely get him killed, of that he was under no illusion.

Because of this secrecy his former friends in the office, Mike included, gave him the cold shoulder. But the transition from agent to principal had been very interesting, and less of a hardship than he'd anticipated. The perceived glamour of being on the client side of the fence wasn't all it was cracked up to be, and if it wasn't for his mission, he concluded that it would have been quite tedious. It certainly wasn't as exciting as he'd imagined. Seeing how it all worked from the client's perspective was eye-opening, and kicked off a steep increase in his learning curve that would stand him in good stead in the long run, after all this was over. But Rupert never forgot the real reason for his presence there and continued to search for any information that might be relevant. This often took him into Simions' office, which was never locked, on a variety of spurious excuses, giving him the opportunity to look through whatever papers were to hand.

Normally his search produced nothing, but one Tuesday morning when Simions was unexpectedly late, he took the chance to sneak another look. Ever watchful, he walked upstairs and closed the door in order to gain as much time as possible if someone caught him unawares. His heart raced on these occasions, ever fearful of being discovered and the consequences hung over him like the sword of Damocles.

He had just finished a frustratingly careful search of all the papers and desk contents that were accessible, which revealed nothing, when a sharp noise behind him caused Rupert to jump and spin around. His heart thudded, but to his relief it was just Simions' fax machine taking an incoming message. He turned to walk away, his heart thumping, but turned back to the machine to see what the message was. He read the first page upside down as it came out of the machine, being careful not to touch it. *Shingler!* The fax was from Shingler.

It was a single sheet with large, loopy handwriting crossing the page:

Paul,

Cargo on board to Rome, due Thursday. Should arrive at Viterbo midday. Deal to be signed on sale of Casa Romero the day after. Hope that's OK, he has your power of attorney for the sale. The proceeds will be distributed as usual. I've found a new notaio, *more amenable, if you know what I mean.*

Speak to you once the deal is done.

David.

Yes, Rupert said to himself. He carefully re-read the text again and decided to copy it. There was no copier in the room, so he re-fed it through the fax machine on 'copy'. Out it came and he replaced the original in the receipt tray as before. He ran from the room grabbing a file as he left. Rupert took two deep breaths, calmed himself and pretended to be engrossed in his file. He bumped into Simions as he came up the stairs.

"Hi Paul, how are you?"

"Don't ask, the traffic was crap. What are you up here for?"

"Just getting this file." Rupert waved the folder and went to move on down the stairs.

"Stay a moment will you? I need a word about the Castle Road deal."

Rupert went back into the room with Simions, trying at all costs to keep his eyes off the fax in the corner. Simions sat down and started to go over one or two points of the scheme, but in the course of the discussion his eyes wandered to the fax machine. He stopped mid-sentence, rose and walked quickly to the machine. Rupert's eyes followed him, while he concentrated on putting a puzzled expression on his face. Simions snatched up the fax, read it and looked directly at Rupert, who felt as if those eyes were burning into his soul.

"Did you see this?" Simions demanded.

Rupert rose as if to come and read it, feigning innocence. "No, what is it? Is it important?" He held out his hand as if to be given the paper. The ruse worked.

"No. It's nothing. Never mind." Simions strode back to his desk and placed the paper in a file where it could not be read.

"Now, where were we? Oh yes." He continued with the other details and finally dismissed Rupert as if he were a schoolboy leaving the headmaster's study. Rupert closed the door behind him and heaved a huge sigh of relief. He left the landing quickly, running down the stairs two at a time and shot into his office. He was desperate to call Webster but too frightened of being overheard.

At lunchtime, he went to a phone box, got through on Webster's private number and explained everything to him, reading the fax sheet word for word over the telephone. "So what do you think?" he finished.

"I think I need to talk to my opposite number in Rome. Where is this Viterbo place, do you know?"

"I do actually. It's the capital of a local province in Northern Lazio, about an hour's drive from Rome."

"Lazio? I thought that was a football team?"

"It is, but Viterbo is a major city to the north of the capital. But what I don't see is how he is laundering the money there, or even getting it there in the first place."

"Neither do I, but it confirms one thing. Shingler is involved, and we now know where to look. While you've been beavering away in your new job I've been doing some checking on our friend Shingler. He was at school near little Italy, and probably knows Claudio Rico, your assailant, from there. I'm willing to bet that Rico is the courier. My sources tell me his bones are mending well. He might walk with a bit of a limp, and I'm sure that hip will ache when it's damp, but it's starting to all fall into place. Well done, Rupert, well done. I will be in touch."

Rupert, now, is it? He thought. *I've been a good boy.* He considered what Webster had said, and thought about the new Italian connection, wondering how it all fitted in. He needed more information on the buying process in Italy. He was convinced that was where the answers lay.

Of course, he snapped his fingers, thinking of the first day of Sheen's introductions around the building: Howard Bruman at the Offices Department at CR. He'd bought a place in Tuscany and he spoke Italian. He called Howard, remembering that he always was keen on lunch.

"Brett! Good god, man, how are you? Doing well for yourself despite a few setbacks, I hear." They arranged to meet at an Italian restaurant just off Berkeley Square.

Howard turned up on time and they settled down into familiar territory, catching up on old times. Rupert steered the conversation towards holidays and Italy and said a friend was looking for a buy-to-let villa out there, and wanted to know the best way to go about it.

"Tricky really. You definitely need a good *notaio*, preferably one who is bilingual." He went on to outline the process of buying and selling.

"But what about taxes, do you have stamp duty?"

"Well, there is the beauty of it d'you see." Howard gave him a conspiratorial smile. "In Italy, the government levies a tax on both sellers and buyers. The Italians feel that it is their duty to dodge these taxes, and both parties have a vested interest in doing so. So buyers and sellers join forces. For a sale of property to take place, a *notaio* must be used; he acts

214

as a kind of official for the government, and he oversees the proceedings. He registers the price of the deal and sees that all the monies are paid accordingly, and that the price and taxes are logged with the central register."

"Sorry, I'm being thick. I still don't get it, Howard."

Howard smiled: "Well, the *notaio* appreciates the position of both parties, and he's in no more of a hurry for them to pay any more tax than they need to, so he settles the price at a lesser level than in the state lists – which work like our rateable value lists – the main difference being that the Italian records haven't been updated for years. So the true price is anything up to thirty or forty percent more than declared.

"What, so you could buy a property for a million and declare only six or seven hundred thousand for tax purposes!"

"Exactly, dear boy."

"And the *notaio* condones this?"

Howard shrugged. "It's Italy."

"But how does the money get to the other party?"

"In cash."

"What, someone turns up with a suitcase filled with half a million quid's worth of Lire? Incredible. And the *notaio* goes along with this?"

"He's paid in cash too. In fact most of them offer discounts for a cash deal. Do you know what every respectable Italian dreads? That one day there might be a universal currency and all Lira notes will have to be handed in. Do you also know that Italy has the highest currency production of any European country because no one uses the banks? They stuff it under their mattresses. The Italians have an innate distrust of banks. They think they're all corrupt," he finished. "And they aren't that wide of the mark." He grinned and raised his wine glass.

"So if I understand all this correctly, it would be very easy for anyone to bury a substantial amount of money into a property deal and launder the money. All done legitimately, right under the nose of the *notaio*."

"Precisely – which is why Italy has the highest tax band in Europe. No one pays any more than they can get away with. It is also why they have no legitimate house pricing guide that reflects rises or falls in the market. It would be irrelevant anyway, as no one ever records the correct price. Now don't tell me your friend actually wants to launder money?"

"What? Oh no, it's just that I find it all so incredible. No wonder the Mafia are so strong over there, in such an atmosphere of corruption."

"They just accept it as the norm. Now, another drink dear boy." He poured another glass of wine for them both as Rupert's brain did mental somersaults. The rest of the meal was spent comparing notes on all things Italian, and Howard answered a few final questions for Rupert. Lunch ended and Rupert thanked Howard for his time and information.

"Anytime, dear boy, anytime – and if you want the name of a good *notaio*, let me know," Howard winked and tapped the side of his nose.

"Thank you, Howard, I will."

So, he thought, *the next bit of the jigsaw is in place, all we need now is the who and where*. Rupert relayed this information to Webster, who had been checking on the movements of Rico. He told Rupert that Rico was working as a courier until he recovered his full strength, and had booked a flight to Rome, and by linking back through the records, the time and place coincided with the information Rupert had provided.

"What we need is someone out there to follow him," Webster mused. "I can find out which hotel he is staying at," he thought out loud, "and–"

"I'll go, get me the information while I'm in transit and I'll call you from the airport." Rupert made up his mind on the spot.

"But what about Simions?"

"I'll tell him I've been offered a late flight to a friend's villa in Spain or somewhere – anywhere that's hot and isn't Italy. I'll see if I can swing it, OK? I'll call you back later this afternoon."

Rupert hung up and went back to the office as quickly as could, his brain alive with possibilities. Surprisingly, Simions was amenable to the idea and told him to grab the chance while he could. Rupert called Webster and it was all set up.

Rupert telephoned Webster again from Heathrow, taking down the name of the hotel Rico was staying at and the name of the local policeman, Webster's opposite number, who would help him in Viterbo. Everything was coming together in Italy. Simions, Claudio Rico, and possibly the sister who had killed Liz.

Maria. Rupert had a score to settle.

Chapter Twenty

The weather had been pleasant enough when Rupert left England, but the heat hit him like a wall as soon as he disembarked from the plane at Rome's Ciampino airport. It was a different sort of heat, he thought; dry, almost sweet, leaving a perceptible taste in his mouth. He savoured it as he walked across the airport apron, passed through customs and out to the car hire centre.

The bright sunlight hurt his eyes as it bounced up from the concrete. In shirt sleeves, he sauntered across the access roads, glad of the canopy overhead that offered him some shade. He hired a nondescript little Fiat from the airport and drove out onto the GRA – the Roman equivalent of the M25, only much more dangerous. Italian drivers conducted themselves with zeal and panache that perfectly matched their Latin temperaments; dodging in and out of the traffic lanes, judging their distances to the merest inch as they did so, horns blaring.

Rupert headed west and then north around Rome and

nearly missed the turnoff for the *Via Aurelia*, one of the oldest and most important transport links in Italy. *Well*, he thought, *if you can't beat them, join them!* He accelerated through a tiny gap in the traffic and was sent on his way by a discordant fanfare of tooting horns. He headed north on the *Autostrada Aurelia* and turned off just before Tarquinia, heading across country eastwards to Viterbo.

The guidebook he had read on the plane described it as the finest medieval city in Italy, with a fully preserved historical centre still bounded by the original city walls. He arrived some two hours later, having stopped off for coffee on the way in the small town of Vetralla.

Approaching Viterbo Rupert thought that it looked like any other large Italian city. A long, straight highway led through a sprawling industrial zone, shabby peripheral warehouses and some low blocks of run-down apartments. But then he found the inner ring road, passing under the huge arches that still guarded the old city gates leading to the inner sanctum, a more historic and better kept area. The guidebook was right; most of the walls remained intact and had been integrated into modern lifestyles and architecture, something the Italians did very well. The crazy one way system confused him at first and he circled the city centre three times before finding his way.

He finally found his hotel, a discreet renaissance building just outside the *Centro Storico*. He parked in the car park at the front and walked into the reception. He wondered to himself, not for the first time, why all Italian hotels smelled the same; a mixture of sweet and savoury overlaid with garlic and floor polish. Wherever he went in

Italy it was always the same, whatever size or quality of the hotel.

He booked in, speaking in broken Italian, but the concierge replied in English. *Better than France, where they pretended not to understand you at all,* he thought. The room was comfortable and ornate, in keeping with the general style of the hotel. He unpacked, called Webster to say he had arrived safely and confirmed the address of the bilingual *notaios* in Viterbo, of which there were only two. There was no hurry; no one would be working now. It was lunchtime.

It was too hot to be hungry, so Rupert dozed in his room, relaxing in the shade on the balcony, absorbing the sights and sounds. At 2.30 he changed into a linen suit. He put on a Panama hat and a pair of sunglasses and headed out into the stark sunlight, making his way towards the main legal centre where the *notaios'* offices were. One of the advantages of his detective work was that he could check regularly with the street map and look like a typical tourist without appearing too conspicuous.

He wandered through the *Centro Storico* towards the main street, which according to his map led to the legal area of the city. The street was cobbled, with small shops set into the older buildings, their narrow frontages looking either dated or a little tacky. There were a few designer shops but no chain stores. *The surveyor never takes a rest,* he chuckled to himself. Only the ubiquitous Benneton and McDonalds gave evidence of any form of corporate presence in Italy. England, that "nation of shopkeepers" boasted the best shopping in the world. Here the shops were old fashioned and boring. Pleasant enough for a few touristy days, but to live here permanently would be very dull indeed, he decided.

He moved through the crowds of tourists, blending inconspicuously with the other holidaymakers and visitors to the city. He found his way to the legal district, noted the various offices of the *notaios* from the list provided by Webster's Italian counterpart, *Commisario* Davide Cappulacci. He worked his way back down the list until he came to the name of the hotel Rico was booked into. Rico was not due in until tomorrow's flight, so Rupert had time to kill and he spent it relaxing, wandering the streets and visiting the local churches, an old central villa and some museums. He tried to contact Cappulacci at the police station, but he had difficulty making himself understood, and was assured (he thought) that the detective would be in the office the following day.

There was nothing to fear at this point, but his mind was constantly on the job ahead, which was fraught with difficulties and danger. Over dinner in a quiet back street *trattoria*, he reflected on how much had happened in the last six months. Despite the awful events of Liz's death, the move to the client side from being an agent had been incredibly profitable and a positive learning experience. Not that this had blunted his desire for revenge, which was as strong as ever. It was just odd how it had all worked out, especially considering his initial fear of leaving the agency background and the good feeling of having a big team around him. Other agents had started to return his calls again – even Mike.

He realised how much he had grown in the last 12 months and how that growth had led him to this – risking his life to play amateur detective, tracking his girlfriend's killers. The strong, local red wine was making him maudlin in the cooler evening air. Looking down at the bottle, he was surprised to see that it was empty. He grinned to himself, accepted the offer of a grappa from the waiter and ordered a double espresso to go with it.

He paid the bill and walked a little unsteadily back to his hotel. As he entered, he did not see the figure opposite, who stopped short of the corner, lit a cigarette and spoke softly into a radio device held in his left hand.

The following morning was bright, sunny and hot. The temperature was already in the eighties and the double onslaught of the heat and a hangover felt like an ice pick in his head.

Bloody grappa, he thought to himself. *It always does this to me, but I never learn.*

He shuffled out onto the hotel terrace for breakfast, sat down, drained a pitcher of iced water and ordered a large cappuccino. He blinked behind his sunglasses against the glare. Two cups of coffee and a brioche later he was beginning to feel human again, and decided he had better make a move before Rico booked into his hotel. He looked at his watch; 10.30. Rico's flight would have landed an hour ago.

Rupert walked through the city, following the route he had rehearsed the day before, and found Rico's hotel. He looked around, bought a two-day-old copy of the *Telegraph* from a local newsagent's and settled himself under a sunshade in front of a small café which afforded a good but secluded view of the hotel's main entrance. Coffee ordered, he unfolded the newspaper and waited. He'd been there over an hour and was beginning to think that he had missed Rico or that something had gone wrong when a car pulled up outside and decanted Rico, who stretched and looked around, scanning each direction. Happy with what he saw, he limped into the hotel with a suitcase and a bag in each hand. Rupert's heart leapt in a mixture of elation and fear.

Rico had looked a little different from the last time they'd met. There were new lines of pain etched into his face, he carried himself to favour that left hip and the limp was pronounced, and from what Fleming had said, permanent. Rupert hunched further behind his newspaper and turned his head to avoid eye contact, despite the sunglasses. Beads of perspiration broke out on his forehead – the cold, sweat of fear. If Rico had known his erstwhile assailant was sitting across the road from him, he'd have come for Rupert in a heartbeat, and maybe luck wouldn't be on Rupert's side on this occasion.

His mouth felt dry at the sudden burst of adrenalin his body produced. His limbs felt heavy and his head felt light, and he asked himself not for the first time if he was doing the right thing, and why he had volunteered for this job. Then he thought of Liz, and reason and determination came flooding back to him. He snapped his paper open once again and kept an eye on the front of the hotel.

Time slid by slowly until Rico finally reappeared. He left the hotel building and paused, studying the streets on either side of the hotel, wary as cat. Rupert left it a minute, then stood, folded his newspaper under his arm and followed.

The medieval city was swathed in deep shadows cast by the midday light, which bounced harshly off the cobbled streets and the buildings. It would soon be the hottest part of the day, and the pedestrianised streets were full of people as tourists and locals started to head for the shade of the cloistered piazza off the *Centro Storico* with its bars and cafes.

Rupert watched as Rico took a firmer grip on the briefcase he was carrying and walked off down the street, stopping occasionally on the pretext of studying a shop window. Rupert knew the trick. Rico was using the shop windows to check for any potential tail, or anyone who might be showing more interest in him than they should be.

Rupert passed him twice, checking back to see that he was still heading in the same direction. He was fortunate in that he looked the way he did. The hat and the sunglasses made him much harder to recognise, and whether he realised it or not, his lack of certainty and the strange environment made his walk less assured and his mannerisms less recognizable. Rico walked right past him without batting an eyelid.

The busy streets and Rico's pronounced limp made the job of following him from a greater distance all the easier. What could be more natural, he thought, than a tourist meandering through the city; looking into windows, wandering into streets in search of the elusive bar or restaurant that would offer comfort, relief from the sun and a hint of exclusivity. The main street split, with one road turning uphill to the left. Rico veered off in this direction, occasionally looking back or stopping at a shop window to glance over his shoulder.

Satisfied, he moved off at a slower pace, as the incline took its toll on his hip. There was no doubt that Rico was heading for the legal quarter, Rupert thought, but where-abouts? Which of the *notaios* was he doing business with?

He was moving smoothly through the crowds and keeping his distance, when Rico made a sudden change of direction, crossing the busy street. It would be dangerous for a pursuer to emulate that sudden movement, Rupert reflected, exposing their position. He took off his Panama as if to mop his brow and left it a few seconds before following Rico into a narrow side street that was gloomy and suddenly devoid of people. Twenty yards in, a large arm reached around his neck and a huge hand covered his face, dragging him into a dark covered alcove at the bottom of some steps, leading to part of the old castellated walls. Reaction kicked in and he struggled, trying to stamp down on the man's instep. But he seemed to be held in the grip of a bear and was dragged inexorably further backwards.

"*Silenzio!*" a voice hissed. "Stop!"

Rupert struggled harder and was rewarded for his pains by a hard blow to the stomach, which knocked all the air from him, causing him to double over. A second figure, the man who delivered the blow, emerged from the gloom and proceeded, with his help of his colleague, to manhandle Rupert up the steps to the old ramparts. They emerged into the scorching sunlight once more, overlooking the street.

"We mean you no harm, signor," the second man said in heavily accented English and produced an identification card with his picture on it. "But you must be quiet and watch." he continued.

Rupert nodded. They let go their hold and he relaxed.

"*Qui, qui! Subito.*" They pointed to where a mature

bougainvillea climbed above the waist-high wall on a large, faded trellis, effectively screening part of the ramparts from the street, allowing any watcher to see but not be seen. His two abductors hustled Rupert behind the natural screen and proceeded to carry on a lively discussion in full view of the street in fast, excited, Italian.

As Rupert watched, a bulky figure appeared in the street below: his dark, oiled hair hung to his shoulders in a curling mullet. He wore sunglasses, a padded leather jacket despite the heat, a white t-shirt and jeans. He had entered the side street at a run, as though he'd been following somebody and had suddenly lost his quarry. He looked alarmed that the street was almost empty and did not contain his prey. He looked back and forward and finally up at the two arguing Italians. He spoke in rapid Italian, demanding to know if they had seen a man dressed in a pale suit and wearing a hat. He was a friend of his, whom he had lost, he explained. They nodded and pointed and away from the direction that Rupert had taken, answering that they had seen him heading in that direction.

"Grazie," the man said. He checked around one last time, smacked the wall with the palm of his hand in frustration and sped off up the street in the direction he'd been shown.

When they were sure that the man had gone they stopped arguing and walked over to Rupert.

"You are very fortunate, *Signor*," The man with the strong arm and the bear-like paw of a hand said. "That man is an enforcer. Whatever game you are playing, it is a dangerous one, and it is also one you are not very good at."

He took Rupert's English newspaper and stuffed it into a nearby bin as if to emphasise the point.

"He hides behind a newspaper in his own language," the other man said, laughing. "I think you had better come with us for your own protection, *signor*." He offered Rupert his hand, which Rupert shook without thinking, his English manners coming to the fore. "I am sorry I hit you so hard," the man said, "but it was the only way to make you shut up quickly. No...no feelings of hard, yes?" He finished.

"No, of course not. Thank you," Rupert replied, grinning ruefully whilst shaking both the policemen's hands. *How many more breaks can I get?* He wondered. It had been a long and dangerous journey to this point, and he was already on edge. A journey that had taken him on a career path of deceit, bribery, corruption, murder and the death of someone he had loved. Someone he might have had a future with. Three years ago he'd been finishing his degree. Now, circumstances had set him on the trail of a criminal conspiracy in a foreign country where his very life was in danger.

Chapter Twenty-One

The two police officers who had waylaid Rupert introduced themselves, showing their identification cards. They suggested that they all leave, return to the police station and meet up with their boss, Cappulacci. Rupert was shocked by the turn of events.

"How did you know, and what happens to Rico? I must find out which *notaio* he uses, I need to follow him," he protested.

"*Calmo, signor. Piano, piano,*" one of the men said.

"But he'll get away."

"Signor, it will be OK, we have the place covered," the other explained. "There is a, how do you say, *cordone*?"

"A cordon?" Rupert hazarded a guess.

"Yes, a cordon. All will be recorded and he will be followed. Come, we will explain." The expansive gesture was plain; it was not an invitation but a polite order.

The police station was a sterile and unfriendly looking building located beyond the city wall on the sun-baked concrete outskirts, surrounded by high steel fencing. As they approached, the steel gates slid back, motors humming as the well-oiled wheels rumbled in their tracks. Cameras followed their movements. Once through, the gates closed quickly behind them and the blue and white Alfa accelerated into the parking area, halting with a dramatic screech of brakes. The cameras followed them in through the front doors, which slid crisply shut as soon as they had entered. A second pair of doors opened as the first shut. Security was tight; it was standard practice in the *Carabinieri*. Guards with semi-automatic weapons watched Rupert's progress with hard, unemotional eyes.

He was finally shown into the inspector's office and was surprised. He had been expecting a typical Italian: stocky and running to fat. Instead he was met by an unusually tall man with rugged looks, curly hair, striking blue eyes and an engaging but slightly crooked smile. A hand the size of a ham grasped his in an excruciating grip. It was not intentional, Rupert decided, the man just didn't realise his own strength.

He said in heavily accented, but good, English, "Please sit down, Mr Brett. I am Commisario Davide Cappulacci. How are you?"

Rupert responded politely, but despite the pleasantries he realised that the Inspector was nobody's fool and his eyes carried a piercing analytical glint that seemed to probe into him. Rupert went on to describe the events of the last few hours and was alarmed to learn that he had been followed from the time he arrived in Viterbo. The inspector shrugged.

"But this is normal in Italy. If a scam is going down, everybody takes precautions. You merely got caught up in the security measures," he finished with a grin. "Fortunate for you."

"Yes, thank God your men were on hand to bale me out."

There was a rapid-fire exchange of Italian and Cappulacci laughed. "The English newspaper, signor. You stood out like... *come un pesce fuor d'acqua*... how would you say? A fish taken from water."

Rupert looked at the floor. *Too many James Bond films and not enough practical experience*, he thought. It was a mistake he would never repeat.

The inspector went on to explain the extent of the surveillance operation that had been carried out over recent weeks in conjunction with Webster.

"Signor Brett, I apologise for making fun. Thanks to you we can put the final piece together, as we know their aim: to launder money from Italy to the international market and ultimately fund drugs rings, here and in *Inghilterra*. The scheme is virtually foolproof and has been adapted perfectly to our," he hesitated, a grin on his face as he sought the correct words, "unusual system of property taxation."

"I am still at a loss to understand how exactly it works in practical terms," Rupert said.

"Well, we have been tracking with the *Guardia di Finanza* the movements of Signor Rico and associated companies run by a *Signor...* Simione?" he raised his voice as if the name held a question.

"Simone? That'll be Simions, it has to be," Rupert exclaimed.

"Yes, Webster agrees. However, it will be difficult to

prove everything without someone confessing or," he hesitated, "a little coercion." Cappulacci went on. "The story began some three years ago," *About the time of the Clifton Bridge suicide*, Rupert thought, "when Simione was bequeathed a large villa by his grandmother. He has since sold and resold countless properties, each time increasing the value or managing to buy two and shelve the proceeds to an offshore company in *Sardegna* – the equivalent of your Channel Islands accounts," he deferred to Rupert and continued.

"The proceeds were then reinvested either through a company or individually; the usual tax evasion loopholes were exploited to release the cash and transfer it to the UK mainland. But the problem we have had until now is timing. We have always been aware, how do you say, after the act?"

Rupert nodded. "Too late to prove anything," he said.

"Just so. But this time we can track him – and if we are lucky we will catch him with the cash, follow the route and persuade him to reveal everything. *Capisce*?"

"Yes, I understand, but if all this is falling into place, how do I fit in and why did Webster want me here if you have it all under control?"

Cappulacci's eyes twinkled as if he was relishing the next statement. "Well, you have served a purpose already. They think you are the only tail, and–"

"You mean Webster set me up as bait?" Rupert exclaimed.

"Bait? What is bait?"

"A trap."

"Ah, yes. I am afraid so. They were aware of you all the

time – but don't worry, we were watching over you." Rupert went suddenly cold. Rico and his thugs had been waiting for him. While Rupert had been playing James Bond, thinking he was so clever, they had known all along. He visibly cringed, thinking of what Rico would have done to get his revenge for the injuries Rupert caused him. This was for real. If the cavalry hadn't charged in in the form of Cappulacci's two sergeants, he could well have been tortured to death by some homicidal Mafioso thug. It was all getting out of hand.

"So, if I have played my part, what more is there for me to do?" Rupert asked.

"Ah, but the game, Mr Brett, is not finished. We now need to assure Rico and, more importantly, his contacts in *Inghilterra*, that you are the only opposition acting independently, all alone and unofficially. Do you see?"

Rupert saw only too clearly.

"If we went in now, we would lose the proof. But if you continue your detective work, he will suspect that no official action is happening. Today he thinks he has lost you, how do you say, he has evaded the pursuit. We take you back to where we found you and you walk back to your hotel looking angry, so if they still watch you, you will look like you lost Rico. But you will follow my instructions and tomorrow, you will be wherever I say when we tell you. OK?"

The choices were limited. Rupert nodded in agreement, the danger suddenly very apparent.

"They think you are here on your own to find the people who killed your friend. Just remember, we will be watching you all the time. Everything will be OK."

The words sounded hollow, like a father reassuring a child just before diving off the top board. Rupert was aware of a dry feeling in his mouth and the raw fear beginning to tie knots in his stomach. He tried to shrug it OK.

"Don't worry, we will be there," Cappulacci said with a grin, but the expression of sympathy went against the thrill of the chase, which was plainly visible by the sparkle in his eyes.

Chapter Twenty-Two

By the following morning the events of the day before seemed like a bad dream to Rupert, who lay in bed waiting for the call that would set his nerves jangling and send him towards an uncertain future. He considered the events of the last few hours and the duplicity of Webster. When he returned to England, policeman or not, he would tell the little shit what he thought of him for setting him up like that. He finally left the comfort of his bed, showered, dressed and packed his bag in anticipation of an early departure. He went down to breakfast, waiting for the call to drop everything and start walking again like the day before. He sat alone to one side of the busy dining room, absentmindedly looking at his other guests.

The sound of cutlery and plates clashing together echoed around the room, accompanying the chatter of voices discussing plans for the day in a variety of languages. The waiters were busy, occupied by a table of particularly demanding Americans. Rupert was considering whether to have a third brioche, washed down with yet another cappuccino, when a waiter came across.

"*Scusi* Signor, telephone for you at the main desk."

He gestured with his arm, and Rupert muttered his thanks and rose to take the call. What he missed was the almost imperceptible nods exchanged between two waiters, a mutual understanding passing between them. The closer of the two passed quickly out of the dining room, following Rupert to the reception area. The concierge at reception indicated the telephone on the front desk and smiled, moving a discreet distance away. As Rupert picked up the receiver and placed it to his ear he heard a quiet click, which he assumed was the call being put through. Cappulacci told him that Rico had made the pick-up, the *notaio* had been identified and was being watched. Rupert was to make his way to the airport as soon as possible. He was told to head for the international departures terminal at Ciampino and put himself in a position where he would be seen by Rico.

"You want him to see me?" he whispered down the telephone. "Why?"

"Calm down, Signor Brett. You will be watched and protected at all times, do not worry. OK?"

The last word was stressed and drawn out in the way Italians do with unfamiliar expressions.

"But why?" he continued.

"Because we need a ... *como se dice* ... *catalitica*. A catalytic. Something to force him to panic. To let him know that you are right on his tail. He will act quickly and carelessly, we hope," he added. "So leave now and get to the airport as quick as you can. We will be waiting. Don't make it too obvious that you are intending for Rico to see you – and," he hesitated, "don't get too close to him. *Va bene*?"

Rupert's stomach took on the now familiar feeling as fear gripped him. The images of the assault in the car park in London flashed before him. It wasn't so much the attack, it was the enraged animal he saw snarling in defiance that made Rupert shudder involuntarily. The memories were not good and would stay with him for a long time to come.

"OK," he said at last. "I'm on my way."

He replaced the receiver and rubbed a dry hand across his forehead. It came away damp with sweat. He collected his luggage, paid the bill and hurried out to his car. He fought his way out of Viterbo centre and onto the ring road leading to the SS Aurelia. The journey sped by, with thoughts flying through his head, panic crashing like a thousand cymbals in an orchestra. When he arrived at the airport approach it came as a shock to him that he had reached his destination so soon; he had little recollection of the journey.

He parked the car, returned the keys and the documentation to the hire centre and entered the main terminal building. It was very busy. The atmosphere, as always, was tense. The presence of so many people on edge, expectant and hopeful never failed to excite Rupert. The tension and the clicking information signs reminded him of the Stock Exchange. He loved airports and always had. The thought of so many people acting out their individual dramas – waiting for friends and lovers, family and business partners; anxiously scanning the arrivals board or checking for delays in departure – distracted him momentarily from the task ahead. He relaxed, collected himself mentally and sought the location of the correct check-in desk for departures to London. He found it at the far end of the line; British Airways, Desk 9.

With his passport checked and ticket issued, he folded everything away, smiled and turned to go. As he turned, he almost stumbled into the passenger behind him. Their eyes met and a sense of dread began to rise up in Rupert.

A horrible smile crept across Rico's face. Not surprise, just a smile of cruel satisfaction. The fear on Rupert's face was palpable. He shuddered involuntarily and made to move off quickly but not before Rico grabbed him by the arm.

"You'll get yours, you little shit! I owe you," he muttered quietly in Rupert's ear, the voice filled with menace. Rico released Rupert's arm and patted him lightly on the shoulder twice. "Ciao," he said, and the moment was gone. Hurrying away as quickly as he could, Rupert found that he was hyperventilating. Fear had settled itself deep in his stomach, adrenalin surged around his system and his legs felt like lead.

Calm down, he told himself, *it's done. You've seen him, he's seen you and you're in one piece.* His breathing slowed as he walked past the group *Carabinieri*, debating whether to report it or not. *No, keep calm, Cappulacci's men were sure to be around somewhere.* As if on cue, a smartly but conservatively dressed man approached him from the group of offices to his left. About thirty years old, the man wore a suit and tie had a world-weary, confident air of authority about him.

"Signor Brett?"

Rupert nodded. "Yes," he replied.

The man smiled benignly. "Sergeant Scibilia. The Commisario sent me. He has been watching the events from there." He gesticulated towards a large window with a mirror film across it. "Please, come this way."

Rupert, suddenly very relieved, followed the sergeant, who hesitated once before finally opening the door to the offices, checking around to ensure no one was paying them too much attention.

"We cannot be too careful, signor," he nodded conspiratorially.

Rupert smiled back, glad of the tight protection they were placing around him. The door opened inwards and the sergeant ushered Rupert into the lit room, empty but for a filing cabinet, two chairs and a door on the far side. The door closed quickly behind him and Rupert sensed all was not well just before his world exploded in pain.

A shocking, numbing jab to his kidneys was delivered by the unseen man behind the door. He struck with his fingers extended, bent at the middle knuckle, palm uppermost just below the ribs. The pain was indescribable. Rupert arched away from the blow like a scalded cat and he instinctively sucked in air, causing more pain.

The sergeant appeared to his right and delivered an elbow strike to his sternum. All the breath left him and it felt as if knives were stabbing inside his chest. He wanted to cry out, but no words would come. A small part of his brain thought in an abstract way – the way the body does in moments of extreme stress – that it was not like in the films. You can't take a punch and then beat the bad guys. It was his last conscious thought before he passed out.

As he collapsed to the floor, the second man kicked him hard in the ribs, resulting in a sickening crack. He raised his foot for a second kick and the sergeant stopped him.

"*Basta!* Our orders are to deliver him in good condition," he said in fast Italian.

The other shrugged. "Rico wants –"

"Forget what Rico wants," the first man interrupted, "Rico is nothing, just a small cog, don't listen to him or it will be you who gets hurt. We need Signor Brett in a condition to talk, we need to know how much they know."

The other man scowled and relented.

They lifted Rupert by his arms and legs, manhandling him through the doorway on the far side of the room. The door led out onto the pavement next to the departures doorway furthest away from the terminal. A dark blue Lancia saloon was waiting, its powerful three litre engine burbling away. The front and back doors on the concealed side of the car were open.

The driver looked around and beckoned them towards the car. They changed position and half carried, half walked the slumped figure of Rupert between them and folded him into the car. Slamming the door shut, the sergeant walked around to the other rear door, got in and straightened Rupert up. It was over in a matter of seconds and no one appeared to take any notice.

The front passenger door closed and the driver pulled away, waiting impatiently for a break in the traffic without wishing to draw attention to himself. After a few seconds he slid the car into a small gap in the traffic. A horn sounded, gestures were exchanged and the Lancia sped off as soon as a gap in front extended sufficiently for the driver to accelerate.

The exit road from the airport was approaching, and the three lanes merged with traffic exiting the car park. The driver checked his rear-view mirror and saw it was all clear. Rupert's head lolled from side to side with the movement of the car as it sped through roundabouts away from the airport, heading out onto the GRA. Away from the confines of the airport, the sergeant urged for more speed.

They continued north on the SS Aurelia and pulled off after 25 km, leaving a cacophony of car horns in the wake of their last minute manoeuvre. The side road led to the coastal town of Civitavecchia, a major port for western sea traffic and the main link to the island of Sardinia. They drove steadily along the front, past the old turreted fort heading down towards the docks.

A large derrick swooped down like a crow's beak, plucking containers from the dockside and putting them into the waiting holds of the container ships. The dock area was a hive of activity, making it the perfect place to move unnoticed.

The Lancia pulled to a halt next to a pile of containers being readied for loading. The only other arrival was a lone motorcycle that cruised along the dockside, dodging derrick legs and containers like a skier on a slalom course. The deep burble of the BMW 850 reverberated off the containers as it passed. It had been half an hour since Rupert's abduction, and he was now bound and semi-comatose in the back seat of the Lancia.

The sergeant left the car to talk to one of the dockers, and a container was opened with a view to loading the car and Rupert inside it. Returning to the car, he saw Rupert gaining consciousness.

"Signor Brett, so glad to have you back with us." He smirked. Rupert gradually became aware of his surroundings, twisting in horror as he saw that he was about to be loaded into a container. "Don't worry, it is only a short trip to *Sardegna*, just two hours, and then you will be out again. You will get plenty of fresh air, no problem. We do not want you dead – not yet."

The threat invoked more horror in Rupert. He knew that once he was on the island, he would never be seen again. Having holidayed there a few years ago, he recalled the rats' nests of hills, hideaways and inaccessible mountains where a body or captive could easily be hidden.

He mumbled incoherently through lips that didn't seem to work properly.

His reward was a smack around the head from the sergeant. Anger and fear at the attack seethed within him. He went forwards with the blow, then jerked his head back straight into the face of the of the man who was leaning towards him. It was a damaging blow, the hard back of Rupert's skull breaking the man's nose and smashing his lips into his teeth, blood spewing out.

"Fica!" the man screamed.

Rupert took the opportunity. He might not get far, but he had to try, if only to attract attention. He jacked his legs outwards, his cracked ribs screaming in pain, and kicked the sergeant in the stomach as he jerked upright. Rupert lurched forward, impeded by his bound hands, and began running away from the sea front, shouting for help as he went.

As he ran, he made the mistake of looking behind and seeing the sergeant scrambling to his feet and pulling a Berretta from inside his jacket. The distance was forty yards. *Getting towards top range for a handgun,* Rupert thought before he tripped on the rough concrete. Unbalanced and with his hands still tied, he landed awkwardly, and as he crashed to the concrete he heard a gunshot and the roar of a motorcycle exhaust.

The sergeant half turned at the sound to face the oncoming BMW. The motorbike did not hesitate and there was a sickening crunch as tyre and handlebars connected with human flesh. Caught in the upper leg and ribs, he was bent in two and tossed sideways into the air, the automatic flying from his hand. He slammed into the concrete and lay motionless.

Without warning sirens pierced the air and a pair of blue, unmarked Alfa Romeo 75 Evoluziones converged from the entrance of the docks, coming to a screeching halt by the side of the Lancia. The driver and one of the remaining guards raised their hands as the police, including Cappulacci, flew from the car, guns pointed at the three men.

The third guard was braver, he raised the stock of his Beretta MP12, snapping off a quick burst before being hit by a wave of bullets fired by the police. His lifeless body fell to the ground, where it twitched for a few seconds before becoming still.

In a matter of seconds the police moved out from behind the cover of their cars and rammed the barrels of the guns hard against the necks of the two remaining men. They shouted fast, staccato commands and the dazed men raised their hands. One of the men checked the body of the sergeant, looked up at Cappulacci and shook his head.

Rupert lay still on the concrete, mesmerised by what was happening around him and shocked at the amount of pain coursing through his body. His chest hurt when he breathed, he could feel the bruising around his cracked ribs. His head pounded and his vision swam. He tried to move himself into a sitting position but the pain made it impossible.

"It's OK, Signor Brett," Cappulacci assured him, kneeling down to untie Rupert's hands. "It's OK, *calmo, calmo*," he said gently. Rupert focused briefly on the concerned face, his own contorted in pain, before mercifully passing out again.

Chapter Twenty-Three

The dim light became brighter and turned into a blazing orb in the centre of the room. Rupert's eyes focused slowly as the room finally stopped spinning. The anaesthetic in his bloodstream was still having an effect and the drip attached to his arm periodically pumped another shot of morphine into his system.

The last thoughts he could recall were of crashing to the concrete, extreme pain, a lot of noise and then nothing. He gradually became aware of his surroundings, and the clinical smell of disinfectant and a smiling young nurse peering over him told him that he was in a hospital. The nurse was very pretty in a very Italian way; her large and expressive almond shaped brown eyes were set against an olive skin, and lips that could very well pout were instead smiling kindly at him. He imagined her buzzing around Rome on a Vespa like an extra in a Federico Fellini movie.

"Signor Rupert?"

He refocused on her face and stammered, "Wherrr,... where am I?"

"*Ospedale*. What you ...? House of sick. You are safe now, Mister Rupert. Don' you worry. There is guard at door and I will now go and fetch the doctor. Be calm." She patted him gently, picked up the bedside phone and spoke quickly into the handpiece, nodding her head and saying, "Si, si."

She replaced the receiver and smiled at Rupert.

"The doctor, he is on the way, don't worry, just rest." She mopped his brow with a cloth that felt blissfully cool, smiled reassuringly and left the room. Minutes later a man appeared in a white coat with a stethoscope around his neck. He walked briskly into the room with a no nonsense manner that was typical of all doctors. Rupert smiled despite himself at the cursory inspection and the taciturn attitude.

"Signor, you are a lucky man," the doctor said, his eyes crinkling into a smile that pulled his nicotine-stained moustache upwards at the sides, taking years off his age despite his greying hair and thick glasses. But the eyes behind the lenses were kindly as he continued. "However, you have some concussion, two broken ribs and a cracked sternum. But you are young, you will be fine. In a week, maybe ten days you can be moved and go back to England," he finished with a dismissive shrug, as though the prospect of returning to England was an extraordinary thing to look forward to when one could live in Italy forever.

"But in the meantime you must rest and take time to recover. Now I will give you some more morphine and you will sleep, and we will see how you are when you wake up." Rupert felt himself drifting into a soft, chemical-induced sleep as soon as the drug hit his bloodstream. He dreamed of a pretty girl with dark curly hair riding a scooter through the crowded streets of Rome, moving from one café to the next drinking espresso and laughing with friends as young men pursued her. Just before the dreams faded the girl became Claire, beckoning him, and then even this vision faded as he dropped into a deeper state of unconsciousness.

Chapter Twenty-Four

London

Two days later, a very different conversation was taking place some fifteen hundred miles away in London.

"Yes, it was in the local paper, *la Republica*, and made a small news item on the radio," Shingler said. "Roughly translated it said that an English tourist was hurt in a police chase and later died of his injuries in hospital. So there's no need to worry. It also says that he was in a coma and never recovered consciousness. Rico assures me that all is well, and that he was not followed either before or since. The *notaio* has made the payment, it is in the offshore account and all is well. Relax."

"So you say," Simions replied. "But I'm the one who carries the can in the end. It's me that has to contend with police knocking at my door, me who has to answer the questions and me who gets put under the spotlight," he shouted. It was a measure of Simions' anger that he had raised his voice at all, but the circumstances merited it.

"Just stay calm," Shingler insisted. "Nothing can be proved. Rico won't talk, you've nothing to worry about. He'll be safely tucked away in Sardinia now telling us all he knows. After that..."

"Fine but look here–"

"No, Paul," Shingler interrupted sternly, harsh tones entering his voice. "You look here for once. We've been here before, remember? Don't make me remind you. And remember it was both of us who ordered the hit on Liz Carmichael and it was me who arranged the 'suicide' in Bristol." The threat hung in the air, more menacing than a raised voice.

Simions was silent, his thoughts turning to the events Shingler was alluding to. His eventual response was a flat snarl that spoke of fear and desperation, like a cornered animal. "Fine, but I won't go down alone, just remember that," he said and slammed down the receiver.

He stared across the office, beads of sweat forming on his brow, and he realised that he was hyperventilating. He held out his hand palm down and looked at the perceptible shake which he struggled to control. He swore harshly in Italian. He thought it was strange that after all these years, it was still the language he cursed in. It seemed to mean more when he used his native vernacular.

How long had it been? He counted four days since the incident at the airport. *Soon*, he realised, *they will come soon*. The *notaio* had signed everything off; the Italian authorities would take an age to register the deal and the Italian police would never follow it up, they would stick with the supposed Mafia connection in Italy if nobody paid them off. It was just the English police that could be a problem. Acting on instinct he rang down to his secretary to check for calls. She told him that a caller had rung twice asking if he was in the building, but had left no name. Alarmed, he rang off and paced the room, collecting his thoughts and working out a strategy, eventually finding a calm place in the eye of the storm. He felt his rational mind take hold. Raising his hand and holding it palm down, there was not a movement, no longer so much as a tremor.

"Let the game commence," he murmured in defiance.

The police arrived a day later. They had of course checked his movements, and the calls they'd made were just to soften him up, put his nerves on edge. They had to an extent succeeded. DI Fleming and DS Brooke were shown up to his offices once again.

"We just wanted to ask you a few questions, to clear up some loose ends that we have concerning one of your employees," Fleming began. "Or perhaps I should say one of your former employees."

"Oh yes. Poor Rupert, I assume? So sad, we were all really upset when we heard..." Simions let his words fade away and looked down in a suitably grief-stricken manner.

"Yes, strange coincidence really, first his girlfriend and now him. It seems that it's somewhat unlucky being associated with you, Mr Simions." Fleming's tone changed through the sentence, became harder and more aggressive.

"I beg your pardon, Inspector Fleming, what on earth do you mean by that remark?" The fluster was part reality, partly put on for show. "I don't like the tone that this conversation is taking, and I certainly resent the insinuation in your last statement. I have lost a colleague and a friend."

"Well, Mister Simions," Brooke said. "We rather suspect that the death of Miss Carmichael and the incident with Rupert Brett are linked, and that you know more about this than you're letting on." Brooke finished abruptly without any further explanation.

"Hang on a minute. Miss Carmichael's death occurred months ago in London; Rupert died in Italy, and you somehow think they are connected? It appears to me that Rupert was grief stricken by Elizabeth's murder and had followed a lead of his own to Italy, where he got on the wrong side of some dangerous people. If you think I am somehow involved in all this, you are clearly delusional, and this conversation is at an end," Simions finished. "If you wish to say anything more, you will have to wait until my solicitor is present. I don't know what the game is here, but I certainly resent the implications you are making. In the meantime if you are dealing with poor Rupert's death I would suggest that, as a pair of detectives, you go off and do just that: detect!"

The staring contest continued for a few seconds, and it was Simions who first looked away. But the detectives knew that they had no concrete evidence with which to charge him, and moved to leave.

Once they were outside the building DS Brooke exhaled slowly.

"He's fucking guilty as hell. But we can't do anything. They're holding Rico in Italy for currency charges – money laundering at best – and he is not talking. A decent lawyer will have him out in no time flat. And him in there," he jerked his thumb backwards, "is guilty of all that as well as murder, corruption and bribery – you name it, and we can't touch him."

DI Fleming shook his head in disgust. "I know, I know. But what can we do except keep the pressure on and hope that something breaks? I'm going to speak with Webster again now that we've seen Simions."

Two weeks passed and Rupert was healing fast from the injuries he had sustained, as all young people do. But while the physical side of the healing process continued in leaps and bounds, the mental strain and trauma of the past few months was becoming more apparent and taking longer to repair.

Back in London, his face had taken on a gaunt and hollow-cheeked look as he ascended the austere staircase to the now familiar office of DS Webster. Rupert's eyes were ringed by blue circles and dark smudges. His summer tan was beginning to fade, leaving a pale and sickly coloured pallor. His ribs still ached a little from the exertion of climbing the stairs, but it was a good sign; they were healing. He finally reached the landing and walked through into the outer office, occupied by the same efficient looking secretary. She offered him a weak smile and motioned for him to sit, before picking up the telephone and announcing his arrival to Webster.

When Webster appeared he was ebullient and smiling, yet managed somehow to produce the sympathetic expression of a man torn between having achieved what he wanted but needing to conserve his position as a caring authority figure. Rupert wondered if he'd practiced the expression in front of a mirror. He extended his right hand towards Rupert and maintained that caring demeanour. "Rupert, so good to see you up and about," he said. "How are you?"

The false bonhomie didn't fool Rupert for a moment, but he played the game, smiled wanly and shook Webster's hand.

"Pretty crap, since you're asking. Being kidnapped, along with cracked ribs and sternum will do that to a man," he finished.

"I am dreadfully sorry that you were hurt. The Italians were supposed to take care of you and they failed miserably. But we did all we could this end."

Rupert's eyes hardened for a moment, then he relaxed through sheer effort of will. Webster motioned him through to his office and followed him in.

As soon as the door closed, Rupert let rip with all the pent up emotion of the last couple of weeks. "You fucking bastard! You knew you were setting me up, you knew I was being followed. I was your stalking horse and you let me walk right into the trap. Getting me beaten up no doubt helped seal the conviction. Is that it? Well fuck you, Webster! I came here to say that, and whatever else you invited me here for can stay unsaid. Whatever you want, the answer is no!" he turned and made for the door.

Webster's bland response followed him: "I understand how you must feel, but what you say is not entirely true. Yes I did–"

"You understand?" Rupert interrupted. "I doubt that

very much. How could you? I'm fed up with being lied to, now I'm leaving."

"You realise that Liz's killer is still at large, and you are the only man who can put her away?"

Rupert paused, hesitating, then forced himself to carry on walking towards the door. "I don't give a shit," he retorted.

"Yes you do, Rupert. You wouldn't be human if you didn't. One more meeting, no violence, I guarantee it."

"Yeah? Just like the last time."

"Just give me five minutes and then you can walk out, OK?"

Rupert's hand was actually on the door handle, but suddenly all the fight went out of him. He saw Liz's face, looking at him over some restaurant table or other. She was smiling, and the felt the touch of her hand for a fleeting second. His shoulders sagged, he relented with a sigh and returned to take a seat facing Webster. But when he left twenty minutes later, the answer was still no.

After Rupert had left, Webster called Fleming. "He still won't do it. Despite Cappulacci getting Rico to talk, we can't get Shingler or Simions without further proof here. We need more conclusive evidence. Brett feels let down by us and Cappulacci. He's no fool, and he knows he was used to spring a trap."

Rupert went home and brooded until early evening, when the painkillers he was still taking made him dozy again. He was brought back to full consciousness by the insistent ringing of his doorbell intercom. He picked up the access phone and looked at the monitor. Claire.

"Rupert? Is that you? Is it really you? For God's sake let me in."

The vision Rupert was met with was a long way from the Claire he remembered. She stood before him with the tears running freely down her face. Her hair was pulled back in a ponytail and her mascara had run onto her cheeks. She looked at Rupert from the doorway, as if she was frightened to come any further, as if he might just vanish in a puff of smoke.

"Rupert, oh thank God. What's happened to you?" Claire seemed to take in his gaunt appearance and the rings around his eyes.

"Claire, what is it? Whatever's the matter?"

"I thought you were dead, you little shit, dead! I've been in pieces. Why didn't you tell me?"

She rushed forward and threw her arms around him, and he winced and protested loudly. "Ow! What are you doing here if you think I'm dead?"

"Oh Rupert, I'm so sorry. Did somebody hurt you?" Claire asked, but gave him no time to respond, as emotional as she was. "Sit down and let me get you a drink. Your mother phoned me out of the blue. She said you were alive, but not well. She was worried sick. Told me you'd been hurt. No one else knows, she told me not to tell anyone. I came straight here. Rupes, talk to me," she shook him gently by the shoulders. The tears had dried, but her eyes had an unnatural sparkle. He read elation, anger and puzzlement in equal measure. "Tell me everything," Claire said.

So he did, everything from the moment he'd left to when he got back to England two days previously. He'd contacted his parents to make sure they didn't believe any news they heard, and he had sworn them to secrecy. It was a measure of their concern that his mother had contacted Claire, who sat in studied silence, listening and wincing or exclaiming in parts, saying nothing. When he finished she hugged him very gently, running her hands through his hair as if she never wanted to let him go. She opened a bottle of wine from his fridge and poured for them both, and sat with him as the world outside grew dark.

"So what are you going to do?" she asked eventually. "I must say I don't like the sound of this DS Webster's scheme. Too many loose ends and you will end up being the fall guy for all their plans – if you haven't ended up there already."

"I don't know. I really don't. I am mightily pissed off but fed up being manipulated by everyone else – whatever side of the law they're on. I spend all my time playing catch up, following or responding to everyone else's actions. Now I feel I need to take the initiative."

"Good for you. I thought you had given up the fight there for a minute."

"Not a chance," he retorted.

"But listen, up until now you have been fighting on everybody else's terms and it has always had a physical end. I don't know how good you are at all this spying and rough stuff. What you need to do is to take the fight to them." She waved off Rupert's proposed objection. "Not physically; from what you've said about Rico you'd come off a pretty poor second anyway. No, I mean use your intelligence. Hell, you were one of the best agents in the West End. You came from nothing to doing £350k a year non-retained. For God's sake, Rupert, that takes some doing and you didn't get it handed to you on a plate. Use your cunning and the streetwise abilities you've learned from Simions and his like. You're always telling me you have an almost photographic memory for facts, numbers and deals. Well, think back and use that to your advantage, not theirs."

It was as though a light had suddenly clicked on in his brain. Claire had shown him the way and opened a door for him to step through. They talked it over while Claire made a simple pasta supper ("Memories of Italy. Way to go, Claire", He'd said, and she'd laughed naturally, the beauty coming back to her face). Afterwards, they made lists of people and events that had occurred over the months before Liz's death and since. As they followed the timeline through, a plan was beginning to occur to Rupert.

If he was right, it could bring down the whole house of cards.

"OK," Rupert said. "First we need to contact Liz's parents and see if they have the notebook she wrote everything in. I really am not looking forward to that, not at all."

"What will you do, telephone them?"

"Yes. I know where they live in West Sussex, a village near a town called Midhurst. Her funeral was there, and I met them – after I was exonerated from any associated guilt, of course. They offered me their sympathies, which I thought was pretty decent of them, all things considered."

"Midhurst?" Claire said.

"Yes, why do you know it?

"Of course, it is the polo capital of the UK. All the pony club championships are held there. I know it quite well. In fact everyone knows everyone there. If Liz was horsey I bet I can find someone who knows the family."

She went off to get her Filofax and started to make a number of calls. Half an hour later she was there.

"Bingo," she exclaimed. "Here we are." She passed over a number and address. "She used to be a member of the Pony Club and this girl, Louise," she pointed at the Filofax, "knew her quite well and still keeps in contact with the parents. Obviously they are still very cut up about Liz's death, so tread lightly."

"Understood."

The call was not easy and Rupert was afraid at one point that Liz's father would put the phone down on him. But he gently persevered and they agreed to help by looking for the black notebook he had seen her reading to Simions all that time ago in Boswells. As Claire said, Rupert had an elephant's memory for detail. Apparently the police had returned it as it was in shorthand and seemed to be just a secretary's notebook. They promised to post it as soon as they found it. Rupert came off the phone visibly shaken.

"That was horrible. Those poor people. I never want to have to do that again."

She rubbed his shoulder affectionately. "Rupes, I have to go. I have a report to draft before tomorrow and it's a mare. Like everyone else, I've spent the last two weeks thinking you were dead, and I haven't been able to concentrate on much else. I left early the minute your mother called."

"Sorry, Claire. I had to keep up the pretence, and I still do. Go on, but for God's sake stay sad." She batted his arm and grinned. "You've done more than enough: thank you so much, and I'm really sorry I couldn't tell you," he said sincerely. "But keep it to yourself, the fewer people who know the better – and that includes Mike and Jemma"

"Of course. Night." She pecked him on the cheek and left, her perfume lingering in the air as a constant reminder of her presence.

Thank you, Claire, he thought. *Thank you.*

Chapter Twenty-Five

Three days later the notebook arrived from Liz's parents. Rupert called Claire, using the agreed pseudonym of Steven Smith – not the most original.

"The package has arrived. Just one small problem, can you read shorthand?"

"It's one of my many hidden talents," she replied.

They agreed to meet up after she left work to finalise their plans. She arrived at his flat and began poring over the notebook. On their own the notes meant little, but taken in context and with the inside knowledge they already had it was dynamite. They hatched a plan and agreed to meet up at a little wine bar off Maddox street; somewhere that was out of the way and perfect for their needs.

Two days later, Claire sat at a table with her secretary Tracey, who had gone off sick when the details of the Golden Triangle scheme had been leaked.

"The point is this, Tracey," Claire snapped, "I know you took money to pull a sickie for two days; that in itself was not too bad, we all call in sick occasionally. But what you didn't realise is that we lost massive amounts of fees on that deal, and it's all down to you."

Tracey responded petulantly, "I don't see how. Two days sick, so what?"

"Fine, have it your way. I know Secs in the City called you, it's on the records," she bluffed. "I also know you were paid a sum of money by them in cash. What you do not know is that Paul Simions of MAS owns that agency. You thought it was just Pauline, didn't you? And the temp leaked secrets to Simions, which is how you lost us money."

"So," Tracey began to look nervous, "...what are you going to do?"

"Well you have two choices: You can do as I say or I go to Personnel and get you fired," Claire said calmly.

"What? No, don't do that. What do I have to do? I will help, but who is we?"

At that point Rupert turned around from the table behind: "It's me, actually."

"What! You're dead! The papers said..." she blurted out, as if she'd seen a ghost.

"You shouldn't believe everything you read in the papers Tracey," he chided.

For Tracey, the conversation went downhill from there. She agreed to help and sign whatever they wanted. After she left, the two co-conspirators smiled, chinked glasses and Rupert commented. "Well now, that went well, didn't it?"

"Right, stage three," Claire replied.

That afternoon she called Secs in the City using a false name and asked if she could come in to apply for temping work, claiming she was fed up working at CR and wanted more freedom. Using herself as the reference, she applied as a senior PA, and she was interviewed by Pauline Wood herself. Claire mentioned that she was hard up for cash and that if any high paid PA jobs came up she would be glad of the money.

"I can invoice you as self-employed, if that helps?" she said. For a moment, she thought she had overplayed her hand, but Pauline Wood latched on to this, her sharp eyes glinting.

"Really?" she said. "And you're a property secretary I see?" She ran a be-ringed finger down the page of the fake CV. "Can you work at short notice?" Claire nodded. "Good. Well we work a lot within the property world and for rush jobs we get paid bonuses, which we are able to pass on as cash, if you know what I mean?" Pauline smiled, and the smile reminded Claire of a hyena; it was not pleasant.

"I'm happy to work on a cash basis," Claire enthused. The hard eyes appraised her again.

"Well, sometimes we get asked to do a little bit extra. It might be –"

Claire interrupted. "Oh, I won't sleep with anyone. I'm not that desperate!" Claire said with mock outrage, deliberately misinterpreting Pauline's meaning.

The hyena laughed, showing even, white teeth. Her double chin wobbled a little.

"No my dear, nothing like that," she assured her. "Just sometimes we like a bit extra done or copied..."

Claire pretended to finally catch on, "Oh yeah, no probs. Anything like that."

And so it was left. The trap was baited and the waiting began.

That evening Rupert and Claire held a council of war.

"So, it went well then?" he queried.

"Yes, she snapped me up. I thought I'd overplayed my hand at first, but the revolting creature was delighted to add another convert to the cause. So now we wait. When do you think we should go to Webster? We're going to need help from him soon to pull it all together, aren't we? Especially where Shingler is concerned."

"I don't know that we will. You told me to use my cunning. Well I have, and I want them to turn on each other. I have the advantage of surprise: they don't know I'm alive. But for every day that passes, that risk becomes greater, then I will really put the cat amongst the pigeons. Revealing myself to Tracey was risky enough."

"Helped though, didn't it? Anyway, I thought we said no risky physical stuff?" Claire asked.

"Don't worry, if there's one thing Simions won't do, it's start a fight, more's the pity. I'd just like one chance to knock the bastard unconscious!" Rupert finished.

A week later Claire was called on her home number. It was Pauline Wood.

"Louise? It's Pauline Wood from Secs in the City. How are you?" The call progressed and she was asked to come in to temp at, of all places, Halpern and Beams in three days' time. The placement was in the Investment Department and she was to collect information on a scheme and a portfolio that was to be released for sale in two weeks' time. She accepted eagerly and put the phone down and immediately phoned Rupert to explain everything.

"So, what's the plan now?" He asked.

"I know Richard Saunders, the head of investment there, really well. I'll go and see him tomorrow. I'll tell him what's happening and tell him to keep it as quiet as possible so that he can help us spring the trap, because I am going to have an accident and I won't be able to work there," she prophesied.

"Hmm. We need the temp to be caught in the act. We also need the complicity of the Personnel Department."

"Don't worry about that. I reckon they are up to their ears in it," Claire confirmed.

"OK then, good luck."

Claire phoned in sick with a badly sprained ankle, saying she couldn't make the temp appointment. Pauline Wood was not best pleased, and offered her very little sympathy.

"Just one more thing Louise. We like to keep certain aspects of our practices quiet and the bosses don't like this sort of thing being bandied about. Do we understand each other?"

"Of course. I want more work, and as soon as this bloody ankle gets better I'll be back. Don't you worry," she reassured her, ignoring the threat.

"Good. See that you are discreet." Pauline rang off.

Claire checked the day before, and found that another temp from the agency had been placed. Richard Saunders had been more than willing to go along with Claire's plan, seeking a little revenge of his own, and the hapless temp was caught faxing some false details directly to David Shingler's office. Shingler would be none the wiser.

Saunders had the temp sign a statement admitting to everything in return for being let off with a warning and no prosecution.

The next day, Rupert arranged to go and see Webster, who looked expectant, hoping that Rupert had changed his mind about working for him. His greeting was a good deal warmer.

"Rupert, how very good to see you again – and looking better, I am pleased to see."

Rupert acknowledged the compliment and told him Webster what he had done and why he was there.

"That was a very dangerous and stupid thing you both did. You're playing with fire, in more ways than one."

"It's not that dangerous," Rupert retorted. Anyway, it's Shingler who calls the heavies in, not Simions."

"Yes, but who do you think orders it?" At that moment, the final piece of how to crack this fell into place for Rupert. "Fair enough. Now, you wanted my help and I'm giving it. If you agree, I'm happy to bow to your knowledge and follow standard procedures, but I would like you to apply pressure on Pauline Wood directly."

Rupert went on to outline his plan.

The next day the police interviewed a very aggressive Pauline Wood, whose bluster and denials changed when she was shown written statements from various Personnel departments, Tracey and the temp who had replaced Claire at Halpern and Beams. She demanded a lawyer and ensured that he in turn spoke to Shingler. At the same time, Rupert was having a Lazarene moment with Paul Simions. Rather than being introduced at reception, he used his knowledge of

Simions habits to ambush him after lunch as he was walking from his car towards the office steps. For Rupert, it was a moment to savour. Simions was looking confident, and had clearly not yet been given the bad news by Shingler as to what had just occurred at the offices of Secs in the City.

He approached Simions, smiling and expansive. "Paul. How the devil? I was just on my way to see you." All smiles, extending his hand to shake with Simions.

"Rupert! What the hell... you're alive. But I thought you...I mean, they said..." he finished completely nonplussed.

Rupert laughed at him, filled with new-found confidence. Simions was no longer the bogeyman. "Do you know, that's probably the first time I've ever seen you lost for words."

"Well, yes... well... But why didn't you call and let me know you were all right? I was trying to get hold of your parents to see when your funeral was," he finished lamely.

"I was in Italy, and I was in hospital, and then," at which point he looked around furtively "I was interviewed by the police and they told me I was not allowed any contact with anyone – especially you or David Shingler." Rupert was delighted at the effect the words had upon Simions. His face fell, and a world of fear and wariness was exposed in a fleeting instant before the mask went back into place.

"I think we had better step inside," Simions said, offering the way with his hand.

The response of the receptionists was just as spectacular. They only let them pass after two minutes of brief explanations. Simions himself was clearly impatient to learn everything. While waiting for the lift one of them called: "Before you go up sir, Mr Shingler is on the line, says it's urgent. He tried your car phone but the driver said you had just left."

"Tell him I'll call him back in a few minutes – and that Rupert is back and with me at the moment," he finished pointedly. "I am sure he will be delighted to hear it."

Upon entering his office he continued, "Now, tell me all about it from the beginning. I really am so pleased to see you," he adhered to his disingenuous alter ego. So Rupert did, slanting the narrative his way and finishing with the premise that the police thought he was somehow involved in a falling out amongst thieves.

"I felt like a bloody criminal," He said. "The Italians even took my passport and told me not to leave the country – and it was me that got beaten up. I don't get it."

"You poor chap, how awful for you."

Rupert waved off the sympathy. "But listen, the real reason I came to you directly is that they think that you and David are involved."

"Why?" Simions snapped.

"Well, it's all to do with this chap Rico. Apparently his sister is the one who may have murdered Liz. She was seen at the apartment block on the night of the murder, and because I was there they think I may still be linked to it all," he continued, watching every nerve of Simions reaction. *I have him hooked*, he thought, so he ploughed on.

"You see, apparently there is a connection between the temp agency you use – Secs in the City – David Shingler, Rico and his sister. The police are trying to do a deal, I think. They wanted me to admit some culpability, anyway, but I wouldn't because it was nothing to do with me. But as you are so close to Shingler I just wanted to warn you, in case you need to cut ties with him quickly. The last thing you want is to get yourself involved with corporate espionage and murder."

The old Simions was back, the lupine eyes regarding him balefully. The temperature in the room seemed to drop suddenly.

"And why do you think that this concerns me?" he asked icily.

"I told you. From what the police have said to me, they think that they have found a connection between you and Shingler. Look, I never liked him much, you know that, but this is serious and I certainly don't want to get any more involved as one of your employees."

Simions responded as Rupert knew he would: with aggression.

"Rupert, I don't know who the hell you think you are, but firstly you no longer work for me – your employment was terminated when we thought you were dead – and secondly it's none of your bloody business. I have absolutely nothing to do with this, and just because David does a lot of work for me, it doesn't mean that we had anyone murdered – Liz or anyone else – is that clear?" the last words were shouted. Rupert had never heard Simions raise his voice before.

Rupert blanched, then let his own temper out, knowing what effect it would have. "Well fuck you! I came here to help – my first call after being freed by the police and this is the response I get? Stuff you, Simions. I don't know what you're involved in, but you won't get any more help from me, that's for certain." Rupert's parting words were delivered as he was half-way through the door, and they shook Simions. "I intend to vindicate myself, and if that involves pointing the finger elsewhere, so be it."

He stormed out, slamming the door. As soon as he was outside he exhaled and grinned to himself. "Yes! Now let's see what happens," he muttered. "You may not like it, DS Webster, but the results could be spectacular," he murmured to himself.

Back in Simions' office the phone rang.

"Paul? It's David. Where the hell have you been, and how come Brett is alive?"

"To answer your points *seriatim*," Simions replied pompously, "I've been talking with Mr Brett, and he is alive because your man fucked up! Now shut up and listen." He told Shingler everything Rupert had said, finishing with the veiled threat.

Shingler was furious and clearly worried, and he told Simions about Pauline Wood's arrest and said that she would probably talk in return for a more lenient sentence. The rats were, in his eyes, clearly leaving the sinking ship but the most worrying problem was the murder of Simions' former partner and Liz. "This all taking a bad turn. The bribing and espionage is bad enough, we could fight that with good lawyers, but the association with murder scares me shitless," Shingler said.

"Just sit tight," Simions replied. "We can rely on Rico being strong enough and not revealing the link between you and his sister."

"That's all very well for you to say. You aren't the one

with all this hanging over your head. Listen, if Rico incriminates me, I will bring everyone down with me, including you. I am not doing time for manslaughter or criminal conspiracy to commit murder. You sit there in your ivory tower," he spat, "distanced from it all but where would you be without me pulling all the levers and making it happen, huh? Fucking nowhere, that's where. So don't patronise me with that 'sit tight' bollocks. We need to think about this carefully and make sure our case is solid. The police have asked to see me tomorrow, but I swear I am being followed already."

Simions changed tack, seeking to pacify Shingler. "David, look, you're right. We're in this together, we will find a way out. We have the best lawyers and we will fight it. As far as the police can prove, it is only a bit of white collar crime and fraud. Difficult to prove in court. They might nor even prosecute, and if they do, we'll fight it."

"Ok that's better." Shingler conceded "I'm going to tidy up in the office. Make sure all evidence has gone and no trail of any kind is left – fax memory, the lot. You do the same, OK? You can be guilty by association, and I don't want any link between us coming out of this."

"Good point. I'll wait for the girls to go and clear everything out that might be in the slightest bit incriminating. We'll speak tomorrow but if anything else occurs just call me. We'll fight this thing."

Shingler, finally mollified, agreed. "Sure we will. Talk later."

Simions turned around in his chair and looked out over the London skyline, lost in thought. Shingler was right. He was the link in all this. Shingler's link to Simions was also his link to Rico, his sister and a whole world of trouble. *Everyone talks,* he thought, *no one is ever loyal.* He made a decision, picked up the receiver and looked up a number in his address book. Thinking better of it, he made a note on a slip of paper and then left the office, telling reception that he was popping out for a few minutes.

When he returned he asked the receptionist if any anyone had called. Nobody had.

"Well just so you know, there are some strange rumours regarding Rupert and his former employment. If the police should call either in person or by telephone, I want my lawyer called directly. You have his number, yes?"

They nodded in assent and he passed on the same message to Gayle, his PA.

Chapter Twenty-Six

After his meeting with Simions, Rupert called Claire to tell her how it had gone.

"Was that wise?" she asked. "We agreed not to push him that far."

"I know, but he just sat there with that smug smile on his face, then he tried the I'm-more-important-than-you tactic. Well stuff him! I really enjoyed rocking his world, second only to smacking him one. I did think at one point he was going to come over the table at me, but as I said, he may be a bully but he's also a coward."

"Well, I hope you know what you're doing. Listen, don't take this the wrong way but would you like to stay at my flat for a couple of days? No one knows where I live – except for Angus, who's long gone – and no one knows I'm involved. You say that Rico could come back to the UK, but it would be even more scary if his sister comes looking for you. If this goes wrong..." she left it hanging in the air.

"Do you know, I might just do that. I'll pick up some

things from my flat and be around later." He rang off and looked into the mid distance. *Claire, Claire, Claire*, he thought.

The next call did not go so well.

"You've done what?" shouted Webster. *Ah*, thought Rupert, *it was obviously the day for ruffling feathers.* He grinned to himself and continued calmly: "Yes, I bumped into him in the street. As you can imagine he was surprised. Things just went from there really," he finished and waited for the reaction. He was not disappointed.

"Rupert, we have just arranged for Rico to be set free as a stalking horse to try to trap them, and you go and blow it. For Christ's sake, have you also considered that they might come after you now they know you're alive? Now we're going to have to put you under police protection," Webster said angrily.

"Are you indeed? Like you did the last time? Forget it. I'll take my own precautions. But I don't see how this changes anything. It will just put them on their guard, and they're more likely to make a mistake."

"Just make sure you stay in touch, whatever happens," Webster snapped.

"Oh I will – except if I'm dead, OK?" Rupert snapped back and put the phone down.

The day progressed without further incident. Rupert picked up spare clothes and essentials from his flat and walked the few streets over to Claire's, feeling exposed despite the busy streets. She had left a key with a neighbour and he let himself in and waited for her to come in from work.

Back in the City, David Shingler was working late. He was the last one in the office and no one was there to witness his ruthless clear-out. He looked at his gold Rolex: 6:50. The cleaners would be here soon, he reflected, putting several black bin bags of shredded documents outside the office door, and by tomorrow all the evidence will be gone. He shredded a few last files and reset the fax machine memory. A noise startled him just after 7.30. The lift doors opened and with it the jabber of the cleaners' voices. *I'm getting jumpy,* he thought. *The police won't come that quickly.*

The cleaners spread out, the din of vacuum cleaners, chatter and the cleaning trolleys moving through the offices. Eventually there was a tentative knock at his door. A care-worn face appeared, clad in a tracksuit protected by a nylon apron and wearing yellow rubber Marigolds. She pushed a large trolley holding a huge plastic bucket laden with cleaning sprays and dusters into the room.

"Can I clean the room, sir?"

Shingler grunted. Looking around the room, he decided that he was nearly finished. He'd get in early tomorrow and do a few final bits then. Most of it would be cleared and destroyed tonight, a job well done. He waved the cleaner in and lifted his suit jacket from the back of his chair. The best thing was that all the money from the drugs and the clubs was either in cash or looked legitimate. It was a good job Simions didn't know what he had been up to in their joint names, or there would be hell to pay. He grinned to himself.

"Come in," he told the cleaner, "and make sure all those bags are cleared away." He motioned to the small stack of refuse sacks.

With a final glance around, he left the room and headed for the lift. The ping of the doors opening drew his attention upwards as another cleaner appeared, pushing the ubiquitous trolley and without waiting, went in front of him, securing a place in the corner.

"Cheers mate," she muttered.

He was treated to a strong waft of cheap, sickly perfume from the cleaner, whose dull bunches of hair fell from beneath a large headscarf. She leant over the apparently heavy cart, pushing in front of him so he was unable to make eye contact.

"No, no, please don't worry," he muttered sarcastically. "After you." She made no response and he then saw that she had wires going to her ears and a Walkman belted to her tracksuit waist. He heard that faint sound of tinny music that was becoming ubiquitous out in the streets as the ghetto-blasters fell from fashion. He shook his head in disgust, ignoring her and pressing his own button for the basement car park. The lift moved and started its downward journey, the cleaner oblivious, swaying to the rhythm of the music in her ears, tapping a foot as she fiddled with her trolley contents. The speaker announced that the lift had reached the basement and the doors started to open. The cleaner turned as if to pull her cart, and Shingler caught sight of her face. The scar, the hard brown eyes and the cracked tooth. His face registered alarm.

"Maria!"

"Paul Simions and Claudio send their regards," she sneered. Her gloved hand came up with a plastic spray cleaner, which she sprayed directly into his face and open mouth. The scent of bitter almonds was overpowering. Shingler gasped as the hydrogen cyanide spray entered his bloodstream, affecting his metabolism instantly.

Never as quick as in the films Maria thought, *but quick enough.* She had pulled down her headscarf to cover her nose and mouth just before spraying Shingler, and now she covered her face with another thick pad held in place by the other gloved hand to be sure. The lift doors slid open. She gave one last spray directly into the face of the comatose Shingler, who was already lying prostrate on the ground, and stepped out into the fresh air, leaving a broom handle to prevent the lift doors closing. She pulled off her scarf and inhaled deep gulps of air once she was a few feet from the lift.

She waited three minutes before returning to the lift. The doors had banged against the broom twice in an effort to call the lift back. She dragged Shingler out by the armpits, propped him against the wall and checked his pulse. It was thready and faint. For good measure she sprayed him again, directly into his mouth this time, closing his lips around the nozzle. Leaving the dying man she fetched a Ford Escort van and opened the rear doors. Returning to Shingler, she noticed that his face had ironically turned a pink, healthy colour. Staying masked, she dragged him over to the van and heaved him head and shoulders first into the back. Shutting the doors she drove off as unobtrusively as possible, leaving the cleaning cart in the car park behind her as the lift doors banged once more into the broomstick.

Rupert was enjoying supper with Claire in her flat, blissfully unaware that his plans had far exceeded his expectations. In his heart of hearts, he knew that Simions would probably take some drastic steps to contain the problem, but he was yet to realise just how drastic.

A bottle of wine later, Claire and Rupert were lying back in each other's arms on the sofa, in a sleepy embrace. The initial tension of the evening had evaporated and they had fallen into a conversation about their plans for the future once all this was behind them – not least of which was what lay in store for Rupert now he was back in the UK.

"It's a very good question," He said, stroking her hair absently. "What am I going to do? I don't really want to go back to CR, and I doubt they would have me anyway; there's still a cloud of suspicion hanging over me there. I don't think anyone – with the possible exception of Sheen, strangely enough – thinks I am entirely innocent. *A man shall be known by the company he keeps*,'" he finished, quoting Aesop. "And that applies especially to my old pal friend Mike Ringham, who appears to have dropped me like a stone."

"Oh don't be too hard on him, Rupes. Jemma is really upset about it all and if Mike suddenly finds out you're alive, I'm sure the two of them will be over the moon."

"Hmm." was all he replied, stubbornly refusing to see the best in Mike, hurt by his reaction to the circumstances Rupert had found himself in.

Changing the subject she asked, "But do you think that you'll become an agent again when all this blows over?"

"Yes, definitely. I mean, being a client was fun and everything, but it's not for me. I like the cut and thrust, the thrill of agency; certainly for the immediate future, anyway."

"And a bloody good agent you shall be once more," Claire said, slapping his chest and turning to smile up at him.

It could have been the wine, the enforced intimacy or maybe just circumstances, but he looked into her large green eyes and kissed her, tentatively at first but as she responded the kiss became a thing of passion, giving him warmth and release from the outside world.

In the meantime, a very different sort of interaction was taking place at the Carlton Club. Simions was comfortably ensconced in a wingback armchair, relaxing after a good meal with two friends and gently puffing at a cigar, a glass of brandy in his left hand. He was still smiling from an amusing story told by one of his friends when he looked up at the face of the waiter who had silently appeared at his side.

"A telephone call for you, sir."

Simions nodded an acknowledgement. "Please excuse me," he said. "My mother has not been well and I have been expecting news of her." He smiled benignly and followed the waiter. Picking up the receiver he answered: "Simions. Is everything alright?"

The woman's voice at the other end of the line answered him. "The first part of the operation went off well. But the secondary investigation showed nothing. Any ideas?"

"That's such a relief to hear. I'm sure Mother will be fine. The secondary bit would, on reflection, be best left alone, at least for now. Too many complications, don't you agree? Best let everything heal naturally, I think."

"Your call. I'm going away for a rest myself very soon. It's all been a bit busy here. I will let you know when I return."

"Very well. Have a good trip, and I will ensure that I pay for all the care, don't worry," he confirmed.

"Good." The call was terminated.

You've either been very lucky or very clever Mr Brett, Simions thought on his way back to his friends. He decided to let things lie now that the worst of the danger was past and the more significant problem had been dealt with. He would probably have to fight a court case, but so be it. It wouldn't be his first or his last.

Claire and Rupert spent the night together, making love gently, exploring each other's bodies with the practice of experienced lovers. It was an exciting and beneficial experience for them both. Rupert woke first, with a smile on his face.

A sleepy, tousled Claire rolled over to face him, her eyes half closed.

"What are you grinning at?" she demanded. In response he pulled her towards him and kissed her.

When they broke apart he started to speak, "Last night was special and –"

Claire pressed a finger against his lips.

"No. Not now. Don't ruin it with words. Just let it be and enjoy it. We'll talk tonight. I have to get to work – some of us still have to, you know," she mocked, grabbing her dressing gown and dashing through to the bathroom. But as an encouragement, she shot her head back through the doorway. "But don't run away will you? Promise?" He grinned and nodded.

After Claire had left, Rupert called Webster, who answered on the third ring.

"Webster."

"Rupert Brett. How are you?"

"Rupert, where the hell have you been? I've been trying to get hold of you."

"Why? What's happened?"

"Shingler has disappeared. Didn't return home last night, no sign of him so far today. He was last seen in his office by the cleaners as he was leaving. Nothing since. We had a man watching his home and he never went there; he's just disappeared into thin air. Talking of which, where were you last night? We had your flat watched as well, and I might it's a bloody good job we did – you had a visitor."

"Who?"

"Maria Rico." Webster let the name hang in the air, and Rupert went cold. "Tidying up loose ends, no doubt. What the hell did you say to Paul Simions? You knew this would happen, didn't you? If I didn't know better I'd say that you orchestrated it: you set them against each other and damn nearly got yourself killed in the process. We need to talk," he continued brusquely. "You had better come in." Rupert agreed to see him later and ended the call.

Rupert jabbed his fist in the air. *Yes*, he thought. Shingler had got his. Liz was avenged, and all without involving himself directly, whatever Webster might think. He realised that all that was left now was to wait and see how things panned out for Simions. Webster had told him that it was doubtful they'd be able to prosecute Simions for murder. *I just want to see his smug face when he's sentenced*, Rupert thought. And as Claire said, it had all been done using cunning and intelligence, with not a blow struck in anger – Shingler's possible fate notwithstanding.

Two hours later, in Webster's office, he got a severe

grilling. "I did not give you information so that you could go off on a one man revenge spree, Rupert." Webster said. "Apart from the fact that you could have got yourself killed, think about your friend Claire Sewell. It would not have been beyond Simions to put two and two together to realise that she could have been involved. Did you consider that? You knew that whatever you said would set Shingler and Simions off, didn't you?"

Rupert looked at Webster, his face a picture of composed innocence. "I had absolutely no idea," he lied. "Like I said, I bumped into him in the street, he invited me into his office, we chatted and the whole story came out, especially the fraud aspect," he answered, shrugging a shoulder.

"I don't believe you. But I can't prove anything, and for what it's worth I'm glad Shingler got what was coming to him. What really pisses me off is that we still haven't got anything on Maria Rico. DI Fleming is going to be very angry with you, Rupert. But one way or another it's a result, and we will nail Simions for fraud, amongst other things. But he's been too clever, and we won't get a conspiracy to commit murder charge to stick."

Rupert risked a jibe. "Yeah? Tell me something I don't know. Do you really think you would have? Do you really believe they would have ratted on each other and you would have been able to persuade a jury to convict one or both of them? For a senior policeman, you can be pretty naïve sometimes." He looked across at Webster, whose piercing eyes looked back at him over the top of his spectacles.

"We'll never know now, will we? But just take care 'til the trial is over, OK? Although if I know Maria Rico she'll be out of the country already, and her brother and their friends will provide her with proof that she was never here when the crimes were committed."

"Noted," Rupert responded noncommittally. "I will take extra precautions and stay away from my flat for a while."

"Good, and keep in touch regularly." Those were Webster's final words as Rupert made for the door. He nodded his assent and left, realising that he hadn't considered that Claire might have been in danger. He knew he couldn't stay with her indefinitely. He thought about heading back to his parents for a while, to recuperate properly and reassure them that he was OK.

That evening they went to a little Italian restaurant around the corner from Claire's flat. Neutral ground was better, he felt, for both of them. Rupert was more nervous about the evening than many of the other situations he had found himself in over the last few months. They settled back after ordering and Rupert tentatively took Claire's hand across the table. She sensed his diffidence, which was a revelation considering how confident he normally was.

"Claire, I've got so much to say that I don't know where to begin. I have so many thoughts and feelings all whirling around in my head..." he gave up, shrugging in frustration.

"Then you should let them all come burbling out and we will understand each other better," she responded gently. "God's sake, Rupes, it's not as if this is a first date and we don't know each other."

He smiled, encouraged by her attitude. "OK, this going to sound really weird but I have really strong feelings for you. I always have, ever since university and even..." here he hesitated. "Even when I was seeing Liz. I thought I loved her, but looking back I don't think I ever did. Is that strange?"

She smiled and squeezed his hand, and that was the moment when Rupert knew then that everything was going to be all right. "No it is not weird, and I am certainly not going to over-analyse it. I think we both owe some debts to our past, otherwise we would not be here. You and Liz, me and Angus."

"Angus? Really?" he interrupted.

"Hah," she mocked herself. "Yes, in a way it was the last time I gave in to my wilder side, when I wasn't sure which direction I wanted to go in. Should I carry on down the path of meaningless affairs and work or consider being a little more stable and probably happier for it. I suppose what I am really saying is that it made me grow up," she gave a humourless laugh.

Rupert felt the pressure on his hand increase as she made this statement, and he knew that it had taken a lot of courage.

"No, you're right," he said. "I had never really thought of it in those terms before. Thank you," he finished quietly. From that point the evening went well. With the barriers down, they both explored their feelings and came to the conclusion that they had a genuine affection for each other.

As they walked home in each other's arms, the tricky subject of accommodation reared its head.

"You're welcome to stay here with me," she offered. "I'm not trying to be pushy or anything, but if it is dangerous to return permanently to your flat in the short term, well..."

"Thank you. But I think that it would be a mistake for

both us. I want this to last, and it would be too much too soon, don't you think? There's still danger as well, and the last thing I want is to see you hurt. I think I'll go back to my parents' for as long as I can stand it: I mean I love them dearly, but weeks on end?" He winced, and they both laughed.

"I know, and you're probably right. Good choice. But you'd better let me come and see you at weekends – and don't bonk any of their friends' daughters while you're there," she chided.

"OK, but that does mean that we can spend tonight together before I go?" he laughed.

Epilogue

It was six months before Paul Simions' trial was over. It was the biggest case at the Old Bailey for months, with vast amounts of speculation and a confirmation in the eyes of the public and the City that estate agents and their like were all little more than a bunch of crooks.

Rupert was called as a witness along with various secretaries, heads of personnel and surveyors – including Pauline Wood, whose evidence proved crucial.

David Shingler's name came up on many occasions, but of course he was never present at the trial. A badly decomposed body was found floating in the river Thames some weeks after his disappearance. Headless and without fingertips, the body was unidentifiable, but the general consensus was that it was Shingler. He was made out to be the fall guy, and with nobody to defend his name much of the blame was placed upon his shoulders, clearly helping Simions' case.

But Simions did not have it all his own way. The jury, for once, was not taken in by his suave ways and his cool demeanour, and he was convicted on three counts of fraud as well as other crimes. The CPS would not consider anything to do with Liz Carmichael's murder: the evidence, they said, was too circumstantial.

Paul Simions was sentenced to fifteen years in jail. Rupert attended the sentencing and enjoyed every minute of it, although he knew what Simions was really guilty of, and he was annoyed that Simions did not get a longer jail term.

Mike and Jemma got married two weeks after the trial ended,. The wedding was a grand affair, held at St. Georges in Hanover Square. The reception was at the Grosvenor House Hotel in Park Lane, and was all that it should have been. The right people were there in all their finery and a beautiful horse-drawn carriage transported the bride and groom from the church to the reception.

Upon learning the news of Rupert's apparent return from the dead, Mike had actually gone around to his flat to apologise for his behaviour, and said that was sorry he had doubted him at all. Rupert had accepted the apology with a good grace, but he was aware that for the foreseeable future there would be a shadow over their friendship.

Claire and Rupert were together now, and had been since Rupert had returned from a month in the country with his parents. During the course of a slow dance at the reception, towards the end of what had been a splendid evening, he asked her if she would move in with him. She replied by hugging him more tightly.

"Oh Rupes, of course I will. I don't know why it took you so long to ask me."

. . .

www.simonfairfax.com

To start book two, A Deal Too Far, click here

A message from Simon.

I know you have over a million of choices of books to read. I can't tell you how much it means to me that you have made time to read one of my books.

I really hope you enjoyed it and that your found it entertaining. If you did, I would appreciate a few more minutes of your time, if I may humbly as you to leave a review for other readers who may be trying to select their next reading material.

If, for any reason, you weren't satisfied with this book, please do let me know by emailing me at simonfairfaxauthor@gmail.com

The satisfaction of my readers and feedback are important to me.

Best wishes,

Simon

Next In Series

A Deal Too Far: Deal Series Book 2

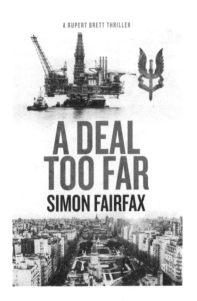

From Property Agent to Government Agent
Autumn 1990 - a deadly challenge awaits Rupert Brett,

as he opens a new office in Buenos Aires and is asked to spy for the UK Government. Finding corruption and the threat of a Falklands invasion, his life is on the line as traitors within his midst threaten to betray him.

He must fight to escape Argentina with crucial data before he and his only ally are found and killed.

A Deal Too Far is the second exciting book in the Deal series of international, financial and political thrillers.

To enter this cloak and dagger world Click Here to read immediately.

Acknowledgments

First of all, thanks to my editor Perry Iles for all his work, advice and encouragement in getting me into line, he added so much to my writing for which I am very grateful. So many others helped me on my first book's journey, either directly or indirectly, providing information, technical help and encouragement. These people include Nigel Beaumont (Purdey & Sons), Frances Campbell, Terence Cox, Michael Ford, Andrew Klein, Scott Murdoch, Patricia Salter, Jamie Salter, John P Smail, Vittorio Scappini, Dave Taylor, Paul Vockins and 'AJ' Webster.

About the Author

— As a lover of crime thrillers and mystery, I turned what is seen by others as a dull 9 – 5 job into something that is exciting, as close to real life as possible, with Rupert Brett, my international man of mystery whose day job is that of a Chartered Surveyor.

Rupert is an ordinary man thrown into extraordinary circumstances who uses his wit, guile and training to survive.

Each book is written from my own experiences, as close to the truth as possible, set against world events that really happened. I go out and experience all the weapons, visit the places Rupert travels to, speak to the technical experts and ensure that it as realistic, as possible allowing you to delve deep in to the mystery, losing yourself in it for a few hours.

www.simonfairfax.com

Made in United States
Troutdale, OR
05/25/2024

20114205R00166